ALSO BY
ROGER ROSENBLATT

Lapham Rising
Children of War
Rules for Aging
Witness
Anything Can Happen
Black Fiction
Coming Apart
The Man in the Water
Consuming Desires
Life Itself
Where We Stand

AN **ecco** BOOK

HARPER **PERENNIAL**

NEW YORK • LONDON • TORONTO • SYDNEY • NEW DELHI • AUCKLAND

Roger Rosenblatt

BEET

A NOVEL

HARPER ● PERENNIAL

A hardcover edition of this book was published in 2008 by Ecco, an imprint of HarperCollins Publishers.

P.S.™ is a trademark of HarperCollins Publishers.

HarperCollins books may be purchased for educational, business, or sales promotional use. For information please write: Special Markets Department, Harper-Collins Publishers, 10 East 53rd Street, New York, NY 10022.

FIRST HARPER PERENNIAL EDITION PUBLISHED 2009.

BOOK DESIGN BY SHUBHANI SARKAR

The Library of Congress has catalogued the hardcover edition as follows:

Rosenblatt, Roger.
    Beet : a novel / Roger Rosenblatt. — 1st ed.
        p.   cm.
    ISBN: 978-0-06-134427-5
    1. College teachers—Fiction. 2. College students—Fiction. 3. College stories. 4. Massachusettes—Fiction. 5. Satire. I. Title.
    PS3618.084B44 2008
    813'.6—dc22   2007028229

ISBN 978-0-06-134428-2 (pbk.)

09 10 11 12 13 WBC/RRD 10 9 8 7 6 5 4 3 2 1

FOR MICHAEL J. ARLEN

husband
(man) wife (woman)
LOVE = Athena   Peace — Olivia
(sister)   ✓
                2 kids
                Beth = 9
                Robert = 7

"Tomorrow we start shutting down the college."
"But Professor, where will the students sleep?"
"Where they always sleep—in the classroom."

—*HORSE FEATHERS*

BEET

CHAPTER 1

"DON'T BOTHER TO COME HOME IF YOU STILL HAVE A JOB," Livi Porterfield called to her husband as he hustled their two groggy children into the 243,000-miles-and-still-rattling Accord, to drive them to school. He blew her a kiss.

The job she referred to was on the faculty of Beet College, forty miles north of Boston, where eighteen hundred handpicked, neurotically competitive undergraduates were joined with one hundred and forty-one handpicked, neurotically competitive professors to instruct them. Beet was a typical small New England college, fortified with brick and self-regard—the sort of place people call charming when they mean sterile.

There Peace Porterfield the youngest full professor in the school's history, taught English and American literature—which is ordinarily enough to mark a person for disaster. If that didn't do the trick, he also believed in what he did, being committed to an academic discipline said to have exhausted both its material and its usefulness, and patronized by institutions of higher learning like a doddering tenant no longer able to come up with the rent. And if those things didn't do him in, he believed in the value of a liberal arts education, and in colleges in general, from whose sacred waters, he further believed, civilization flowed. Need one glaze the duck? He believed in civilization.

The same may not be said of the redhead knockout Olivia Weissman-Kelleher Porterfield, M.D., Peace's wife of thirteen years and mother of Beth and Robert, their bellicose progeny of nine and seven. Livi had the face and temperament of a despotic ingénue. While she gave an occasional nod to civilization, she thought of colleges and universities as—how did she put it?—fucked up beyond belief.

She waved good-bye and wished him "Bad luck, Candide!"— what she called him when she was especially exasperated by his even temper. He needled her by adopting the nickname.

Voltaire probably pictured someone like Peace. Eyes as blue as daylight, hair the color of damp sand that flapped over his forehead. Six foot one, give or take. An athlete's careful lope. And a stoic expression, created and often tested by the name his 1960s-generation parents had burdened him with. His less respectful sister Love, a parole officer in Newark, legally changed her name to Athena. Peace was more naturally serene, which came in handy at times as tense as these.

And why were these times tense? Because the board of trustees of Beet College was threatening to shut the place down. Since eight o'clock that morning, they had been meeting in the Temple, the imitation Parthenon atop College Hill, under the leadership of Joel Bollovate (known as "the man in the iron belly" to his colleagues, competitors, and to his family as well), chairman of the board and CEO of Bollocorps, the largest developer in five of the six New England states. And why close the college? Because Chairman Bollovate reported that Beet's $265 million endowment had been reduced to nothing, and the school was going broke.

"Jesus, Mary, and Moses!" Livi would say as often as she could. "A two-hundred-and-fifty-year-old American institution down the toilet in three short years. The Bollovate legacy."

Livi lacked what is known as the patience of a saint. When the Porterfields had first arrived at Beet, she could find no openings

Nathaniel Beet

job

nearby in her specialty in hand surgery, and was forced to cool her heels working in the ER at Boston North. That diversion, she hoped, would be as short-lived as her husband's employment. She looked for any opportunity to free her family from what she called "the graves of academe."

But she was right about Beet's distinguished place in American history. Given every advantage at its birth in 1755, the college profited from the shortcomings of institutions of higher learning that had preceded it. Harvard College was founded in 1636, but in 1718, at the urging of Cotton Mather (whose urgings were rarely ignored), a group of New England conservatives who felt Harvard's standards were slipping decided to found Yale. A few years later another group, who felt Yale's standards were slipping, decided to found Princeton (1746). Not long after that yet another group, detecting more slippage still, created the University of Pennsylvania (1749), then Columbia (1754), until the groups of roving college founders felt standards had slipped so much and so rapidly, they could no longer find them. It was around that time Beet came into being.

rumor of founding

focused on religion & animal husbandry

That was thanks to a gift of Nathaniel Beet (1660–1732), an American divine and the wealthiest pig farmer in the New England colonies. Beet bequeathed his library of one hundred books (half on religion, half on animal husbandry) and his pigs, which were of much greater dollar value, to establish a "Collegium for Young Men in the Service of Almighty God and Livestock"—thus the college motto, "Deus Libri Porci."

motto

Beet was to be God's beachhead on a pagan continent, created to produce the sort of young man that England and her motley intermarrying kings and queens had failed to produce since 1066—a learned, ruthless Christian who knew the value of a penny. Small wonder Beet was where the term "capitalist pig" originated, though not as a pejorative. negative

goal of Beet

"Love ya, Dad!" Beth and Robert shouted as Peace dropped them off, just before they shoved each other in the small of the back when Dad drove away. Then he too headed off to school, as he had done his whole life, from the age of three to thirty-six—St. Paul's,

Harvard A.B., B.Litt (Oxon.), Harvard A.M., Ph.D.; a year teaching poor and neglected kids in Sunset Park, Brooklyn (where he and Livi met); his first job, at Yale: school, school, and more school.

He drove down the dirt road, which became the macadam road, which became Main Street of the town of Beet, and he winced. If the college closed, so would the town. Everything in it—the This Little Piggy Muncheonette with its fourteen-by-twelve-by-ten-foot fiberglass shocking pink pig standing at happy attention on the roof; the Pig Out Diner; the Pen and Oink Bookshop; the Bring Home the Bacon butchers; Marty's Swine & Cheese; the Pigs-in-Blankets Bed 'N Breakfast and its High on the Hog Lounge; and businesses with similar stage names, too many, all except the town bank, which had rejected the most obvious name for fear of appearing breakable—relied on the college for its survival. As did its citizens, who, with not much to do, depended on Beet's extension courses to teach them ceramics, photography, macramé, origami, quilting, quilling, and the sketching of nudes.

A fork left, a quick right, and onto the interstate that exited at the county road that exited at the old horseback highway in the woods that wound round to the high black iron gate at the college entrance. Past Gregory, the barely intelligible security guard, who welcomed him with "Flingle!"; past the clusters of students in jeans, sweatshirts, and baseball caps; down into faculty parking. Four years this had been his routine. When the Accord's engine finally stopped wheezing, he tried to deny the accompanying sinking feeling, and applied his natural buoyancy, explaining to himself that his wave of depression was due merely to the cumulative effect of any of life's habits.

He settled in his office to work on the latest batch of student papers. Mrs. Whiting, the department secretary, sat at her desk and sorted mail. They were the only two in the building doing what they were being paid to do. The other department members, ten in number, were gathered at the windows like winter houseflies buzzing and banging themselves against the glass, peering up at the Temple on the hill.

Standing at the Temple window, Chairman Bollovate looked

down. "Are we agreed?" he said. He had the taut mouth of a ne-crophagous animal and spoke with paratactic abruptness ("I go. You stay") but without the courtesies often implied by the style, and he never sounded as if he were asking a question even when he was. "Are we agreed?" was heard by his fellow developer trustees as "We have a deal." They laughed like gunfire, especially Beet's President Lewis Huey, a born picaroon who, once he determined a certain reaction was permissible, reacted with extra oomph. Then the board shook hands all round with greater gusto than the situation seemed to call for. "Who'll tell them?" Bollovate asked and de-clared.

"You do it, Joel. It was your idea."

So Bollovate walked from the building and proceeded down the hill with a jouncy royal gait, such as the gait with which Henry VIII undoubtedly had waddled, or perhaps one of Nathaniel's prize pigs, down toward the campus, which spread before him like a vil-lage ripe for sacking.

Directly below lay the quadrilaterals of the two Pens, Old and New, like two large stockades with five-story brick buildings occupy-ing the four sides of each, and square lawns in the centers. The Pens contained the academic departments, classroom buildings, and Ba-con Library—not a pig joke; it was named for Francis. They were joined (or separated, depending on one's perspective) by College Hall, a long gray structure where President Huey and the deans kept their offices. Student dormitories clustered east of the Pens, and beyond them the parking lots and college gate. To the west lay the athletic fields, hockey rink, tennis courts, track, and gym. On a terrace to the north were the college museum, the Faculty Club, Health Services, the Campus Store, and frame houses for sundry societies and extracurricular activities like the student newspaper, the *Pig's Eye*. To the south was Lapham Auditorium, where concerts and readings were given, speeches delivered, and plays played.

"Plotinus!" thought Bollovate. Isolated names and words from what he defined as his "wasted four years" at college haunted him whenever he found himself on campus. He shivered with horror and contempt. "Who the fuck was Plotinus?"

The Old Pen presented itself like differentiated functions of the mind—History, Classics, Languages, Philosophy, Mathematics, Physical Sciences, Biological Sciences, Chemical Sciences, Government, Economics, Peace's own English and American Literature, and so on. Nathaniel's Tomb, the size of a toolshed, was squeezed between Philosophy and Economics.

"Tiresias? Who the fuck was Tiresias?"

The more recent disciplines had homes in the New Pen, and their names were painted on signs rather than carved into stone, so that they could be replaced at a moment's notice. Ephemeral or not, they brought in the dollars, though apparently not enough to forestall closure. They included Communications Arts; Native American Crafts and Casino Studies; the Sensitivity and Diversity Council; the Fur and Ivory Audiovisual Center; Ethnicity, Gender, and Television Studies; Little People of Color; Humor and Meteorology; Bondage Studies; Serial Killers of the Northwest; Wiccan History; and the I Am Woman Center, connected by a walking bridge to the Tarzan Institute, which housed the Robert Bly Man's Manliness Society. Bliss House—not a department but a counseling service for students and faculty, described by its curator Professor Donna Dalmatian as "a safe haven where the mind meets the heart"—stood off by itself.

The New Pen was what the college had become in the Bollovate/Huey years. Before them, the Beet curriculum was like that of any self-respecting college—boring but harmless and offering a general education that allowed the more motivated students to enter the outside world relatively unimpaired. In contrast, the new curriculum presented an array of courses and programs specifically designed for popularity. In this effort, certain members of the faculty—particularly those who deemed themselves hip to the sensitivities of undergraduates—cooperated, though unwittingly, by mounting a curriculum meant to draw greater numbers of students by bucking up their self-esteem.

"Postcolonial Women's Sports?" Livi erupted when she'd heard of the latest. "Are you shittin' me?"

Two results ensued, both unfortunate: The outside world

showed not the faintest interest in bucking up the self-esteem of anyone, so the student who was prepared for four years to think well of him- or herself did not get a job or soon lost one, causing an extreme drop in self-esteem and the onset of lifelong psychiatric attention. And the college lost money anyway, which would have been less upsetting had anyone recalled that the institution was supposed to be nonprofit. Bollovate himself had no such recollection. More than once he told President Huey, "The property alone is worth more than anything the deep thinkers are doing, or ever did! Ha ha ha!"

Peace continued to grade papers in his office, until his friend Derek Manning blustered in.

"I told you so," said Manning. "The bottom line. As soon as that phrase crept into the language, country was cooked." He strode back and forth in front of Peace's desk.

Manning held the Samuel Beer Professorship in Public Policy, and like the Harvard scholar for whom the chair was named, was the straightest of shooters. He was built like a boxer and had a boxer's nose—earned legitimately when he was growing up, or trying to, as the one Jewish kid on an Italian block in Providence. The fight of his life, however, he'd lost two years earlier, when his thirty-three-year-old wife Margaret died of Creutzfeldt-Jakob disease, akin to mad cow. It caused an encephalopathy, beginning with headaches, moving to disorientation, then loss of motor function and body function. Her dying took eight months. The terrible suddenness of the disease, mixed with the mystery and futility, gave Manning a look that seemed grim and combative at first glance, but when one searched it, showed fear. Yet he had a proleptic gift for argument and a forward tilt that read: Do you really want to start with me?

Usually Peace did not—he liked him too much—except on the basketball court, where the younger, taller Professor Porterfield creamed the forty-six-year-old Manning one-on-one, four out of five.

"Will you please sit down! You're freaking me out."

"Look at them, will you?"—continuing to pace and pointing to the office window. "Our esteemed colleagues panting like dogs, waiting for a sign from Joel Bollovate to tell them about the rest of their lives. The Day of the Bollovate. A hundred and forty-one people study and overeducate themselves for decades, only to wind up at the mercy of a man like that." He sang, "Money money money money money."

"Stop!" Peace covered his ears.

"Tell me," said Manning. "Do you really think anyone would care if Beet went out of business? And that's the way most people would think of it—going out of business. Would anyone care if every college in the country went out of business? I mean honestly. I know what people always say, what they tell the pollsters about the importance of education. 'Our number-one priority.' But if you gave them the choice of tearing down all the colleges and putting Starbucks in their places, or better still, offered them one hundred smackers for every college torn down, don't you think they'd line up around the block?"

"I do not."

"Really?" He rubbed his thumb and index finger together in the gimme sign. "There are four thousand colleges in America."

"Boethius!"—Bollovate shuffled on—"Who the fuck was Boethius?"

Beet occupied no more than 210 acres, but within its precincts it became an inescapable maze. The Pens were enclosed, the classroom and department buildings nearly touching. The dorms were rectangles, the length of one bisecting the breadth of another, and creating an alphabet of horizontal T's with the two lines unattached. Once autumn arrived, one could barely see daylight—for the trees, and for the high chimneys, many to a building, which seemed to serve as lookouts for attacks. Even when high noon was blasting all the rest of Massachusetts, Beet remained a network of penumbral corridors that went everywhere and nowhere, there being many more paths than destinations, as if they had been laid in anticipation of every possible walker's itinerary, with several extra thrown in to confound them. It was a world unto itself, equipped with its own sun, which never blared brighter than a platinum haze, and its own moon, which was russet and wore a veil.

"I don't get you," said Manning. "You sit there as though you had nothing on your mind but those papers."

"Because I can do something about them."

"Oh, yes. I forget. You're the pure teacher. But it's not natural. Where's the gnashing of teeth, the cursing out of the pricks?"

"You handle that."

From the year of its establishment, darkness seemed to have found a home in Beet College. Dark pink for the brick buildings, dark green for the doorjambs and the benches, dark iron for the hinges, dark stone for Nathaniel's Tomb; darkness in the piceous roots of trees that broke through the earth like bones through skin. Darkness in the impermeable forest surrounding the college, and in the Atlantic, too, three miles to the southeast yet audible at night.

Livi loved the sound of its churning. "Like traffic going somewhere else," she sighed.

Darkness even in the Temple, whence Bollovate made his slow descent and which, though composed of alabaster, seemed to absorb the light and turn it to the color of tarnished silver. High on the hill it squatted, with its frieze of piglets on the tympanum above the cornice, and its acroterion made up of a three-foot-high pig on its hind legs, the entire structure looking like a proud white pig itself, yet still emitting that haughty gloom the Puritans gathered up from the smoke-choked huts and cottages of the seventeenth-century English countryside and brought to the New World to guarantee its continuity.

"I knew it, I knew it! They're definitely closing us down," said Manning, as he traced the trustee's leaden steps. "If they had intended to keep us open, they would never tell the faculty first."

That was the general opinion of all who flattened their faces against the windows of Beet that morning, including the dither of deans (the collective noun was coined some years earlier by a professor of Romance languages named Wilcox, who ran off with a wild and brilliant sophomore named Maud). Many grew excited.

Hungry for honors, no matter how dubious, they sought even this one—to receive the bad news personally and be the first of the last people standing.

And yet, as usual, the Beet intelligentsia misjudged the situation. For if Bollovate planned to deliver the announcement of Beet's closing, he never would have bothered to tell the faculty himself. He held an even lower opinion of Beet's professoriate than he did of the administration. He held a very low opinion of Beet altogether. When President Huey appointed him to chair the board, he'd asked what exactly a college trustee was entrusted with. Was the board supposed to keep the college going no matter how much money it was spilling? Or was a trustee one entrusted to make the hard, unsentimental choice of getting off the pot when the pot was leaking shit? (The metaphor was his.) Actually, he asked those things as second thoughts. His first was, "What's in it for me?" Huey had heard the question as rhetorical.

"Governments are shaped by pretenses, my boy. Noble pretenses." Now Manning leaned over Peace's desk. "If you studied something practical, if you didn't bury that fair-haired head of yours in the airy-fairy land of 'literature' [slowing up so as to pronounce every letter], you'd see what I mean. America announced ambitions like liberty, equality, all that glorious crap, so we could try to live up to them. But set the bottom line as the goal of the country, and what do we become? A nation of pork bellies." He pointed to the window. "And there it is now, fat and sassy, rolling down the hill."

"You and Livi ought to get together. She hates the college as much as you do."

"In a heartbeat. Will you keep the kids?"

By now Bollovate had directed his royal progress toward the Old Pen—professors in the New Pen moaned and sighed—and had limited his possibilities to three pathways, a choice of one of three departments at which to make his announcement.

But just as History and Social Anthropology were working themselves into a tizzy, he swung the iron belly toward English and American Literature and entered. The department members coagulated about him like rock star groupies. He scanned his surroundings, as if calculating square footage.

"Professor Porterfield?" he asked the crowd. They pointed to a closed door. He did not bother to knock. "Professor Porterfield?" Manning shook his head. "Professor Porterfield?"—addressing the right man at last.

Peace stood. Manning edged toward escape.

"I'm pleased to tell you," said Bollovate, "that the trustees have decided not to close the college just yet. You know how much the place means to us all. [Manning coughed.] But given the empty state of the endowment, we cannot survive beyond the end of term unless we can turn things around in a hurry. So we voted to use the remaining weeks to ask the faculty to come up with a new curriculum. Something bold and different [two more coughs from Manning]. Attract more paying undergraduates, more grants, more alumni gifts. [He frowned as if sincerely.] Of course, it also has to be intellectually worthwhile [three of Manning's loudest coughs]. If the faculty can produce a curriculum like that, we might stay open indefinitely."

"Aren't we at capacity right now?" Peace asked.

"Technically, yes," said Bollovate. "Depends on how you define capacity. The board sees the college as a growth industry. We figure we can take four to five hundred more undergraduates without straining the system."

"How will you house and feed them?" Peace asked.

"Leave those concerns to us bean counters," Bollovate chortled. He reached up and clasped Peace by the shoulders. "Think big, Professor!"

Peace said nothing but wondered if it were possible to raise the numbers and hold the standards. Yet the prospect of a new curriculum intrigued him.

"We still have time to save our asses," said Bollovate.

"That's great, Mr. Bollovate," said Peace. "But what does this have to do with me?"

"We want you to chair the new curriculum committee."

"Me?"—a squint mixing surprise with suspicion. "But there are so many better people. People who have more experience. Like Professor Manning here"—who suddenly was not here, but half-way out the door, smiling sadly with his back turned.

"You're the one the trustees want," said Bollovate. "And you're the right man for the job. Everyone says so. They say you have ideals. Do you have ideals, Professor?"

"Oh, does he ever!" said Manning, walking away.

"Ideals. They're so important," said Bollovate. "Don't you think so?" He gave Peace his I'm-very-concerned look. "I'd like to say think it over, Professor. But there's no time. Yes or no? In or out?"

Afterward, Peace phoned Livi at the hospital.

"So it wasn't bad news. It was worse," she said. "By the way, we're having goose for dinner. How do you like it cooked?"

Matha Polite
poet

CHAPTER 2

"SHITSHITSHITSHITSHIT!" SAID THE POET MATHA POLITE (pron. "Pole-eet") when she learned of the trustees' decision and of Professor Porterfield's assignment to save Beet from extinction. This knowledge came to her approximately two minutes after it had come to Peace himself, since nothing moves faster than a rumor in a college, even when the rumor proves true and is not about sex.

Matha first shouted her reaction to herself, then to the group of her fellow student radicals gathered in her dorm room in Chillingworth. (All the dorms had names that froze the blood—Chillingworth, Fordyce, Snowe, Coldenham, Sleeting, and Frost.) They lolled on the floor and on the bed, under posters of Che, Dr. Dre, Oprah, and Simon Cowell, and listened to their leader. "Shitshitshitshitshit!" she said again. This turn of affairs represented a catastrophe.

"Okay." She rubbed her hands together. "If they're not going to close the college, then we'll do it for them!"—met with murmurs of assent and one or two yeahs.

If ambition had a face, it would be Matha's. It was small and tight about the skull, masked by an expression blending mere competence with want. Her hair was the color of mixed nuts, worn

Martha descrip.

short and close like a helmet. Her eyes were brown and burned like coals in ash, but without light until she had need of it. Her mouth looked poised and loaded like a crossbow; the whole head pushed forward as if about to fire. It was her stridency that accounted for her appeal, both sexual and political, and her gift of fury. In high school she tried out for Lady Macbeth but lost the role because she was too ruthless. IRONY

"Matha! Did you hear? Profesor Porterfield is going to save the college"—a shout from outside the dorm, directly below her window.

"Is that Akim?" asked Peter Bagtoothian, the one bona fide thug in Matha's group. "May I go down and kill him?"

"He's just hot for me. We have more important business."

Matha was a transfer student from Magnolia Blossom College in Balloo, Virginia, her hometown, and reigned as Queen of the May Flowers, the highest honor Magnolia Blossom bestowed. At her coronation she'd worn a pale blue antebellum ball gown with yellow rosettes at the breasts and spread her hoop skirts on the college green like Arabian tents, as ladies-in-waiting dried the beads of perspiration on her brow, waving wide white pleated fans. In those days, she was a different Matha Polite. She kept horses, owned an impressive collection of expensive pearls given her by various beaus of excellent if profligate local breeding, was elected social chairperson of her sorority, and looked forward to a life in a big white pillared Georgian house in Balloo similar to that of her mama and daddy, where she would decorate dinner party invitations with floret embossments, prance to church on the arm of her handsome chosen husband-to-be, Dawb Dubelle, and primp her daughters for their comings-out at the Balloo Cotton Cotillion, where she too came out, as had her older sister Kathy, her mama Luelle, and her grandmamma Bluelle before her.

At the time, she also spoke with a thick-as-custard southern alto, with which, it was said, she could coax the male birds from their nests, and often did. "A girl like you could sell a man anything, honey," her father, Beaulieu Polite, the most successful real estate broker in Virginia, told her more than once. "I'd hate to think where I'd be if you were my competition, girl!"

"Oh, Daddy!" Matha would trill and laugh and stand on her tippy toes to give her father a kiss on the cheek. "I leave all that to yourself, and of course to dear Kathy. No one could ever compete with you. And besides, what would a teeny little thing like me know about the man's world of big business. Real estate! I swan!"

"Matha!"

"Akim!" She opened the window. "Shut the fuck up"—and slammed it down.

Her suitor stood his ground and pined.

Akim Ben Laden was the official campus nutcase. Born Arthur Horowitz, he'd changed his name and other things in rebellion against his father, a conservative rabbi from Scarsdale who had beaten his son in chess relentlessly ever since he taught him the game at the age of two, with nary a smile, either sympathetic or gloating. He also insisted they play every night after supper, sitting across from each other at the dining room table cleared of kosher plates, where Akim would grow grimmer and grimmer year after year, and his father would sit statue-still wearing a green eyeshade beneath his black yarmulke. In the last game they were ever to play, so intent on his winning streak was the humorless if focused rabbi, he'd failed to notice that his son was wearing a white kaffi-yeh, a blue terrycloth bathrobe, and green talaria sandals with little leather wings at the ankles, which became his signature outfit.

Shortly afterward, Akim founded the Arab League at Scarsdale High School, along with the Loyal Sons of Mohammed and the OPEC Social Club. Of all these extracurricular groups, he was the only member, as even the Muslim students at Scarsdale were leery of him, especially after he called himself a half-Sunni and half-Shia Iraqi, and was given to kicking in the door of his own locker. He was also tossed out of several mosques because he'd never figured out the correct way to face Mecca. At graduation, he received a sound beating at the hands of a bunch of Arab and Jewish boys, the only such cooperative venture in local memory.

"Matha! My love!"

"I'm not kidding, Akim!"—opening and slamming the window again.

Matha hated her sister Kathy, the most aggressive real estate agent on Long Island's East End, which was saying something. But in her hidden heart she envied her sister's success in business and hoped to eclipse her. She was nineteen years younger than Kathy. Beaulieu and Luelle, once they'd observed the development of their firstborn child, had been reluctant to create another. Their second daughter was named in the hospital, when Luelle was watching the *Today* show. She was suffering from postpartum depression, which accounted for her emotional reaction to the appearance of the up-and-coming Martha Stewart. Luelle was overcome with admiration for the pies Ms. Stewart was effortlessly baking, particularly the peach, and she hoped that if she named her baby Martha, the girl would grow up to be someone of equal stature and importance.

"We'll close down this place tighter 'n shit!" said Matha, who never uttered what Daddy called cuss words back home but, liberated at Beet, cursed a blue streak. Only sometimes she would get overexcited, and the words were misapplied. "Tighter 'n shit!"

So, she'd transferred in her junior year, shortly after the unfortunate business with Professor Portebelloe of Magnolia Blossom's Comparative Literature Department (the scandal drove Dawb into solitary despair in an A-frame in the Blue Ridge Mountains, where he carved pickaninny dolls from balsa wood and beheaded them). Portebelloe was kicked out, but Matha got a note from her doctor, her uncle Delray explaining she was afflicted with gerontophilia, and was not accountable for her actions.

A fistful of pebbles rattled the window. Bagtoothian was startled. "Couldn't I kill him?" he asked Matha. "It'd only take a minute."

Until her arrival at Beet she had never set foot north of Port Deposit, Maryland, and yet it took her no more than two weeks to shed—or, as it turned out, to temporarily place in storage—her southern accent, replace it with a shrill and clipped Yankee voice, start writing poetry, and most important to her, call herself Matha, a name of her invention that seemed both hard and precise and feminine too—the female Math, a bouquet made of numbers. Not only was the name exotic, it was worlds removed from the name she was born with. (What would those sophisticated northern intellectuals make of Martha Stewart Polite?) She insinuated herself into Beet's student radical movement, which she could tell required leadership. It had appealed to her at once, since she could see that underneath their scowls, the students were not all that different from the ones she'd left behind at Magnolia Blossom.

The Beet radicals of today, a much smaller group than the radical students of the 1960s, had no Vietnam to march against. They were uninterested in Iraq because they could not be drafted to fight there. They had no minorities to defend, because they didn't want to.

From time to time the radicals would amuse themselves by testing the sympathy limits of the faculty or simply stirring the pot. They'd tell the people at the Robert Bly Man's Manliness Society *poet* that Marigold Jefferson of the I Am Woman Center was entertaining its members by screening *Deliverance*. They compared everyone they disagreed with to Hitler. It was Matha's group that agitated for the latest entry in the course catalog—Nippocano Studies: Where Tokyo Meets Tijuana. They'd meant it as a gag, but once established, it was oversubscribed. *looking for the easy way out*

Their favorite faculty sympathizer was Tufts Godwin, who headed the Sensitivity and Diversity Council and who was known as Professor Sensodyne behind his back. They would come to him with some concocted grievance against another professor, any other professor, whose tongue slipped, causing him to say Miss rather than Ms., or who referred to a woman as beautiful. They would get Professor Sensodyne to insist that the insulting party make a public apology on the lawn of the Old Pen or take a course in sensitivity training. They would show Godwin their appreciation, but with niggardly zeal. Last spring, BWAP (Beet Women Against Pigs) voted him the "Professor Most Sensitive to Women's

Issues." But when he showed up to accept the trophy—a plaster-of-paris bust of Rosie O'Donnell inscribed "Noli me tangere"—the women refused to allow him into the meeting because he was a man. Professor Sensodyne said he understood perfectly.

"He's such a shithole!" said Matha.

Then there was the matter of "niggardly zeal" itself, which phrase had been used in a lecture by a careless astronomy professor a couple of years back, and which almost got him fired for his vocabulary. Like all such incidents, this one flared from dustup to furor in less than a day, mainly because rather than letting bad enough alone, the accused made the grave error of trying to explain himself by calling a public meeting to which he brought Webster's Dictionary to supply the correct definition of *niggardly*. The black students at Beet, all eighty-seven, weren't bothered by the professor's usage, and had not raised an eyebrow, much less a voice, against the man. But the Beet radicals, all white, and all five of them, arrived at the meeting in blackface, called for the professor's head, and nearly got it, showing niggardly zeal.

"Matha! Come down! Live with me. I'm moving to a cave! We can be happy in a cave!"

None of these issues was sincerely meant because the students' passions went elsewhere.

What the new radicals at Beet wanted to do was nothing—not to attach themselves to any existing political movement or party, not to do public service and read *Harry Potter* to blind kids, or teach "The Wheels on the Bus" to old people with spittle on their faces, not to put up a Habitat for Humanity house for "some dimwit in New Orleans who couldn't understand a weather report," not to go help some struggling mosquito-ridden country in Africa, or some bird-flu-infected country in Asia, not to build new democratic institutions or to infiltrate existing institutions or companies and radicalize them from the inside or to take the antipodal direction and live on communes, make babies named for vegetables, and smoke dope. Their aims were at once minimal and anarchic. Since in their estimation there was no cause worth marching for and no America waiting to welcome them to its employ, they figured why not simply

Dickie Goldvasser

stop—quit classes, quit college, and if possible go home and live with one's folks? That vision plus the pleasant prospect of doing nothing with one's life is what the students were willing to fight for.

"Or do we want to spend another year on *Will and Grace*?"

She invoked a recent cause célèbre. A Beet graduate had complained in a lawsuit against the Department of Ethnicity, Gender, and Television Studies that, upon applying for a position at Microsoft, he'd presented his honors thesis, "No Transgender Asians on *Will and Grace*: An Oversight or an Insult?" The human resources official not only laughed out loud but called in her coworkers and bosses, Bill Gates among them, to share the fun. "Okay," said Gates after the laughter had subsided. "What did you really study?"

abird

Akim tried to sound adamant. "I shall stand here until you love me!"

Matha filled an ice bucket with hot water from the bathroom, reopened the window, and hit her suitor bull's-eye, drenching his kaffiyeh.

"I am yours forever!" he yelled back.

The nihilistic line appealed to Matha mightily; essentially it was what she'd practiced at Magnolia Blossom, minus the ball gowns and the flowers. Writing poetry was new for her, though, and something of an afterthought. She soon realized looks and southern charm were not the appropriate tools for advancement at a place like Beet. To call oneself a poet, on the other hand— which was all one needed to be one—worked out just fine. Her poetry was marked by synecdoche when it was not marked by catachresis or plain impenetrability, which is why she'd avoided Professor Porterfield's courses, or any of the advanced writing workshops where the students were serious and might give her stuff close reading. On the narrow territory of Beet's outer fringes, however, Matha was the It girl, and on a morning as momentous as this one, it was to her that Beet's radicals turned for direction.

"What do you like mean?" asked Dickie Goldvasser, sole heir to the Goldvasser tungsten fortune in Elko County, Nevada, and who hoped family connections might one day get him into law school. He had hair like shredded carrots and a fearful and astonished gaze. "Like what do you mean, we'll do it for them? Close the college? May I ask how?"

"The tried-and-true approach," Matha said. "We'll disrupt the place. Today is October 16. We've got a little over two months to create time-wasting disturbances."

"Let's kidnap Latin," said Bagtoothian, meaning Latin the Pig, the school mascot, a picture-perfect Large White who was taken to escaping his pen, galumphing around campus, and peeing everywhere with the range and power of a golf course sprinkler. "If he pisses on us we'll kill him and eat him."

"We're not killing anybody," said Matha, to Bagtoothian's distress. She considered. "We'll occupy a building! If the tactic was good enough in the sixties, it's good enough for us."

"But it *wasn't* good enough in the sixties," Dickie protested. "It never worked. Not at Harvard, not at Columbia, or Berkeley. Kids just got themselves like beat up by the cops." His voice quavered. "I don't want to get like beat up."

"Me neither," said Betsy Betsy, a jittery sophomore who was small enough to fit into a case for a sousaphone, and had Betty Boop eyes without the allure. Effervescent at eighteen, in her fifties she would be a dead lightbulb hanging in a basement in Bridgeport.

Betsy feigned loyalty to the party line of no gainful employment, but secretly wanted to forge a career as a media reporter. She rationalized her treachery by concluding that media reporting would not really be working.

"Couldn't we just walk around yelling things in unison?" she said. "I like it when we do that."

Jamie Lattice, a junior, said nothing, but his tiny old man's face twitched at the thought that if he went to jail he might never realize his membership in the New York literati. What he most wanted was to be a New York Public Library Literary Lion, and he was debating whether to write a how-to book or a cookbook to win the honor. Before coming over to Matha's room he'd spent twenty minutes at the mirror, practicing a look that combined Age of Innocence promise with fin de siècle despair.

"For shit's sake!" Matha exploded. "They're not going to beat us up. In the sixties, the colleges didn't give a shit about their shit-ass image because they weren't worried about money. But now they're all going broke, and they're oh-so-careful about how they come across on TV. These shitheads are not going to call the cops, I promise you. They'll call the incident 'unfortunate' or 'disturbing' or 'sad' or some fuck like that." Then she added: "You have to remember: The professors of today were yesterday's protestors."

"But I still don't see why we have to close the college," said Betsy.

"It's a statement," said Matha, who was about to add "shitnose," but held back because she knew Betsy would burst into cartoon-size tears for little or no reason. "We close down Beet College, dear old much-sought-after Beet College, to show the world that college is useless. Who needs it? I mean, look at the situation this morning. That ass-shit Bollovate and his brains-for-shit trustees were about to close the place for a few bucks anyway. What difference does it make who shuts the college down? What is college for? Zip! And what do we do when we graduate? Make indie films about sex in Tribeca? Tread water in graduate school? An M.F.A., for fuck's sake?" The group guffawed. "We're toast! That's the statement we want to make." She considered a moment. "You know what? I think we're the lost generation. That's what I think. We should call ourselves The Lost Generation."

Her comrades were confused but aroused. "That's a great name," said Jamie. "The Lost Generation." He thought of using it in his inaugural essay for *Harper's*.

"What building do you want to take?" asked Bagtoothian, who was watching Akim out the window, still itching to get at him.

That required some discussion. If they took the administration building, it would not mean much because the dither of deans would vacate their offices gladly and await instructions from President Huey. If they took President Huey's office, he would vacate gladly and await instructions from Bollovate or from anyone else with instructions. If they took a departmental building, that would do no damage at all because the faculty members were always ready to turn against the administration on the slightest provocation, or none, or to turn against one another.

Pity, the one professor whom Matha and her cohorts could not count on to betray either the administration or his colleagues was the same Professor Porterfield to whom the salvation of Beet College had been entrusted. That dismayed Matha. In seeking to close Beet down, she was in reality on the side of the trustees, who, the natural businesswoman in her surmised, would rather dump Beet and cut their losses than keep it going. If Peace Porterfield saved the college, said Matha, the radical movement would be no more, since closing the college was their one true cause.

"So let's take Porterfield's office," said Bagtoothian, who merely wanted to push someone down a flight of stairs.

"No. He's too well-liked," Matha said. "It's not a matter of singling out an individual. We have to occupy something that is central to Beet, and better still, central to a liberal arts education in general, so when the rest of the country sees what we've done, they will know that not just Beet College but higher learning itself has been brought to its knees."

"Let's take the Free Speech Zone," said Goldvasser. Everyone chortled. *bah*

The Free Speech Zone, a twelve-by-twelve-foot plot of lawn at the far west end of the campus, was the area in which anyone connected with the college could voice an opinion. It was created in response to complaints, mainly from faculty members, that things were being said in the dorms and the classrooms, on the pathways, and in the bathrooms as well, that offended some people, or could be construed as offending some people, or might have offended some people had the remarks been heard. The first speaker to make use of the new area was a sophomore from Pennsylvania who stood dead center in the grassy square, cupped her hands to her mouth, and shouted that she had mixed feelings about the Quakers.

The students considered, then all five said it at once. "The library! Let's take Bacon Library!"

"The library!" said Dickie.

"The library!" said Betsy.

"The library!" said Bagtoothian, who had not yet set foot in one, but looked forward to the adventure.

"The library?" asked Jamie, who anticipated he would be ill the night of the takeover.

"So it's the library," said Matha.

It was an impeccable choice. How better to put an end to institutions of higher learning—perhaps even to learning itself—than to pull down the very warehouse of learning, the time-honored repository of the best that was ever thought or felt, and keep it from future generations? Bacon Library was the lifeblood of the college. Matha and her comrades had hit upon a course of action at last, and yet an action that would effect inaction, the great work stoppage of the mind.

Not only that: the library displayed the Mayflower Compact—a document, in terms of pure rarity, even more valuable than the Declaration of Independence or the Constitution. Though the original compact did not exist, the William Bradford copy in Bacon was a treasure in part because *Mayflower* passenger Bradford was the first governor of the Plymouth Colony. The document, dated 1630, was signed by John Alden and Miles Standish, among other notables, and was the first written American expression of the intent to "combine together in a civil body politic."

"Damn!" said Matha. "We bring down the library, we bring down the college, we bring down the country!"

"Is that like a good thing?" said Goldvasser.

They looked to one another, but no one knew for sure.

"When do we go? Tonight?" asked Bagtoothian.

"No," said Matha. "It's got to be planned out. I think we should wait till Porterfield's committee is about to make its report to the faculty. There's a meeting on December nineteenth, which is probably when they'll do it. If we go in on the eighteenth, that should shit things up, or fuck them up, or something."

"What do we do in the meantime?" said Lattice, hoping that in the meantime they'd drop the plan.

"Small stuff," said Matha. "Minor annoyances that get in the way of the committee."

The group was happy and high-fived one another to prove it, and low-fived one another as well, and bumped chests and fists. Most of their courses demanded no intellectual effort. But a series of disruptions? That was something they could sink their teeth into.

"Use for the useless!" cried Matha, not entirely sure what she meant.

"Use for the useless!" cried the others.

"My darling! My sweet! My heart is breaking!" Producing his iPod, on which he'd recorded a medley of Syrian love songs, Akim sang along with "My Sheep Are in the Pasture."

Matha nodded to Bagtoothian. "Now."

take over Library instead of kidnap

CHAPTER

3

LIVI WAS ON A TEAR AGAIN. HER EYES BLAZED GREEN, AND she yanked at her hair, which looked on fire. "Keelye Smythe? That snake in the grass? You appointed Keelye Smythe?"

"I can handle him."

"That's what you always say. Jesus, Mary, and Moses! I married a babe in the woods!"

"I know what Keelye is, but he's also smart."

"Everybody's smart. But not everybody's good."

"Well, pickings weren't exactly cherse."

"Because the only people who want to join committees are jerks."

That was their conversation of the previous night, when Peace told Livi whom he had named to the CCR, the shorthand by which Peace's committee on curriculum reform was now known. He'd used the two days since the Day of the Bollovate to select the members. He knew he might have done better, but he was pressed for time—two months to come up with a plan to save the college— and while it may have been hard for Livi to believe, the six he'd come up with appeared to be the best of the applicant pool.

Pickings from Peace's own department had been the slimmest. Apart from Smythe, applicants included the minor poet Willa

willa ~~Bee~~ George   Johnny   Larry
                         Claque   Gunderson

George, founder of the Beets, a local group in the 1960s who re-
belled against Kerouac's bunch, pooh-poohed jazz, ridiculed Zen,
said no to drugs, and wrote blank verse; Johnny Claque, the only
independently wealthy department member, who'd struck it rich
with a bodice-ripper, and was said to be one; and Larry Gunder-
son, the Shakespearean who could recite the 128th Sonnet in 5.3
seconds, and could not be stumped on questions about Edmund
Spenser, no matter how hard one tried.

Manning had told him so—"I told you so"—earlier in the day,
when Peace was putting his committee together. "This assignment
will bring you in contact with every mad dog in the college."

"Very helpful. Instead of being so all-knowing," said Peace,
"why don't you serve on the CCR yourself?"

"Because I only *look* crazy."

On the morning of October 17, Peace crossed the quad of the
Old Pen toward the CCR's first meeting in Bacon Library. He was
already beginning to feel he'd entered a new world, and in some
ways he had. He had never served on a major committee, much less
headed one, either here or at Yale, where a lowly assistant professor
was not accorded the honor. One of the less substantive reasons he
was so well-liked at Beet was that he had not been involved in its
business. All he knew about being a professor was ~~students,~~ teaching, and learning, and this skewed and narrow prospect of academic life deprived him of the full, rich picture.

"Down with Beet! Close the college!" chanted Matha and her
band of revolutionaries. They stomped back and forth on the
lawn.

"You want to close the college?" Peace asked them as he walked
past. But they kept chanting and drowned him out.

Reaction from the faculty to the news of his assignment was as
swift as Matha Polite's. It ran the gamut from sneering contempt to
indifferent contempt. As long as young Professor Porterfield kept
his head down, there had been no reason to anoint him with the
traditional loathing reserved for the prominent. But, as the Japanese say, the nail that sticks up is the one that gets hammered. On

the other hand, Peace's sudden celebrity, however shaky, opened the path for others to share in it. So the outward response of his colleagues—save Manning, of course—was boisterous bonhomie, which gave Peace the willies.

But the sight of Bacon was always reassuring to him. One of the few structures not built in the small-college idiom, the library filled the south end of the stockade of the Old Pen, grand and solid, its dusty Ionic columns crowned by volutes curled downward like inverted scrolls. Something about the height of the steps and the stylobate made the building appear even larger than it was, and when taken in from a distance, it seemed forbidding, like a bank vault. Perhaps for that reason, some years earlier an anonymous wag chalked a notice on the outer wall that read: "This is not the library. The library is inside."

"Professor Porterfield?"—Peace was about to mount the steps. "We've never been formally introduced. I'm Professor Marigold Jefferson—of the I Am Woman Center?" She wore her hair in tight blond curls, which though real, looked like a wig. And she had the half-sloshed eyes of a giraffe, and seemed as tall. Peace nodded. He knew little about her, save that the previous spring she'd written and performed a one-woman play at the Beet Theater Club, called *Yeast,* in which she dressed as the infection. Reviewers found it "vile yet brave."

"I hope you won't find this presumptuous," she said. "But I just wanted to say that whatever curriculum you come up with, it should feature the work of Mariah Carey. Don't you agree?"

"I'm not sure I understand you," said Peace. Jefferson was the sort of person he feared most from his childhood—sixties-generation friends of his parents who used a stare of aggressive innocence to coax others into crazy and dangerous situations.

"You know my work on Mariah Carey?" she asked.

"I'm afraid I don't."

"It's considered seminal. I've been writing a book-length essay on Mariah as the nexus of American song and dance. It would fit into the new curriculum beautifully, don't you think?"

Not knowing what to say, Peace smiled faintly and continued on, but had not progressed three steps when the radicals' favorite, Tufts Godwin—Professor Sensodyne of the Sensitivity and Diversity Council—called his name. Godwin had hair like a thatched roof with no house under it, and the vague and hulking form of a woolly mammoth. Peace had successfully avoided his company for four years, but, as Manning had predicted, after the Day of the Bollovate there would be no avoiding anyone.

"A word, Professor Porterfield?" His eyes seemed to peer out from pallets of fur, with the sharp and brainless scrutiny of an animal. "I'm sure you must be sensitive to this, but you and your committee have a great opportunity to do something for the plagiarists."

"What are you talking about?" That came out more harshly than Peace intended.

"Well, you know how poorly they are thought of, I mean still, right now, as if we weren't living in the twenty-first century." Peace kept waiting for a signal to laugh. "We at S and D have come to think of plagiarists as our last civil rights issue. For God's sake, some Neanderthals still treat them like lepers."

"But they *should* be treated like lepers," said Peace. "They're thieves." It came to him that Godwin chaired a committee that had let off a sophomore charged with plagiarizing Emerson's *Self-Reliance* word for word, changing only "whoso would be a man must be non-conformist" to "whoso would be a person with human feelings." The student had explained his work as an *homage*.

"I guess I should have realized," said Godwin, turning on his heels. "They would have appointed a conservative."

Out of nowhere, Dean Wee Willy Baedeker rushed up and pressed a sheet of paper into Peace's hand. Baedeker, whose life's ambition was to appear on public television, was sort of a reverse centaur in miniature. He had the body of a small man and the head of a pony. "Read it," he said. "Give me some feedback." He trotted away.

Peace read:

Ferritt Lawrence

"Professor Porterfield?" Now it was Ferritt Lawrence, a reporter
on the *Pig's Eye*, the college ("Beet is Our Beat") daily. Lawrence
had a brilliantine head and a face on which curiosity battled with
ignorance, and lost. He was majoring—or concentrating, as it was
called at Beet—in communications arts, and was writing his senior honors thesis, "The Media: Has It Lost Its Credibility?" Naturally, he was pursuing the story of Peace's committee. "Rumors
were swirling," he wrote in his notepad. "They are spreading like
wildfire."

"What can you give me?" he asked. "I was hoping for a far-
ranging interview."

"Nothing," said Peace. "The committee is meeting for the first
time this morning. Even so, it wouldn't be a good idea to talk until we really have a plan"—with the smile he'd given Marigold Jefferson.

"The people have a right to know, Professor."

Entering Bacon at last, Peace was tempted to cry "Sanctuary!"
and had just tossed Baedeker's memo when he noticed Akim Ben
Laden seated at a carrel, his head in his hands. He'd had the boy
in a seminar on Conrad the previous year, and though Akim was
loony, he was also bright and sweet-natured. Besides, it came as
something of a relief to encounter a nutcase who knew that he
was one.

"What's the matter?" Peace asked, realizing the question might
be too open-ended.

"Homeland Security, Professor Porterfield."

"It's interfering with your work as a terrorist?" He indicated he
was kidding.

"No. It's the only concentration I could get into. And it's awful. I can't find a single professor to talk to because all the courses are online. Besides, I think there's only one professor in the department."

"Why not switch out?" Peace had only just learned about the Homeland Security department. It was dreamed up by Bollovate and Huey over the previous summer, when no faculty were around to vote it up or down. The brochure (online) advertised Homeland Security as "the nation's leading growth sector," and said the concentration would lead to careers in law enforcement, public safety, SWAT team memberships, and hazmat expertise. Homeland Security required no classrooms, none of the paraphernalia of real courses, and only the one professor mentioned by Akim, an ex–New York cop named Billy Pinto, who was kicked off the force for firing his weapon at a slow-cooking steak on a grill during a police department barbecue in Ozone Park, Queens.

"I can't switch," said Akim. "The other concentrations are all filled. I wanted Communications Arts, but I was rejected by Professor Lipman's How to Write for the *New York Times* course—the prerequisite for the concentration."

"I thought you were a straight-A student."

"I am. Professor Lipman said the *Times* only wanted straight-A-minus students."

Peace gulped. Joan Lipman, a former editor of the recently instituted *Times* Young Gay and Straight Celebrity Styles section, was on his committee. He'd put her there because if he hadn't included someone from the New Pen, he would have been accused of reactionary traditionalism. "Why is she looking for A-minuses?"

"She said it's the only acceptable standard for the paper. She said a record of straight A-minuses indicates a student will give back just what the teacher says but with some special words included in the pieces to add flair. The *Times* favors 'brio' and 'luminous.' I told her I wanted to write arts criticism. I mentioned Bernard Malamud. She said, 'Who's that?' I said, 'Who's Bernard Malamud? Only one of the two or three greatest writers of the twentieth century.' She said, 'There you go, Akim'—assuring me that she had only the warmest feelings toward Muslims—'everyone knows it's Philip Roth who is one of the two or three greatest writers of the twentieth century. The *Book Review* said so.' Then she said, 'I've never heard of Mr. Malamute'!"

"I could take you in English," Peace said.

"No thanks, Professor Porterfield. The English have done too much harm to my fellow Arabs." He glanced about. "You haven't seen Matha Polite today, have you?" Peace shook his head. "You know, I'm deeply in love with her, but she told me that if I went near her, she'd mace my balls."

"Why don't you find another girl?"

"Better than Matha?"

BY THE TIME PEACE CLIMBED THE SHORT FLIGHT OF STAIRS to the conference room, he'd hoped the mad dogs of the day were behind him. But when he opened the door, there was his committee. They were seated around the refectory table, each face turned toward him like a heliotropic plant. He surveyed them counterclockwise: there was Penny Kettlegorf from Fine Arts, Heine Heilbrun from the Theater Department, Molton Kramer from History, John Petersen Booth from Chemistry, Keelye Smythe, his English Department colleague, and Joan A-minus Lipman. At Peace's appearance, all six broke into applause, and Kettlegorf, who tended to express her thoughts musically, sang "We've Only Just Begun to Live."

"Professor Porterfield," said Kettlegorf, "I believe I've come up with a new curriculum that should solve all our problems!" She was a gangly brunette with a face full of aimless enthusiasms, a serrulate mouth, and hands like fronds, which she would flap rhythmically in states of excitement, which were frequent. Unmarried, she claimed to have given her heart to a ship's captain who never returned from sea, and for whom she had pined as a younger woman and paced a widow's walk wearing widow's weeds. The story was undercut by the fact that she'd grown up in Lawrence, Kansas, but no one bothered to make much of it.

"That's great, Penny," said Peace. "We're eager to hear it."

"But Professor Kramer has a plan, too," said Heilbrun. An epigraph without a text, Heilbrun, a bachelor, expressed himself in tones that yoked fear with stupefaction. His hands were hairless, and he was so devoid of definition that had he perished in a blaze, no one could have identified the teeth. Yet he dressed theatrically, usually in Edwardian outfits. Today he was wearing a Wedgewood—navy tailcoat, plain blue waistcoat, and striped trousers.

"I have a plan, too," confirmed Kramer, whose wife kept a mother-of-pearl-plated revolver under her pillow. His echolalia was mitigated by his tendency to repeat himself.

"We'll hear both plans," said Peace.

"Me first," said Kettlegorf.

"I don't have a plan," said Booth. "Is that all right?"

"Of course," said Peace.

Booth's face bore the austerity of a Viking king, though one on the verge of surrender. He camouflaged his smell of sweat with Rugby Players cologne, but only half successfully. "Will Mr. Bollovate know whose plan is adopted?" he said. He had not met Bollovate personally, but once sent him a complimentary note (as he did to everyone at Beet at one time or another), and he had long been of the opinion that when it came to self-advancement, one well-placed complimentary note was worth a thousand real accomplishments.

"I have a few thoughts as well," said Smythe, who was everything Livi said he was. He was in his early sixties, and looked like an enlarged altar boy—not grown up, just bigger. His face was an aquarelle: sandy hair, mottled with faint grays and whites; pale aquamarine eyes; limpid skin around the cheekbones; and the broad expanse of forehead often indicative of candor and nobility, and sometimes not.

Of all the faculty at Beet, Smythe had most successfully mastered the art of academic acceptability. In the 1960s, he marched in every student protest, including one against his own department. In the early 1970s, he grew his hair long and wore a Nehru jacket to formal events. He also picked up the guitar, albeit a few years late, so he put it down shortly thereafter. In the 1980s, he attached Save the Whales stickers to the fenders of his Volvo, which were replaced by Save the Seals in the 1990s and Save the Children in 2004, which he attached to his Prius. He knew all the right initials and said them frequently—TLS, PBS, NPR, SUV. He said poetic things about the Red Sox. Perhaps the surest sign of his social skills was that he showed just the right proportions in expressing contempt for his colleagues when they were in trouble—three parts sanctimony, one part understanding.

"I'm so very sorry about Margaret," he'd told Manning weeks after her funeral.

"Don't make it worse," Manning said.

Smythe's wife Ada was a Lacoste. Her fortune assured her husband, whose parents had run a poorhouse in Eau Claire, Wisconsin, that he'd never set foot in one himself, along with a lifetime supply of shirts. Behind her back he remarked that Ada was so boring, even if she murdered him the police would not consider her "a person of interest." Then he would laugh.

"I'm keen to hear your plan, Keelye, whatever it may be," said Professor Lipman. She had a voice like desiccated fruit, and was said to be married to a submariner in New London who spent four-fifths of the year underwater and had reenlisted nine times. "Of course, I'm keen to hear all the plans."

Lipman was uncomfortable in academic surroundings, and hoped the other committee members would recognize her as an intellectual as well as a journalist. Manning had once remarked to Peace that she had the mind of a Hallmark bereavement card, but less feeling.

"I would like to say, however," she went on, "that whatever we propose, Communications Arts should stand at the center. Not only is it the most profitable of the concentrations"—Smythe eyed her enviously—"communication itself is so essential to the community these days. Without people communicating what they have to communicate, where would the community be?"

"Shall I proceed?" asked Kettlegorf. All nodded. "You know, students love to perform. Sing. Act in plays. Dance. I used to do that as a girl. Dance and dance!" She sailed into a shrill rendition of "I Could Have Danced All Night," whirling in her seat and heaving with jactitations, to which the others responded with dead stares. "Anyway, we could devise a curriculum in which all the disciplines are converted into performing arts. Instead of merely reading *Paradise Lost*, for instance, we could turn the poem into a mime show. Or an old Harlem tap-dance competition. Or a hippity-hop concert with El Al Cold Jay. Think of it! History as opera! Botany in folk songs! Why, I'm composing a country-and-western song about Gregor Mendel in my head right now!" She became a coliseum of exclamations. "And then . . . and then . . . as a sort of final project for the entire college, we present a mixed-media *mélange* performed on the lawn of the Old Pen, in which students dress up as disciplines and sing, and all the disciplines begin in a cacophony of self-assertions, as if competing for dominance, and then, merely by rearranging the clashing notes, suddenly explode in pure harmony. All of learning coming together in a better world! A brave new world! Parents in the audience, the trustees, the deans, our colleagues, on their feet and applauding a revolution of thought bursting into existence right before their eyes!" Her own were like a spooked horse's. "Why, it tires me out to think about it! I'm pooped!"

"Me too," said Smythe. Heilbrun smirked. Lipman looked around to see how to react.

"My plan involves the great battles of history," said the military historian Kramer, taking advantage of the silence. His eyes were fogged goggles. "It's simple, really. We give lectures on the major clashes of a war, then the students go to the gym, where they divide into armies and move toy soldiers around the gym floor to simulate actual battles. And they could dress up as soldiers, too! Fusiliers could carry real fusils! Once the students really got into playing with toy soldiers, they would understand history with hands-on excitement."

To demonstrate his idea, he'd brought along a shoe box full of toy doughboys and grenadiers, and was about to reenact the Battle of Verdun on the committee table when Heilbrun stayed his hand. "We get it," he said.

"That's quite interesting, Molton," said Booth. "But is it rigorous enough?"

At the mention of the word, everyone, save Peace, sat up straight.

"Rigor is so important," said Kettlegorf.

"We must have rigor," said Booth.

"You may be sure," said the offended Kramer, "I never would propose anything lacking rigor."

Smythe inhaled and looked at the ceiling. "I think I may have something of interest," he said, as if he were at a poker game and was about to disclose a royal flush. "My proposal is called 'Icons of Taste.' It would consist of a galaxy of courses affixed to several departments consisting of lectures on examples of music, art, architecture, literature, and other cultural areas a student needed to indicate that he or she was sophisticated."

"Why would a student want to do that?" asked Booth.

"Perhaps sophistication is not a problem for chemists," said Smythe. Lipman tittered.

"What's the subject matter?" asked Heilbrun. "Would it have rigor?"

"Of course it would have rigor. Yet it would also attract those additional students Bollovate is talking about." Smythe inhaled again. "The material would be carefully selected," he said. "One would need to pick out cultural icons the students were likely to bring up in conversations for the rest of their lives, so that when they spoke, others would recognize their taste as being exquisite yet eclectic and unpredictable."

"You mean Rembrandt?" said Kramer.

Smythe smiled with weary contempt. "No, I do not mean Rembrandt. I don't mean Beethoven or Shakespeare either, unless something iconic has emerged about them to justify their more general appeal."

"You mean, if they appeared on posters," said Lipman.

"That's it precisely."

Lipman blushed with pride.

"The subject matter would be fairly easy to amass," Smythe said.

"We could all make up a list off the top of our heads. Einstein—who does have a poster." He nodded to the ecstatic Lipman. "Auden, for the same reason. Students would need to be able to quote "September 1939" or at least the last lines. And it would be good to teach "Musée des Beaux Arts" as well, which is off the beaten path, but not garishly. Mahler certainly. But Cole Porter too. And Sondheim, I think. Goya. Warhol, it goes without saying, Stephen Hawking, Kurosawa, Bergman, Bette Davis. They'd have to come up with some lines from *Dark Victory*, or better still, *Jezebel*. *La Dolce Vita*. *Casablanca*. *King of Hearts*. And Orson, naturally. *Citizen Kane*, I suppose, though personally I prefer *F for Fake*."

"Judy!" cried Heilbrun.

"Yes, Judy too. But not 'Over the Rainbow.' It would be more impressive for them to do 'The Trolley Song,' don't you think?" Kettlegorf hummed the intro.

"*Guernica*," said Kramer. "Robert Capa."

"Edward R. Murrow," said Lipman.

"No! Don't be ridiculous!" said Smythe, ending Lipman's brief foray into the world of respectable thought.

"Marilyn Monroe!" said Kettlegorf.

"Absolutely!" said Smythe, clapping to indicate his approval.

"And the Brooklyn Bridge," said Booth, catching on. "And the Chrysler Building."

"Maybe," said Smythe. "But I wonder if the Chrysler Building isn't becoming something of a cliché."

Peace had had enough. "And you want students to nail this stuff so they'll do well at cocktail parties?"

Smythe sniffed criticism, always a tetchy moment for him. "You make it sound so superficial," he said.

"Shall we move on?" said Peace.

But his committee looked deflated. They just sat mum and buried their heads.

"Okay," Peace said. "Don't worry. It's only the first day. We'll get there." And they adjourned.

On the way back to his office, he broke into a run.

Max Byrd

CHAPTER 4

SO IT WENT FOR THE FOLLOWING TWO WEEKS, WITH STU-
dents and faculty growing more edgy, Peace more anxious, Manning more bitterly amused, Matha more strident, Ferritt Lawrence
more journalistic, Akim Ben Laden more frustrated with the Homeland Security Department, and the CCR more feckless, meeting after fruitless meeting. Oddly, the one who seemed least agitated by
the situation he'd set in motion was Joel Bollovate, and thus Lewis
Huey was calm as well.

stress

calm

Livi was not calm. At night, after her husband's reports of another day of failure, she'd go upstairs and surf the Net for openings for hand surgeons, preferably in the Boston area, but not
exclusively.

Then, on the day after Halloween, and just before two o'clock
classes, a senior named Max Byrd noticed something unusual
about the Henry Moore *Two Piece Reclining Man* that had com-
manded the lawn of the New Pen for five decades: It was gone.
Where the two pieces had reclined lay depressions in the earth
bearing their imprints—soft, damp, wormy, and vacant. It seemed
very odd that no one had noticed the disappearance of the vast
object earlier in the day, as the New Pen was heavily trafficked. But
Max, a self-confessed computer geek—who attended Beet on a

Herb Sherman Scholarship awarded to an undergraduate deemed "nice, normal and bright" (and difficult to win because of the first two qualifications)—yet one of Professor Porterfield's sharper students, was an observant young man, able to see absent as well as present things.

He had hair the color of a Hershey bar, and wore round rimless eyeglasses and a thick mustache with a neatly trimmed beard—all of which could not disguise his boyish face or an expression that bore a rapturous love of learning. Max was from Lindaville, Alabama (pop. 4,600), where his father owned the feed store. Until he'd arrived at the Beet train station, he'd never taken a taxi before. Until he met Professor Porterfield, he'd wanted to take the taxi back. Max was encumbered with a tendency never to say a thing he didn't mean, but was otherwise suited for college life. When he went to report his discovery to his favorite professor, he recalled the Wallace Stevens lines he'd learned in one of Peace's classes, about the nothing that was not there and the nothing that is.

"You're kidding," said Peace, who thanked the boy for the tip about the Moore and headed from the English Department to the New Pen to see the nothing for himself. How to explain it? The abduction might have been a Halloween prank from the previous night, though the prankster would have had to use a crane and two large flatbed trucks, one for each reclining half.

Thinking he was the bearer of news, Peace strode toward College Hall and into the president's office. The door read DR. LEWIS HUEY. The "Dr." was honorary, awarded by Huey to Huey at his inauguration.

"You won't believe this," Peace said to Huey, who did. The missing Moore did not at all come as a surprise to the president, who explained that upon conferring with Joel Bollovate (*conferring* being his word), he'd had the sculpture removed and taken to Rockport. Peace asked why.

"To sell it," said Huey, as blithely as if he'd been asked why beavers build dams.

"Sell it? Sell a Henry Moore? How could you do that?" The question was not merely accusatory. Apart from the absurdity of selling an invaluable work of art, how, legally, could the college make a profit off what had been a munificent gift? The Moore had been donated in 1954 (when alumni were still making munificent gifts to Beet) by a local wealthy mortgage broker who never liked it, and quipped during the transfer that he'd just had the thing lying around. College officials chuckled politely and grabbed up the sculpture.

Moore sculpture

"Oh, the legal stuff is taken care of," said Huey, leaning back in his chair, his arms cradling his head like a pair of angel wings, and looking both in charge and scared witless. "Joel Bollovate explained it all to me. Actually, selling the Moore was Joel's idea [as if Peace needed to be told that]. I think the college is going to realize $14 million, before Joel's commission."

"He took a commission?"

"Business is business." Huey could rearrange his face, which had the folds of a shar-pei's, to suit any situation. This one called for the look of an insider. "That's what Joel said."

"Great," said Peace, who saw nothing more could be accomplished by talking to Huey.

The selling of the Henry Moore was but the latest in Beet's commercial ventures since Bollovate had taken over as chairman of the board. Last fall, the college launched an effort to sell various parts of the campus—not to be removed, as was the Moore, but rather to display the names of the donors. Their efforts had been impeded by the first faint whispers about the college's closing, suggesting that the trustees were advertising immortality but selling obsolescence.

They began by offering whole structures that bore no names as yet, from the departmental offices to the indoor garage to the field house and the football field itself, where for one million dollars one could have one's name carved permanently into the fifty-yard line. Since the teams, both home and visitors, rarely made it as far as the fifty, the donor's name was likely to remain pristine.

When there were no takers for the million-dollar names, the college offered individual slabs and bricks in the buildings for anything from $10,000 for a brick to $25,000 for a slab. But again, no buyer was interested. They tried to sell the paving stones on the pathways for $500 apiece, calling it a "Walk of Fame," and were rejected even by Donald Trump, whom Bollovate called a "close personal friend." (Bollovate was called the same thing by Mr. Trump.) Finally, they offered the parquet floor tiles in the vestibule of the student center for $5 a tile. Here they made a sale. Gregory, the security guard, bought one for four one-dollar bills, three quarters, two dimes, and two pennies (the college forgave the difference). After his name was inscribed he would sneak away from the front gate, stare at his purchase, and murmur, "Rhandor."

There even was talk of making Latin the Pig available for branding. The Bring Home the Bacon butchers offered $500 to have its name burned into Latin's hide. But when the students got wind of it, they staged an "Ightnay orfay Atinlay in which the pig was paraded back and forth, albeit carefully, and was cheered lustily with "Avesay Our Igpay!" They took up a collection and raised $500 to keep Latin brand-free. The honoree spewed his gratitude all round.

On the cost-cutting side of the ledger, Mrs. Whiting was told that her workweek in the English Department was to be limited to three days, and her salary reduced proportionately. When Peace learned of it, he offered to help her out with extra work. She declined with thanks and a what-can-you-do shrug.

If there were a third side to the ledger, it would show that the college continued to accept applications for the following year— and more to the point, Bollovate's point—application fees. Manning observed to Peace that while other colleges were competing for students by offering discounts, laptops, and other swag, Beet had its hands in their pockets.

"And if we close shop," said Manning, "there won't be enough lawyers in Massachusetts to handle the lawsuits. Wait and see."

There was more: "Did you know Huey is requiring quarterly reports from the departments?" Manning asked Peace. "No, of course you didn't. You live on a higher plane."

"Quarterly reports on what?"

"Enrollment. Income from tuition. Price points. Yields. In

short—" Peace started to make the time-out T. "Yes! The bottom line. I keep trying to explain this to you. It's simple. Ask for an accounting every three months, and the employees—you and I—start to run scared. We have to meet expectations, like any Wall Street–driven company. We have to *produce*—In an institution where the product isn't visible. The goal is money, man, and make it quick. So, what does one do to show a gain every quarter? Lower! Lower quality, lower standards. You think you're going to draw new students without diluting what little we have left?"

"I'm going to try," said Peace.

"Well, good luck, my boy. But the fact is, we've plunged straight to the bottom line and are headed down from there. Did I ever tell you my theory about that?"

The way things were going, Peace was not very hopeful he would persuade Bollovate the sale of the Moore was ill-advised, as some of his colleagues might say, or as Livi might, crooked, stupid, and wrong. Nonetheless, Livi's Candide decided to give it a shot and make the one-hour drive to Bollovate's office in Cambridge, in one of the new high-rises near Harvard Square. After all, he reasoned, only two weeks earlier Bollovate had said the college could be saved by a new curriculum. Why sell off valuable property?

But Bollovate had a previous appointment in Boston, and only a minute to spare. He was just finishing a large bowl of succotash, his favorite dish. On his desk lay antique paper pressed between glassine sheets.

"Are those surveys?" Peace asked. "They look old. Colonial?"

"Yeah. I'm interested in property lines."

"For developments?"

"Yeah. For developments."

Peace scanned the office. The walls were covered with framed bank checks, the trophies of a lifetime of real estate deals. One dated back to a Lego set Bollovate had sold to a schoolmate at the age of nine. He'd cleared $4.25 on that one.

On either side of Bollovate's desk stood flags on poles. One was the American flag; the other, the standard of Bollocorps, which was bright green and showed a smiling house with a sign on the lawn reading SOLD! In a corner leaned a gold-plated shovel bearing the legend "To J.B., Man of the Soil."

Bollovate scraped his bowl clean and stood to leave, saying merely that the sale of the Henry Moore was a sweetheart of a deal, that the buyer, whom he called a sucker, grossly overpaid, that Beet needed the dough, or hadn't Peace noticed, and good-bye.

"If I were you, Professor Porterfield"—leading Peace down the elevator and out the door—"I'd focus on curricular reform, and leave the fund-raising to the trustees, who know what they're doing. Us bean counters—remember? Temporary fugit. Carpet diem. Time's a-wastin'. Come to think of it, how's your committee coming along?"

"We're getting there," Peace lied. "But is losing a Henry Moore a smart way to raise funds?"

Bollovate settled the iron belly into the black pleather of the back seat of his Cadillac Escalade and motioned his driver to move on. He waved to Peace like the Queen. The tinted window rose shut, leaving the professor standing on the sidewalk in front of the Harvard Coop confronting his own reflection in the dark glass, and looking like, well, a professor.

Yet Bollovate was right; time was a-wastin'. And after nine committee meetings so far, Peace was seeing a lot more waste in his future. For the hell of it, he'd again asked Manning to join the committee. Manning ducked as though a missile had been aimed at his head.

"That's what you do," said Peace.

"What's that?"

"Duck."

Manning shrugged.

Faculty members not on the CCR were free to carp about it, which they had done for the past two weeks, and which they did about most things that did not require their direct participation. Their glee at what they supposed would be the committee's destined failure was somewhat compromised by the fact that when it failed, they'd be out of work.

Not that the pedagogical life at the college came to a stop during this time, or even a pause. Courses in the Old Pen limped on as ever. Students found them adequate (barely), yet the traditional courses seemed country cousins compared with the New Pen offerings. Tried-and-true concentrations like English, history, and government had perhaps grown too tried-and-true—not because of any overt failings so much as because professors had lost confidence in them. They were too aware of the hipper classes occurring on the other side of College Hall, even though the crowds of students were often attracted to the New Pen because the courses were both easier and loopy. To be fair, this was not true of them all, or of all the parts of any one. Still, professors in the New Pen smirked at those in the Old, who smirked back at them for opposite reasons. It all came out even. Students bored to tears with the traditional offerings produced tears of rage or derision at the new ones, as Akim Ben Laden did regarding Homeland Security. Until or unless an interesting curriculum might be devised (did anyone really think it would happen?), the status quo remained in less jeopardy than the college.

Undergraduate organizations continued to solicit new members, though they had a hard time persuading their fellow students to join up when the college was about to buy the farm. Hardy nonetheless, they set up their booths in the Pens and waited—the Beet Buddhist and Karate Club, Bengalis Unite, Berliners for Rebuilding the Wall, WPIG, Jacobean Bloodletters, Brothers for Lynn Cheney, Baptists for Fornication, Equestrian Hillel, Christians for Jesus, Pre-Raphaelite Readers (James Lattice, pres.), Haitian Ballroom Dancing, Fuck Foucault, Chicana Frisbee, and Up with Goats. Only a handful of students stopped by the booths, which sagged like a bazaar after a rainstorm. Even the usually oversubscribed Future Animated Sitcom Writers of America and Future Network Presidential Historians drew no one.

In the wider world, news of Beet's predicament was seeping into America without incurring too much agitation, at least initially, supporting Manning's prediction about public opinion on American colleges. On October 20 the trustees had sent out a press release about the possible closing, and the proposed solution to the problem. But it was phrased so positively, the papers that picked it up featured the story as little more than a filler. Other American colleges were in similar fixes, even if the loss of a whole endowment was unusual, but who pays attention to the autarkies of non-profits?

Still, the arthritic Beet alumni distributed over the country at the Beet Club of Cincinnati and the Beet Clubs of Bismarck, Kalamazoo, Walla Walla, and elsewhere, cocked their heads when they read the item on page 7 or page 8 below the fold. The news especially irked the oldest Beet families, whose New England names were on the dorms and whose frowsy scions dwelled in mansions with peeling paint near Brattle Street in Cambridge. They hobbled around unpolished floors on aluminum canes, wore cardigans with holes at the elbows, cooked popcorn on hot plates, and watched black-and-white TVs with rabbit ears that rested on piles of unopened bills. Their thermostats were kept at 60 degrees. At the Beet commencements, they hailed each other in loud patrician voices, usually in the middle of someone's speech.

But they were not to be trifled with. When they recalled the locations of their Remington typewriters, they fired off furious letters. They yelled in surround-sound. What the hell was going on? And who was this Bollovate anyway? A JEW? A WOP? A NEGRO?

Slowly the world of education was becoming riled as well. Beet College no more? Coca-Cola no more? The Ford Motor Company no more? Some institutions simply represent the breed. And Beet was one of these. When people wanted to indicate natural intelligence, they would say, "Well, I may not have gone to Beet, but . . ." Lesser institutions would identify themselves as "the Beet of the South" or "the West." High schools judged it an official "reach" college. And those who did get in were hated for it all their lives.

Perhaps the surest indication of its catbird seat among American colleges was that Beet undergraduates never admitted they went there. Instead, when asked, they'd say they went "to school north of Boston" or (rarely) "to school southeast of Derry, New Hampshire." Everyone knew what they meant thus, to avoid saying Beet outright was doubly irritating.

Jerry
Jejunum

The disappearance of Beet was unthinkable except to those who thought about it. So the college turned to its head of public relations, Jerry Jejunum, who'd been picked for the job because he was born with an indentation in the parietal lobe that made him incapable of telling the truth. Jerry composed a form letter assuring all concerned not to be concerned; "Dear old Beet will soon be on its feet." He hoped his mantra would catch on nation-wide.

But Manning was right about the parents of Beet undergraduates, who, not so easily gulled, asked, "Why exactly am I paying forty thousand?"

November now lay upon the campus like a painter's drop cloth splotched with zinc grays and badger grays and destroyer grays. The month marked the onset of New England's murder/suicide season, in which Homer, tired of staring at the back of Jethro's head for the past thirty years, decides to blow it off, followed by his own. In this season, one recalls only one's mistakes and wrongdoings. Large quantities of sleeping pills change hands, as do copies of *Ethan Frome*. Phone calls are placed to high school sweethearts of years past. Viewers are glued to C-Span.

Driving back from Bollovate's, Peace figured he had seven weeks to fulfill the trustees' assignment—less than that, actually, since the Christmas holidays started on December 21, and final exams were the week before that. The board had asked for the report before the end of term. Counting backward, he calculated it had to be ready for the full faculty meeting scheduled for December 19, as Matha Polite had guessed, when it would be voted up or down. Yet in this case, down would not be acceptable. Down meant down for the ship. The new curriculum, whatever it might be, not only had to win the support of the Beet College faculty, but the support had to be all-out—a daunting task, since there were more political constituencies on the faculty than professors.

Parents Weekend was coming up, along with Veterans Day. Then, too, there was a whole set of new college holidays that would intervene between now and the end of term, and on which no committee work, or work of any kind, could be done.

Sensitivity Day, always scheduled for early November, was established to memorialize the community triumph in 1998, when especially sensitive college faculty, students, and Beet citizens (the number totaled eleven)—led by Professor Sensodyne—won their bitter fight against the town council to replace the Slow Children street signs with Please Be Careful As Younger People May Be Entering the Roadways signs. The group determined that the former signs conveyed a "hurtful insult" to mentally disadvantaged youngsters everywhere, and, after a five-year battle of attrition, prevailed. For the council there were two issues at stake. One was that the proposal was "horseshit," and the other, that the extra words on the warnings would increase the size of the signs and the steel and paint used in their manufacture, and would cost the town an additional $28,000 a year. But the opposing group asked, "What price sensitivity?"

The answer turned out to be, "Higher than you think," since the additional $28,000 had to come out of the fund for a special wing for the mentally disadvantaged at a nearby children's hospital.

"It's my favorite holiday," Manning told Peace every year. "I celebrate by torturing small animals in front of toddlers, and vice versa."

On Sensitivity Day some years back, Manning counted how many times Hitler's name had been invoked. He'd reckoned it was twice more than during the Third Reich.

There were panels on reparation payments proposed for any people ever harmed by the U.S. government. The list of injurees began with African-American descendents of slaves and was soon expanded to include Koreans, the Vietnamese, Granadans, Panamanians, Bosnians, Cubans, the French and Indians, the British, and as an afterthought, the Germans and Japanese. There were seminars on how to address older people, shorter people, taller people, and lately, poorly-thought-of people who heretofore had been overlooked, such as dentists, lawyers, airline employees, congressmen, senators, cable TV installers, building contractors, and insensitive people themselves. Journalists were on the list initially, but Professor Lipman persuaded the group that to call journalists not-well-thought-of would be "hurtful."

Dr. Bucky Lookatme

On Sensitivity Day this year, Manning once again planned to press his motion to add white Protestants from New Canaan, Connecticut, to the poorly-thought-of list, which had been tabled last year for being "frivolous." He was delighted to learn it was expected to pass with enthusiasm. And a protest was awaited from the Robert Bly Man's Manliness Society against the event itself, which the Bly group condemned as "sissyish."

The day was known by its celebrants as "S Day," and had its own hand signal, like the victory V. Since forming the S required the use of both hands touching at the thumbs (the left held below the right, so that the letter would be backward to the ones who made it yet correct for those facing it), one could not give the sign while holding packages, or holding anything. That sometimes made for physically awkward moments as books, groceries, and occasionally babies had to be laid on the ground before the signal could be given. But since fewer than a dozen faculty members, and no students, remembered either the S sign or how to make it, the inconvenience was deemed minor.

Also on the school calendar was How to Prepare for the Holidays Day—"my second favorite," said Manning—always held the week before Thanksgiving, the components of which were so complicated and muzzy, the problem that once occupied a mere town meeting on Sensitivity Day now required a day of its own. The activities included formal debates regarding public displays of religious symbols such as "The Crèche: Pro or Con?" and "The Menorah: Yes or No?" along with panel discussions of "Atheist Rights," which involved the suggestion that the baby Jesus be removed from the Nativity scene. The panel "Should We Place a Menorah in the Crèche?" was the most successful.

The highlight of every How to Prepare for the Holidays Day was a sermon in the Temple by Dr. Bucky Lookatme, the college chaplain (a full-blooded Cherokee who had been converted to Christianity by Billy Graham himself, when the evangelist's train had made a whistle stop at Lookatme's Arizona reservation), on the ever-popular topic "Godspeak." Lookatme had tobacco-colored skin with a birthmark stain on his forehead in the shape of California.

At the pulpit, he appeared less pastor than apparatchik, and with the backing of Bollovate and Huey had taken to selling his Sunday sermons for fifteen dollars apiece, with a fifty-fifty split for the college. His best seller was "On the Highway to Heaven, What Are You Paying for Gas?" His perennial issue was nothing as simple as whether God should be addressed as He, She, or It, but rather, Should God be allotted divine superiority as compared to humans? Chaplain Lookatme had come up with this problem all by himself, but once he stated it, several of the faculty agreed it was crucial. The point was, said Lookatme, that God Him-, Her-, or Itself would not wish to be thought of as existing on a higher plane than mortals. He or She or It was more of a Friend.

Manning intended to participate in this discussion as well. He was going to propose abandoning such archaisms as the opening of the Lord's Prayer, and substituting "Our Buddy Which art in heaven."

While only one-sixteenth of the college and community observed either Sensitivity Day or How to Prepare for the Holidays Day, the events were fully incorporated into official college life, and foreshortened the term. Some hours were also eaten up by Matha's radicals, who continued to pace in the two Pens with placards reading "The CCR Will Not Go Far." Goldvasser wore a sandwich sign that read, "Free the Des Moines 7," but no one seemed sufficiently interested to point out his errors.

All this made a difficult schedule more so for Professor Porterfield, who, after the first weeks of meetings of the CCR, was beginning to wonder if any amount of time, extended or shrunk, would accomplish what everyone wanted. Ideally, when the new curriculum was presented, the faculty would rise to their feet, every man and woman, cheer, sing the college song (whatever its words might be) and weep openly that in its darkest hour in the darkest season, good old Beet had been rescued by its own resourcefulness and goodwill.

On the road leading to his house, he drove past other professors' houses, which looked much like his own. Past the cords of wood and the mounds of mulch and the separated garbage. Past the swirls of smoke from the chimneys. Past the conversations in those houses, which, when they diverted from the threatened closing of the college, focused on an upcoming trip sponsored by the Boston Museum of Trips, or on the incomparable can-you-believe-it spaghetti squash at the Natural Nature Food Shop, or on the antique birdcage in the shape of a pagoda acquired at last Sunday's Isn't This Precious! Flea Market, or on the latest "fascinating if plodding" book they all were reading; or on one another.

Peace took a wrong turn, the first time that had ever happened.

"Sold the Moore?" Livi said at an early supper that evening. "Jesus! They really must be strapped. I must say, I really don't get it. I mean, it's okay by me if they close the joint tomorrow. But I don't see how a college can go out of business like a falafel stand."

Whenever they looked forward to a rare night out, they pushed up the family dinner hour so they could dine with the children.

"I think it's losing too much," said Peace, as he passed the brussels sprouts to Robert, who made the gag-me sign and passed them to Beth, who pretended to vomit.

"Eat right or die," said their mother. The pair were now attempting to cause each other's water glasses to topple over by kicking the table legs.

The children were still fuming over the previous night's Halloween costume fiasco. Weeks earlier, they'd planned to go trick-or-treating as Sherlock Holmes and Dr. Watson. Beth, the elder, naturally assumed she would be Sherlock; besides, she looked beyond cute in the deerstalker cap. But Robert too thought he would be going as Sherlock, precisely *because* Watson was the elder. In the end, after a shouting match that lasted an hour, they both went as Sherlock, each pointing out the other to their trick-or-treat patrons as an impostor.

At least Livi had not contended with the Concerned Parents of Beet, which annually published a list of unacceptable and inappropriate Halloween costumes. The offensive outfits were hobo, witch, gypsy, old man, old woman, devil, and Indian princess. Last Halloween Livi threatened to dress up herself as a half-Jewish princess, but Peace persuaded her to let it alone.

"Tell me something," she said to her husband, attempting to ignore the brother-sister act at the table, which now consisted of each plunging a pencil into the other's mashed potatoes. "What difference does it make if the college carries a deficit?"

Peace admitted he did not understand the complexities of the matter, or very much at all about college finances. He had no knowledge of discounted tuitions, earmarked donations, or fund accounting, and until lately, had never supposed he needed any. All he knew was that Beet had an operating budget of around $60 million, which depended on sustaining an endowment of $265 million, which had held steady until Bollovate, Huey, and the new board came in. But now the trustees complained that more money than ever was going toward scholarships. Health care costs were up. Equipment—everything from computers to staplers—was way up.

"I guess it's easiest to think of the college as a mom-and-pop store," he said, unhappy to make the analogy. "With zero in the endowment, there's nothing left to invest. All the profits, which pay the bills, come from tuition and gifts. We need more students and more gifts."

"How do you lose $265 million in a couple of years?" Livi asked. "That's a hell of a lot of staplers. And what will the esteemed board of trustees do if it should turn out that Beet is sunk?"

"Sell the property, I guess."

"To pay the bills?" Livi crossed her eyes. "And how could they sell something as old as Beet College? Who owns the land?"

Peace ate two brussels sprouts, chewing very slowly. Should he have paid more attention to money matters?

"Well," said Livi, "if the CCR's dumb-ass report is supposed to save the place—something I must tell you I find hard to swallow— why don't you write it yourself? Let your committee yak away, you create the report out of your own good mind, then tell 'em they did it."

"They're not stupid," said Peace.

Livi said nothing.

Beth and Robert were approaching the end of a breath-holding contest, and glowed like radishes. "Out!" said Livi, to the children's satisfaction.

"Besides," said Peace, "it's not playing fair. The report is supposed to be a collective decision."

"Ooo la la, M. Candide! I love collective decisions," said Livi. "Love love love!"

She examined her husband's troubled face. "Have you ever heard of Dupuytren's contracture?" she asked. "It's a disorder of the palm. Thick tissues, like a scar, develop under the skin. It takes a while to grow and eventually it restricts the motion of the hand, causing one finger to drop involuntarily. The condition starts out invisible, with no pain, and winds up very serious."

"This is a metaphor?" Peace asked.

"Could be." She gave him her business smile. "There's only one way to get rid of Dupuytren's contracture."

"And what is that, Doctor?"

"Surgery."

CHAPTER

5

THE OCCASION OF THE PORTERFIELDS' NIGHT OUT WAS THE visit of B. F. Templeton, known as The Great, the most popular poet in America, there to give a reading in Lapham Auditorium. The hall was named for the funder, the inventor of the asparagus tongs, who was also a Gilded Age press lord and amateur cornet enthusiast lampooned by political cartoonists of the day, including Thomas Nast for blowing his own horn. Lapham sat six hundred in the orchestra, and two hundred more in the loge—the necessary capacity for the throng expected for The Great Poet Templeton. That was how he was always billed, as The Great Poet Templeton. Friends and critics sometimes referred to him as Templeton and B. F., but fans knew him as The Great.

"I suppose we have to go," said Livi when they finished their meal, hoping Peace would hear that as a question.

"You don't, honey, but if I didn't show up, that's all the committee would talk about at tomorrow's meeting."

"Fascinatin' group," she said, adopting her best Jean Harlow. "So cultchered, don't ye know? So refoined."

Cindy the sitter appeared at six, as promised. Beth and Robert hooted and cheered.

"Don't let them get the best of you," said Livi as she put on her parka.

"I came armed this time," said the teenager. "A .38, a .45, and an Uzi."

"You're sure that's enough?"—the parents in unison.

No one was more thrilled by The Great's appearance than Matha Polite, who had selected herself to introduce the reading. This was The Great's second visit to Beet, his first occurring over twenty years ago when he was just starting out, yet recognizable as a rising literary star. His poetry—even his detractors and competitors had to concede—was very good, a concatenation of colloquial Frost and mythological Seferis, with the mathematical precision of Empson and yet the boisterous lyricism of Dylan Thomas. He had much of Thomas in him, including a distant Welsh ancestry (though he had been born and reared in Point Pleasant, New Jersey). He drank as lustily as Thomas had, and lunged at as many undergraduate breasts as well, and as well. And he looked a bit like Thomas—shortish and fattish with a thick raddled nose and chirpy eyes that seemed to preemptively beseech everyone for forgiveness. His God's gift, though, was his voice. If anything, it was even more musical than Thomas's—so bell-like and equipped with its own echo, listeners would rotate their heads and sway to it in a demi-swoon, as they might sitting on a lawn at a Chopin piano concerto drifting over Tanglewood.

Because The Great's speaking fee was $20,000, Bollovate, upon learning of the event, attempted to have it canceled. That is, he got President Huey to try to call it off. But The Great's reading had been set in stone a year in advance, and his contract called for full payment, even if the college backed out.

"Twenty grand for poetry?" said Bollovate. "And what do we get out of it? I'll tell you what. Poetry!"

The students, especially those in English and American Literature, were delighted at the prospect of sitting at The Great's feet, which were usually covered in woolly bedroom slippers worn even in the snow, as he suffered from gout. And the faculty too wanted to gain as much reflected glory as the poet would radiate. Smythe was the most enthusiastic, which is why, as soon as the date was nailed down, he'd volunteered to give a cocktail party to kick off the evening. When The Great stood on the threshold of Smythe's house just off campus, he was upright and sober, and at first few people recognized him.

"Sir! We welcome your return after a long and eventful journey as Penelope welcomed Odysseus," said Smythe.

"Not in the same way, I hope."

Smythe's house was a gingerbread job so laden with rounded shingles and frosted shutters that the place looked edible. The walls were decorated with little prints of English churches and photographs of famous authors—all staring lifelessly into the camera like gulag prisoners, with Smythe at their sides, wearing a satin smile. In the parlor, Ada Smythe, who understood very little of the literary life but knew how to throw a party, had set up a full bar including a life-size ice sculpture of the Lacoste crocodile to honor her family. She asked her husband how he liked it. He told her, "Boring."

By the time of The Great's late arrival, most of the faculty were present, standing like flamingos in a swamp, holding glasses and making burbling sounds as student-waiters, among them Max Byrd, presented trays of midget asparagus and new potatoes stuffed with cheddar. Until Professor Porterfield got there—somewhat after The Great, as at the last minute Livi had to be driven to the hospital to extract a bullet from a kid who'd accidentally shot himself with his father's Glock—Max was the only person in the room who had read all the works of B. F. Templeton, excluding The Great himself.

On the way to the party the Porterfields were talking about what they'd been talking about, off and on, for a year, and more intently lately, with more pain than progress.

"It isn't that I don't want you to go back into practice. You know that," said Peace. "But the timing is lousy, Liv. I need you here."

"If something turns up in Boston, I'll be here. It's only a forty-minute drive. But it's been four years. I'm going to lose everything I've trained for."

"What if it's New York?"

Her voice was soft, controlled. "Then it's New York. Look, darling, this place may not *exist* in a couple of months. And in any case, there's no sense in *both* of us doing the wrong job."

"I'm not doing the wrong job."

"Of course you are. These people don't deserve you."

"They'll come around."

"When pigs fly."

Peace wasn't as confident of his high opinion of his colleagues as he sounded. But he did believe in the value of saying he was. As the Chinese put it, "If you want to keep a man honest, never call him a liar." Peace would have substituted "make" for "keep."

"The students deserve everything, Liv. And the faculty isn't what you see. Most of them are better than you think."

"I sure hope so." She looked out the car window at a clump of dead trees. "You were happiest in Sunset Park. You were doing something there."

"I'm doing something here. And don't romanticize Sunset Park. That was no picnic either, babe, if you remember."

"I won't romanticize Sunset Park if you don't romanticize Beet." She touched his elbow. "The trouble with you is you're a hero."

"I'm not. I just want the college to realize what it is."

"To realize what it is! Oh, Jesus! You *are* a hero!" They rode in silence the rest of the way to the party.

In the atmosphere of Smythe's home, envy was as palpable as smog but, since it was also laced with longing, revealed itself in manic gaiety. All crowded around or edged toward The Great. Lipman clung to him like ivy, as did Jamie Lattice. "It must be wonderful," he said to the poet, "to be part of the New York literati!"

"The New York literati? You mean journalists?" said Templeton, at once flinging the boy and Lipman into deep yet separate funks.

No one hovered as close as Smythe or expressed his admiration more lavishly. Among other social skills, he was the undisputed master of the standing ovation, a skill he'd perfected some years earlier when Steven Spielberg visited the campus. He knew exactly how to begin the clapping, when to rise from his seat, how to extend his arms in an incomplete circle. He was certain this evening would afford the opportunity to strut his stuff.

For his part, The Great was in his element—"a pig in shit," he shouted to no one in particular as he tossed down his first neat Bushmills of the evening, not realizing that porcine references came out as less hilarious at Beet than elsewhere. He was much more comfortable surrounded by professors and students of literature than he was among his fellow writers. Lost in their own orbits, writers would spin away from him, whereas he drew a college crowd to him with centripetal force. Because he produced the works they merely researched or criticized, he understood that most of the faculty wished him dead. But he also divined that he was indispensable to their health, that without an occasional visit from him or some other of his ilk, their bitterness would turn inward and gnaw on its own tail. Grandly would he accept their flattery. Grandly would they flatter. They laughed too loud, and so did he.

"So you're the one who's going to save the college by Christmas," said Templeton, when Peace was introduced to him.

"We're going to try."

"'We' means a committee?"

Peace nodded.

"Ah well," said The Great, in a rare lapse into sympathetic seriousness. He looked up. "You have an innocent face."

"So I'm told," said Peace, who was growing sick of his face.

So full of light and cheer was The Great on this occasion, one hardly noticed the surly brunette who seemingly was soldered to his side. She had bulbous black hair and the face of a Fascist but without the beliefs; and though half The Great's age (of who knows? Fifty?) she seemed to have been through more than one mill. A Leica dangled from her neck.

"This is Sandy, my photographer," said The Great, at last recalling her presence, as if everyone had his own photographer. In any case, from that day forward at Beet, the definition of a photographer expanded considerably. Following her subject at three or four paces, Sandy said not a word as The Great do-si-doed from fan to fan, pausing at only the choicest breasts on his trips to the bar.

"Bushmills, barkeep, if you please!" he cried, gulping his second drink, this time a double. "You can have your fuckin' Dewar's. And your malt shit too, as far as I'm concerned. It's Irish for me! And the only Irish worth a warm fart is Bushmills!" Everyone thought he was right, a few expressing their support by slapping him on his fleshy shoulders.

When Peace stood in the parlor with Livi on his arm, he looked disoriented, as if he had blundered into the wrong party. This was his society. They were his colleagues and their wives and husbands or partners or special friends, his people. Why then did he feel as if he had come upon some Russian bath or Turkish church, a place with strange customs, floral dishes piled with unrecognizable food, samovars, bejeweled troikas, people speaking a language that sounded like none he knew (and he knew several)? The men were spinning like dervishes; a wonder they did not dizzy themselves and crash to the floor. The women tilted from side to side, their faces gleaming under pellets of sweat. Every trail of sound, no matter how loud, seemed to conclude at the word "exactly." All anyone seemed to be saying was "exactly," which struck him as funny because he was feeling peculiarly inexact, out of focus.

"Professor Porterfield?" He looked down to his left upon a head of brilliantine.

"Oh, hello, Mr. Ferritt."

"It's Lawrence. Ferritt Lawrence," said the reporter darkly. Peace wasn't the only one to make that mistake, though he was the first to make it unintentionally. "I'm still hoping for an interview with you," said the nineteen-year-old in a robotlike voice that he hoped sounded menacing.

"I'll be glad to talk with you," said Peace, "and with everyone, when the committee is ready."

"I should tell you," Lawrence drawled, as if harboring a secret no one wanted to know, "I've had off-the-record conversations

Dylan Thomas   Max Byrd

with several committee members already. They say that you're not open to new ideas."

Examining Lawrence as though he were an uninteresting virus, Livi said: "We'd love to stop and chat with you, Mr. Ferritt. But you know how it is—so much time, so little to do." She guided her husband away by the forearm.

The Great, having progressed from two Bushmills to many, stuck his head playfully into the maw of the ice crocodile, while giving Matha the once-over for the third time, thus drawing a steady glower from his personal photographer. When Matha responded and ushered her breasts in his direction, Sandy swung an elbow like a bad-boy NBA forward, catching her opponent on the collarbone.

"Sorry," she said.

"Sure," said Matha, contemplating throwing a punch. The women squared off and sized each other up. Observing the playlet, Ada Smythe rushed over, stood between them like a ref, and offered both a Cosmopolitan.

Quoted lines of the poet were bouncing off the walls as though the room had turned into a squash court. It appeared everyone had a favorite line or phrase or couplet or quatrain, which required reciting at high volume. An oral Bartlett's was created on the spot, with The Great joining in and quoting his own lines, more and more of them, louder and louder, until he remained the only one speaking, and all were standing about him in numinous wonder. At one point he spoke for three minutes straight, then looked around with a bewildered expression. "Someone's boring me," he said. "I think it's me!"

Much laughter followed, rising higher when he added that was the one line he did not write; it belonged to Dylan Thomas, his drunken muse. Max Byrd wondered why poets, even the better ones, had to play clichés. Peace watched his student watch The Great, knowing what the boy was thinking. Max and students like him were his reason for teaching, he reminded himself, discouraged that a reminder was necessary.

But everyone could not have been merrier, and in that state

they left Smythe's house at the appointed hour and gathered themselves into a street pageant, worming down the blustery, leaf-blown pathways into the college, their shoes clacking toward Lapham Auditorium. Smythe took one of The Great's arms, Matha the other. The photographer trailed the revelers, clicking her Leica ratatatat.

As Peace took in the parade of his colleagues from the rear, lagging back and increasing the distance between them and himself, a short story of John Updike's came to mind out of the blue. It was about an old man who keeps a piece of land deep in the sticks, principally so that his extended and unwieldy family will have a spot for their annual reunion picnics. The story involved the latest picnic, and Updike describes the scruffy crew in detail—the sneaky cousins, the dim-witted in-laws, the drug-snorting children, a coarse stewardess brought as a date by the married ne'er-do-well nephew, and so on. While the rest of them play softball on his little piece of land, the old man takes a walk to the top of a nearby hill, from which he looks back and surveys his family. A word comes to him: "Sell, sell."

"Where are you?" Livi studied him. Peace shook it off.

The auditorium was swaying and murmuring like a synagogue in full daven. Not a seat was empty except for the two rows up front reserved for the English faculty and some selected students. With a magician's flourish, Smythe unhooked the red felt cord from its stanchion, and the professors and students took their seats.

Peace saw Manning a few rows behind him. "What are you doing here? This is literature"—pronounced with Manning's derisive emphasis.

"I'm doing what professors do. Stand and sit. Tonight I sit."

Onstage, The Great fumbled with the arms of a green leather wing chair, turning the chair this way and that, and finally figuring out how to sit in it. Matha walked to the lectern and began her introduction of him as "one of the few male poets who really understood the female temperament." Heilbrun whispered to Kramer that not only did he understand it, he incurred it. They shook with soundless chuckles.

Matha continued—one minute, four, five—evidently having decided beforehand that this would be an opportune occasion not only to detail The Great's place in the scheme of American poetry, but also to rail against the countless injustices at Beet College and call for the resignation of President Huey and the board of trustees as well as the immediate dissolution of the Committee on Curricular Reform, which was "illegitimate."

"Close the college!" she said, hoping it would spark a chant. It did not, perhaps because the audience detected a logical contradiction in closing the college and sitting at the poetry reading.

But her remarks were met by the approving outcries of her radical band, along with the intense, noncommittal stares of most of the students and faculty. The bloodshot eyes of The Great rolled from side to side with impatience and Bushmills, as the rest of him tottered in his chair like a beach ball.

So worked up did Matha become, she began to lapse into her southern dialect.

"Ahm disgusted with this College! Ahm fed up! Bring the school down, Ah say! Bring it down!"

When she finally finished her introduction, she neglected to announce The Great's name, ending instead on a call to arms. As a result, there was no applause until the poet stood shakily, kicked off one of his woolly bedroom slippers, and with one good foot and the gouty one bare and pink-purple, limped and wobbled to the lectern, from which he cast a longing and sodden look at Matha's departing bottom.

"Thank you so very much, Mary," he blurted into the mic, the blast causing several people to jump in their seats, his eyes never straying. "Your introduction was ferry vlattering." He hiccoughed and wheezed asthmatically. "I felt like a real big shot. But you know," he said, leaning forward and taking the audience into his confidence, "I'm really known as Fuckface to my friends." Smythe laughed raucously. Others found their own ways to indicate their appreciation.

The Great opened three slim volumes before him, and began the reading. It was an effectively planned sequence of poems. Peace cast off the earlier shadows of the evening, and he—and Livi, too, to her surprise—relaxed in the pleasure of good poetry read well, indeed beautifully. For twenty minutes or so, the audience seemed blown into by a verbal afflatus (afflatus being the word many would have used), each one, including Max Byrd, hoisted away from the banality of the occasion—a poet, a reading, a college—to that moment of the release of the poem itself, when the lines, long considered, hit the air for the first time. It was a particular treat for Max, who took to poetry less naturally than to his Apple, and thanked Peace for broadening his world. None of them suspected that The Great, drunk as he was, had been operating on automatic and was about to become creative.

For then, in mid-sonnet—a Petrarchan piece about love and loss that engendered tears in half the audience—The Great stopped cold, his bloodshot eyes searching the first rows and alighting at last on the idolatrous face of Matha Polite.

"I'm going to pause here," he told the throng. "And instead of reading something old, I'm going to compose something new and original, right here, on the spot." In the audience, frisson mixed with terror. "This will be a poem," he continued, "no, an ode, no, a paean, no, an encomium, no, an epithalamion, no, a *hymeneal* to the young lady who introduced me this evening in so lovely a way, and who, incidentally, is a poet herself!" Matha broke into the widest smile in Dixie, showing every one of her teeth. Sandy also showed her teeth, though not in a smile. "For Mary, then," said The Great to not a sound in the hall, not a clap, not a cough.

"An Ode to Mary's Ass," he announced, and the gasps had not dissipated before he began to recite.

> I don't think I shall ever cast
> An eye on anything like Mary's ass.
> An ass to bump, an ass to grind.
> O may I mount it from behind?
> Poems are made by me, alas.
> But only God can make an ass.

"Amen to that," said Livi, who stood at once and stalked out of the auditorium. Peace was right behind her. And a dozen students and teachers did the same, including Manning. Livi saw him shaking his head.

"Hey, Manning," she called out. "How'd you like his bottom line?"

Most of the crowd remained dead still, like bank clerks told to drop to the floor by a robber in a ski mask swinging a tommy gun, everyone expecting something even worse. The Great now clung to the lectern, which swayed under his weight, as though he were steering a ship in a typhoon. Matha was torn. On the one hand, he had treated her like a piece of meat in public, and got her name wrong to boot. On the other, the most honored poet in America had just composed a poem to little ol' her. She sat and stared. Everyone sat and stared, eyes swelling in their sockets. It may be said of that moment, with the possible exception of what remained of Nathaniel Beet himself, nothing in the history of Beet College had ever been so completely, definitely, quiet.

Outside, Livi stopped in her tracks, listening for something.

"What are you doing?" asked Peace.

And then she heard it. At that moment, as he did so often in his life, and with success assured by practice and virtuosity, Keelye Smythe rose to his feet, extending his arms in an incomplete circle, and the night exploded in a standing O.

CHAPTER

6

WHILE NEARLY EVERYONE WHO WAS ANYONE AT BEET COL-
lege had been sitting in the thrall of The Great in Lapham Auditorium, Akim Ben Laden was trudging across campus, about to put
the final touches on furnishing and decorating his cave. Over the
past two weeks he had scavenged in the trash bins of the school,
which mainly yielded the books of scholars, inscribed copies
thrown out by Beet faculty who were sent them by the authors as
gifts and who had sent back complimentary notes including a
phrase or two from the text to suggest they'd read the book before
tossing it. There was little of value to Akim. Better hunting was
available in the town of Beet, from whose castoffs he had garnered
a ladder-back chair with three missing rungs; an orange Barca-
lounger circa 1965, whose color remained unfaded; a standing
lamp made from a harpoon; a child's roll-top desk from F.A.O.
Schwarz; and the lower berth of a trundle bed with a decal of
Apollo 11 on the side.

For decor, he took a few favorite possessions from his room in
Fordyce—a photograph of Charles van Doren as he had appeared
on the TV show *Twenty-One*, a plaster bust of Batman, a lute, a red
scimitar he'd made of cardboard, and a computer-generated
photo of his father the rabbi, sitting before a chessboard with his

white king toppled and his hands raised in surrender. Generally Akim eschewed material goods. His prize good he kept in his wallet. It was a Matha Polite villanelle, published in the radical broadsheet *Scream*, with the repeating lines, "My phone is ringing off the hook / My cunt will not answer."

Peace was leaving Lapham Auditorium with Livi when he noticed Akim, which was not difficult given the boy's outfit and the fact that he was both carrying and pushing a small mountain of stuff. Before him he rolled a grocery cart laden with books and pictures, an Etch-a-Sketch and a large stuffed panda, a childhood gift from his mother. He bore a backpack so overloaded, it spilled part of its contents every few steps. Under his left arm he tucked a laptop. And around his right shoulder coiled a great many extension cords, two hundred if one were counting, trailing behind him like a long tail and stretching back to Fordyce and up the stairs to his room.

"Wait a second, Liv. I see a student I know. I'm worried about him."

"I can see why. How long will it take?"

"You go on ahead. Cindy has to get home." They kissed, but she could tell he was still sore at her for her evaluation of his colleagues. She hoped it was because he suspected she was right.

Something about a New England college at night—the buildings blazing but deserted, the gaunt trees, the shadows, the puddles of light from the streetlamps covered with rime, the slap of the wind. If a murder or two did not occur in such a place at such a time—preferably by dagger—it would seem a waste.

"What have you got there?" Peace approached Akim as breezily as possible. He pointed to the boy's shoulder.

"Extension cords. I need to connect them to my room. There's no electricity in the cave."

"You're living in a cave?"

"I'm moving in tonight. If it's good enough for Osama, it's good enough for me."

"You admire Osama bin Laden." It interested Peace how crazy people always dictated the terms of their conversations.

"Not the killings part. But the hat and the beard are awesome."

"How's Homeland Security coming along?"

"Don't speak of it, Professor Porterfield. I'm taking three online courses, all taught by Billy Pinto, whom I've yet to lay eyes on." He held up his laptop. "If I were still speaking to my father—may piranhas chew on his liver—I'd tell him what he was paying tuition for. Would you like to hear my fall line-up? A course called 'Emergency Management: What If They Come by Sea?' Another called 'Tunnel of Love or Death?' And a seminar called 'If You're My Mother, Where's Your ID?' I can't even get through to the department by e-mail.

unique courses

"Did you know," he asked Peace, "that Pinto teaches a class called 'Police Brutality—Is It Always Wrong'?"

He tripped over the straps of his talaria and lay spread-eagled on the ground, forcing him to cry out in, and then upbraid himself for, a Yiddish curse. Peace picked him up by the shoulders.

"The brochure calls the department 'asynchronous,' meaning that students are not required to be in a particular place at a particular time," said Akim. "Trouble is, I am in a particular place at a particular time. But who cares?"

Of course, Peace had not been privy to the conversations of the previous summer that put the Homeland Security Department in place. Not only had Bollovate and Huey made the virtual classrooms available to undergraduates, they also opened them to outsiders, for $5,000 apiece. When the revenue started pouring in, Bollovate squealed, "It's a cash cow!" Then he said, "A cash pig!" delighting himself with this singular example of wit. He'd asked, "Why couldn't we run the whole college online? From one building! From a Quonset hut! From a lean-to, for chrissake! An outhouse!" He was on a roll.

"You mean, no regular classes?" said Huey.

"No classes, no offices, no food, no services, no Pens, no overhead," said Bollovate.

"There are schools like that now, Joel. But they're sort of low class. No college of Beet's reputation has ever gone online."

"Ah! That's just the point, Lewis. Who wants an online degree from Podunk? Beet, on the other hand . . . Not only that. Let Beet actually prepare you for a job! Shorten the time it takes to get a degree! Get on the fast track!" Bollovate was approaching ecstasy. "The top of the line online. And money in your pocket, too! What's wrong with that?"

"Well, there's tradition," said Huey, in whose oubliette of a mind a taper of decency could occasionally flicker before he snuffed it out himself.

"Tradition," said Bollovate. "Oh, I see. The tradition of going under." They had been sitting in Huey's office, with Bollovate stuffed into the president's chair behind the desk, and the president, hands in lap, on the visitors' side.

"It's hard to imagine," said Huey. "Beet College without Beet College."

"Isn't it!" said Bollovate. "What a shame! What ever would we do without the sniveling, complaining, lily-livered faculty, and that—what's it called?—dither of deans, and those darling children chasing their hormones until they graduate and drain the economy? What *would* we do?"

Once Bollovate got hold of an idea involving money, there was no stopping him.

"Why couldn't we get commercial sponsors for our online courses?" he'd asked/told Huey. "If everything else in America is 'brought to you by' some shit or other, how about Homeland Security getting sponsorship from companies selling alarm systems, gas masks, weapons? You know, Lewis, if I'd been put in charge of this dump years ago, the History Department would be brought to you by the History Channel right now."

"Are you being serious, Joel?" asked Huey, who was wondering if yet another adjustment of life principles was in order.

"Nah," said the fat man. "It was just a thought."

Peace walked on with his student. He tried to sound upbeat. "You know, Akim. I'm sure there's still time to change your concentration."

"To what? Dominican and Video Games Studies?" In fact, the

concentration had appealed to him, not for the Dominicans, who had joined with the Jews and Arabs in his harassment in high school, but for the video games, one in particular that involved Crips and Bloods carrying pipe guns and chasing rabbis into alleys with no exits. But he'd applied too late.

"Why not take Government with Professor Manning?"

"I sat in on one of Professor Manning's courses last semester, and I actually learned something. But he scares me. He's Jewish."

"So are you."

"That's why he scares me. One day he looked me over and said, 'When are you going to cut the crap, Arthur?'"

Peace accompanied the boy across the baseball diamond and toward the woods surrounding the college. He offered to help carry some of his load, but Akim insisted he could handle it all, just as a toby in the shape of Paul Revere's head fell from his backpack and smashed on a rock near second base. Peace was trying to ascertain just how cuckoo the boy had become since he'd seen him two weeks earlier in the library. Clearly the rejection by the How to Write for the *New York Times* course—and by Matha, too, he guessed—had taken its toll.

"Have you tried contacting Professor Pinto online?" he asked.

"I've been doing nothing else for two weeks. Every time I clicked onto Homeland Security, it showed THIS SITE CURRENTLY UNDER CONSTRUCTION, or PLEASE TRY AGAIN, or—which drove me up the wall—MAKE SURE ALL THE WORDS ARE SPELLED CORRECTLY. Then, the night before last, in a fit of exasperation, I hit the keys with my fist—bang bang bang—and something new appeared: ENTER SECURE PASSWORD."

"A secure password for a college department?" Peace wondered if Akim were making this up.

"That's what I thought. A little strange, huh? So I got myself an alphanumeric generator so I could hack into the department code. All it took was a phone call. I wrote a do-loop program. That way, I wouldn't have to watch the screen all the time. The letters and numbers would just keep churning. I dialed into the sign-on, and waited."

"And?"

"Nothing yet, Professor Porterfield. There could be hundreds of levels of codes. But even if it takes weeks, I'll get in there. Don't you worry. And when I do, I'll find Professor Billy Pinto and look him straight in the eye, and tell him Homeland Security is bullshit! What do you think of that?"

What Peace thought of that was to walk the boy over to the infirmary. But in truth, Akim did not sound crazier than usual. Yet he was. He just didn't want to discuss a particular sphere of craziness with Professor Porterfield.

"I'm fine, Professor. You really don't need to walk me the whole way." Peace stayed with him anyway.

Akim was trying to shake his companion because he had to concentrate on his other new mission—along with cracking Homeland Security—which was to blow himself up. A suicide bombing, he'd concluded, was the only sensible thing to do. The event, if intelligently plotted and occurring in the most advantageous circumstance, would gain him the attention that eluded him in life. He would not explode in a crowd, because he did not like crowds. This would be a solitary act, noteworthy and symbolic. And it would be filled with poetic justice, one of his favorite things, because by blowing himself up he would undoubtedly get in the *New York Times*, an opportunity denied him by Professor Joan A-minus, I-know-what-the-*New-York-Times*-is-looking-for Lipman. He would aim his act at her, at stupid Beet College, at the scornful Matha, and at Rabbi Horowitz. For the past few days he had been fiddling with a suicide note that made several puns on the word "pawn."

Because of the nature of his intentions, he was afraid the Homeland Security faculty, under whose one nose he was plotting, would root him out. But since Pinto's nose remained virtual, he thought he might be okay. The problem (or Akim's interpretation of the problem) was that he knew nothing about making a suicide bomb. He did not know what explosives to use, he did not know where to acquire the ingredients, he did not know how to strap the contraption to his body, or what clothing to wear to conceal it, or how to handle any of the other technical difficulties faced in similar circumstances by crazy people worldwide. At least he knew what he did not want, which was to become a suicide car bomber. He did not possess a driver's license, and the only vehicle he had ever driven was a bumper car in Coney Island when he was nine, and even that he did ineptly, never bumping into anyone.

"You can go back now, Professor Porterfield. I'm in good shape."

By now the trees had grown so dark and thick, they disappeared into the sky, which was starless and moonless. A screech owl performed a nosedive very close to the two of them, causing Akim to stumble again and catch his robes on the underbrush. Yet he remained careful to unravel the extension cords.

"I'll go with you as far as the cave," said Peace.

Akim breathed easy. He had a night of studying ahead of him. The Web site, kaboom.com, had not been all that helpful. It contained the biographies, albeit brief, of the more well-known suicide bombers, along with the long rambling prayers and speeches they delivered before blowing themselves up to Allah. In nearly all the cases cited, it was to Allah and an indeterminate number of celestial virgins that they propelled every last morsel of their existence, Arabs having pretty much cornered the market on suicide bombings. The basic information and the links were not only about Arabs, they were written in Arabic, which Akim could not read, except for the numbers.

It had taken some research, but little by little he'd acquired the necessary information for completing his mission. The weapon of choice for suicide bombers was acetone peroxide, which, he was relieved to learn, could be made from common household supplies—paint thinner (acetone), bleach or antiseptic (hydrogen peroxide), and one of the more powerful drain unblockers, such as Drano (85 percent sulfuric acid). One could secure these ingredients at any hardware store or beauty salon. In the proper mixture, they would produce white crystals of acetone peroxide—triacetone triperoxide, or TATP, for those in the know.

Yet how would he place his order, say, at Pig Iron Hardware in Beet? He would come in with a list of things to buy that included

71

the bomb ingredients, but also innocuous items such as a double-twist sugar bit, a spiral ratchet screwdriver, a ball-peen hammer, a cable ripper, a track and drain auger, a lug wrench, and an extended-pole branch trimmer. That's what he'd do. Then he would oh-so-casually add, "And give me some paint thinner and Drano, will you?" No one would suspect. And the Some Pig! Beauty Salon? Why would he be shopping there? He would be picking up things for his mother or his sister. A lip brush, an eyelash curler, a kohl pencil, cream blush, a brow brush and lash comb. That's what he'd tell them. He hoped they wouldn't think him effeminate— though he realized that upon seeing him, it was probably not the first thing people would think. Only he learned TATP is highly sensitive material and that its instability led to the deaths of forty terrorists handling the compound en route to blowing themselves up. The Web site compared these occasions to premature ejaculation, which would have made the boy laugh had he ever been inclined to. If there was one thing Akim Ben Ladin did not want to be remembered as, it was a sloppy suicide bomber.

The indispensable piece of information conveyed on kaboom.com was that most of the ingredients could be obtained on Main Street in Beet for under $200. As soon as Akim amassed under $200, he'd be all set.

He and Professor Porterfield had gone about half a mile into the woods. Akim had very few extension cords left. He drabbled in a puddle and slipped down a muddy declivity. They stopped. Before them, like a giant's yawn, was Akim's cave, set in a massive granite wall. From the black hole came the grating of a sort of music.

"It's a Syrian love song," said Akim. "I left my iPod on, in case I couldn't find the cave in the dark."

"What's the song called?"

"It's called 'Where Go My Sheep?' They're all called something like that. Would you like to hear it from the beginning?"

"I guess I'd better get back"—still not sure whether or not to knock the boy out and carry him to a doctor. "Don't you think you'd be more comfortable in your room?" Peace asked.

"One must make sacrifices for one's beliefs."

"And what are the beliefs you're making sacrifices for?" Akim had to admit the professor had him there. "Well, good luck with your project." Peace smiled.

Akim stiffened. "Oh, yes," he said, relieved to realize which of his projects Peace was referring to. "I'll hack in sooner or later. You'll see."

Peace bade him good night with some residual reluctance, but he had too many burdens of his own, and at least the boy didn't look as if he were about to harm himself. He turned to go back.

Akim screamed, "Yaah!"

"What is it?"

"It" was a pair of pink eyes about four inches apart and a foot and a half off the ground, glowing like rose-hued pencil flashlights from the center of the cave's blackness. There was a rapid rustling like paws scraping the earth. There was a low grunt. There was a louder grunt. And a snort and another grunt, followed by a phthisic wheeze.

Akim ran to Peace, who swept the boy behind him so that he could face the beast that now, very tentatively, emerged from the dark.

"Latin!" said Akim.

First came the snout, then the ears and eyes, then the hooves, then the whole white luminescent body and the ridiculous corkscrew tail.

"He must have escaped again," said Akim. "Perhaps he was drawn to my cave by 'Where Go My Sheep?'"

"Let's get him," said Peace.

They dove for the frightened animal, which made a deft sidestep, leaving his pursuers prone on the turf. Even an ungreased pig can move, and Latin was about to make a panicky dash into the woods. Akim rolled in front of him and blocked his way, and Peace tackled him around his very hard midsection—the first tackle he'd made since his senior year at St. Paul's. Latin squealed and squirmed, but Peace and Akim hung on until the subdued mascot lay quavering in their arms, his heart thumping, and breathing hard in muffled snorts. They petted him till he was quieter, then all three rose, the men muddier than the pig.

Latin tried to bite Akim, but Peace smacked his snout.

"Thank you, Professor! You saved my life!" *exupo*

"I don't think he was going to devour you. In any case, it would have been the first time treyf ate a Jew."

The boy nearly smiled.

"Well, you won't believe this." Peace called Livi to tell her the story of his evening walk. He'd returned to his office after half-dragging Latin back to his pen, and using one of Akim's extension cords as a leash. As a parting shot the prisoner took a leak on his captor's shoes. "I'd better spend the night here. It's too late to hitch a ride."

"Sure," said Livi. "You didn't hurt Latin, did you? He's my favorite member of the staff."

"I've had enough of Latin's staff for one evening."

"Are you angry with me?"

"Furious. I hate women with minds of their own."

"Me too," said Livi. "Good night, sweetheart."

Peace stretched out on the couch. God, am I wiped! he thought. Luckily he was about to get close to forty-five minutes' sleep.

CHAPTER 7

MATHA POLITE HAD RETREATED FROM LAPHAM AS SOON AS the standing ovation began to peter out. The Great had made an unsuccessful lunge for her from the lip of the stage, stubbing the big toe of his naked scarlet foot and nearly keeling over in the effort, and had shouted her a slurred and toothy invitation to accompany him to his room at the Pigs-in-Blankets Bed 'N Breakfast, to discuss the merits of her poems. Tempted as she might have been on another occasion, she declined. She had not brought any of her poems with her on that evening, thus any discussion of their merits might prove abstract. Also, photographer Sandy might burst in on the two of them during their abstract discussion and crown Matha with one of her catadioptric lenses.

But mainly Matha sought to elude The Great's grasp because she had bigger fish to fry. What had sailed over the heads of the audience at the reading was a particular and deliberately timed moment during her introductory remarks when she called for the resignation of President Huey. That exhortation was a signal to Betsy Betsy, Goldvasser, Bagtoothian, and Lattice to rise from their seats and leave the auditorium. About the time that Akim had begun his trek into the woods, they had proceeded under cloud cover and that of darkness to the New Pen and MacArthur House—the building donated as the home of the Communications Arts Department by Arthur MacArthur, the gossip-newspaper publisher, and earmarked for the study of social life and celebrities in journalism. They jimmied the lock of the front door, and occupied the building. It was a test, a dry run to see how the administration and professors would react, and the first of the major disruptive incidents planned by the group. The occupation of Bacon Library, their main target, was on the calendar for seven weeks hence. The MacArthur takeover would also eat up more time, which was precious to "that shit-fucking CCR."

Unlike Bacon Library, MacArthur House was not acknowledged by the faculty as an intellectual center, and it certainly contained nothing as important as the Mayflower Compact. It was roundly looked down upon by the other departments, except on those occasions when the Communications Arts faculty threw a cocktail party that included people who appeared on television. Then everyone commented how indispensable Communications Arts was to the life of the mind. In making his gift, Arthur MacArthur expressed the hope that in addition to gossip, students would address the question: "With no other assets but money, how does one make it to a seat at the tables of power and influence?" It was the only question that interested Arthur, and the sort of problem MacArthur House was known to tackle.

"But it's perfect for us," Matha had exulted. "The right size, the right location, and near the president's house—so even that brains-for-shit Louie Huey couldn't help but notice what we did."

MacArthur was a clapboard structure no larger than a three-bedroom suburban home. Easily manageable for the occupiers, its entrance was also its exit, "so we can keep the ass shits out forever." And it was where the Communications Arts Department stored its treasury of old newspapers with historically momentous headlines, as well as its library (a shelf, really) of books published by department members with titles like *Is the Media Fair?* and *Who Is Destroying the Media?* Its walls also displayed photographs of world leaders standing next to department members, and little framed notes of thanks from working journalists who visited Beet, including *visitors*

Connie Chung, Al Roker, Tim Russert, and Larry King. In short, everything Communications Arts most valued was housed in Mac-Arthur, whatever others might think of it, or of Communications Arts itself. If the building were taken out of commission, reasoned the radical students—since Communications Arts brought in more tuition revenue than all the other departments combined—"there'll be a fuckstorm from the bean counters."

When Matha approached the door of the building, her comrades had already tacked up a bedsheet on the outside wall with red lettering in poster paint reading, "Power to the People!" This and other slogans they picked up from history books about the 1960s, their principal sources for the symbols, language, and tactics of their protests. Matha knocked three times, then waited, then knocked twice more. The door opened cagily, like a speakeasy's. "It's me, you shithole," she said.

"Password?" said Betsy Betsy. Matha had forgotten it. So had Betsy Betsy.

Matha shoved her way in. "Well!" she said to her little group. "We did it!"

"Fuckin' A!" said Bagtoothian. He looked up from his reading, *An Illustrated History of Sparta*, which he proceeded to grangerize.

They surveyed their conquest and fell into a silence. There were two reception rooms, one containing a cheap nineteenth-century American grandfather clock donated by the Classics Department to give the place, as the classicists told one another, "a touch of gravitas, but nothing meaningful," along with the little library of books about journalism; another room that held the files of newspapers; a private dining room; and three offices for department members. A framed portrait in acrylics of Arthur MacArthur, a small man with an angry face, who wished to be immortalized as he played the oboe, hung in the vestibule.

Matha and her friends looked at everything, then at one another. They sat Indian-style in a circle on the floor of the main reception room and waited five minutes, ten, half an hour.

"Anyone hungry?" Matha asked. The others, not knowing how to respond, didn't.

In spite of herself, she suddenly felt the urge to bake pies. This happened from time to time, in situations that seemed to require a domestic touch, and the impulse terrified her even more than the fear of her fellow radicals discovering her true name. She believed—irrationally but deeply—that in some mystical process at her birth she had absorbed the characteristics of the woman her mother had admired on TV, the DNA passing from the *Today* show into her own baby body. And she recoiled at the vision that one day she would actually become Martha Stewart. Sometimes she had to quash the desire to decorate the margins of her poems with daisies and bluets, and, as in this instance, to bake pies, particularly peach.

"When do you suppose they will like come for us?" asked Goldvasser of Matha.

"Never. No one knows we're here," said Betsy Betsy. All realized at once that their revolutionary gesture would remain unrecognized until daylight unless they did something to call attention to it.

"Maybe we should leave," said Jamie Lattice meekly, as he said most things. He was afraid that if he were kicked out of college, no one in New York would invite him to a book party, which suggested how much he had to learn.

"I'll go outside and yell, 'We've got MacArthur!' said Bagtoothian. "'What are ya gonna do about it!'"

"To whom?" asked Betsy Betsy. "Everyone's gone home. Look out there. The students, the proctors, the administration, everyone's asleep."

Matha reached into her backpack and produced a bullhorn. "Let's wake 'em up, then," she said, and stuck the bullhorn out the front window. "Beet College!" she shouted, "We are the . . ." She turned back to the others. "Do we have a name?"

"The MacArthur Five," said Goldvasser, who blushed at his own ingenuity.

Matha continued: "We are the MacArthur Five! We have taken over MacArthur House to express our frustration with the system." She'd read that sixties students used the word *system* to mean the enemy. "We will remain in this building until our demands are met! Join us, comrades!"

Startled out of his forty-three-minute slumber, Peace thought he'd been awakened by a nightmare. "Join us, comrades!" Where the hell was he? He went to his office window, peered into the night, but saw nothing. All had gone quiet again in MacArthur. He went back to the couch, but not to sleep. "Join us, comrades!" It *must* have been a nightmare.

The comrades regrouped and sat in their circle. The grandfather clock ticked away.

"Matha?" asked Betsy Betsy, after a while. "What *are* our demands?"

"You're right," said Matha. "We don't have any. Let's make some up."

They huddled for a few minutes and came up with a list, but it wasn't easy. Since the sixties, all the conventional demands made by erupting college students had been acceded to, indeed anticipated, not only at Beet, but at practically every institution of higher learning in America. The MacArthur Five could not think of a single ethnic or gender or sexual orientation studies program to ask for that was not already in place. In some instances, the college had come up with a course of study based on a group that did not yet indicate its existence in, much less its anger at, the wider society. The most recent was a lecture series on the Boopa, a stationary race of Bolivian pygmies who have no words for hello or good-bye.

In contemplating their list of demands, the student radicals supposed they could always call for a reversal of contemporary trends and demand a return to the traditional dead-white-males curricula of the 1950s, but they knew that the faculty—many of whom had been students in the 1960s—would accept the revisionist program at once because it represented a usurpation of the current curricula and would sound revolutionary. What good are demands, the students asked themselves, if they are readily met?

"Does Beet have like ROTC?" asked Goldvasser. "What *is* ROTC, anyway?"

They could always protest the presence of the U.S. military on campus, an evergreen of campus disruptions for forty years. But here again such a demand would be difficult. For one thing, there was no such presence to speak of, on Beet's campus or anyone else's, except for the service academies. (Oddly, a few antimilitary protests had occurred at those institutions, but they met with scant success.) The draft was history. And there was the other impediment regarding this issue—that more than a few students actually wanted to enlist these days, going so far as to say that serving in Iraq might be preferable to sitting through another two years of classes on Latina pride (mainly a complaint of Latino students).

"How about demanding they get rid of the Old Masters in the college museum?" said Betsy Betsy.

"Why do that?" asked Lattice, who was paying more attention to an open window.

"Because they're all men," said Betsy. "Where are the Old Mistresses?" Bagtoothian asked Matha if he could kill her.

As for siding with the workers—another ripe issue of the sixties—there simply weren't all that many workers around Beet. The town was principally composed of professionals who provided employment for other professionals, of retirees, and of bored people, who covered all the strata, and who counted upon the college to relieve their monotony. The only involvement they sought from Beet College were the adult learning courses, and for the older male adults, the sight of girls in short skirts about whom they could daydream of leading new lives in seaside shacks on the Maine coast. This is not to say there were no workers around at all. Last year Goldvasser tried to unionize two plumbers who worked in the college maintenance department. He was wearing a hard hat at the time, which the plumbers offered to drive straight up his ass.

Making a list of demands in the contemporary world, the MacArthur Five determined, was not what it used to be. But then, as Matha reminded them, their goals had changed as well. They wanted to close the college, bring it down so they could party day and night, and for as long as possible avoid seeking the jobs unavailable to them anyway. Ideally, the demands they came up with would be so out of reach for the administration and the faculty, they would never be considered seriously. When that happened, they reckoned, the rest of the students would get angry and stand with them out of the usual undergraduate ennui and a mounting contempt for their elders brought on by their excessive attention to the students' wishes. And this marshaling of support would be essential, because at present the student radicals at Beet constituted 0.27 percent of the undergraduate population of 1,800, which is to say, five.

So the band of revolutionaries finally produced the sort of demands they knew no one at Beet would accept. They were:

1. Buy back the Henry Moore! Pay higher than the selling price if necessary, but get it back! [Bollovate and the trustees would never go for that.]
2. Fire Louie! [They would not do that either. Huey was the perfect titular leader for the trustees' purposes— though equally servile and incompetent, he could be difficult to replace.]
3. Fire Bollovate! [Out of the question.]
4. No more pigs-in-blankets in the school cafeteria! We're sick of them! Off the pigs! [A deliberately mad-cap demand to appeal to campus libertines.]
5. Dissolve the CCR! [Matha feared it might actually do something under Professor Porterfield. It had to go before it saved the college.]
6. [And consequently] Fire Porterfield! [Their ace in the hole, because they knew it could never happen.]

The list was completed at dawn. Matha moved to the window again and read the demands in an overexcited southern accent that made them sound more like a schedule of playtime activities announced by a games steward on a cruise ship. She waited and watched. At first, not a single Beet student emerged from the dorms. Then from out of the woods an Arab figure ran toward them, shouting ecstatically. "I shall join you, brothers and sisters! Let us destroy this house of Satan!"

Matha opened the door a crack, saw who it was, said, "Not you, Akim. We only take earthlings," and slammed the door shut. Akim sat on the cold grass in front of MacArthur, attempted to face Mecca, eventually gave up, and slunk back to his cave.

In his room, Ferritt Lawrence toyed with the idea of infiltrating the group so that he could report the takeover firsthand. He could be embedded with them—yes, embedded. But then, realizing he would be more like a real journalist if he reported the event as he reacted to it emotionally, he stayed put. The other students waited for Matha to finish reciting the demands and returned to sleep.

That was not an option for Peace, who now understood that what he'd heard earlier did not come out of his beleaguered mind. The lone faculty member on campus that night jumped up and jogged toward MacArthur. Still at the window, Matha called to the disheveled visitor.

"What's the matter, Professor Porterfield? Did your wife make you spend the night on the couch?"

"What are you doing, Matha?"

"What does it look like? We're taking over a building."

"To accomplish what?"

"You heard our demands."

"You can't be serious. The faculty is trying to save the college, and you people are occupying a building?"

"Matha," Lattice whispered to her. "Maybe he's right. Maybe we should leave." Bagtoothian asked if he could kill Lattice.

"Go away, Professor Porterfield. Go meet with your little committee. See where it gets you. Don't you know they're going to close the place anyway?"

She slammed the window shut. Peace went to phone Huey. Next he called Manning, whom he reached on his cell. This was a Tuesday, and Manning was paying his weekly visit to Margaret at the Beet village cemetery. It was approaching eight o'clock when he arrived and stood beside Peace. "Who's in there? The Junior League Madame Defarge?"

Peace looked over his shoulder and saw Huey and Bollovate descending the steps of College Hall and walking hurriedly into the New Pen toward the occupied building. Other faculty members trickled in—three, ten, fifty.

"Will they call the cops?" Lattice asked.

"If it were up to Bollovate," said Matha, "they'd be loading the rubber bullets right now."

Among the faculty members gathered, only Professor Lipman was noticeably upset. Her office was in MacArthur, and she blanched at the thought of the students riffling through her stash. Hidden away were secret memos from the *New York Times*, lists of favored and unfavored politicians, editors, artists, and so forth that would prove embarrassing if made public. Her treasury included two photos signed by *Times* critics concealed under stacks of manila envelopes in her bottom desk drawer. One was signed, "With luminous admiration, Chip." The other: "All my brio, Ben."

The rest of her colleagues stood dazed and perplexed, blowing smoke in the cold air. For some, the takeover was like a hookah dream. It had been many, many years since any of the professors saw an occupied building, and they were trying to recall how to react. After conferring with Joel Bollovate, President Huey did nothing. So did the dither of deans. The students, still sleep-headed, remained in their beds, though Akim tried once more to stand with his beloved Matha, and again was turned away.

"We have added one more demand!" yelled Matha over the bullhorn. "Amnesty for the occupiers!" The MacArthur Five cheered from inside.

That addendum jogged the professors' memories, and at last some of them recalled how to react to the takeover. They would join it. One by one in a growing line of ten, twelve, and more, they marched up to the door of MacArthur, knocked, and shouted, "Open up! We are with you!"

"Are you people nuts?" Manning called to them. He and Peace stood with several members of their own departments, who said nothing as others approached MacArthur House.

Now it was the MacArthur Five's turn to be uncertain as to how to react. All they knew of student protests came from books and movies, none of which was clear on the matter of responding to sympathy. Bagtoothian said, "Let them in!" And so they did, with Professor Godwin leading the troupe and shouting, "Right on!" as he entered.

All of Peace's committee joined in except Smythe, who hung back to see which way the wind would blow. Professor Booth marched right behind Godwin. Professor Heilbrun repeated "Right on!" then Kramer. Heilbrun had on a Beckbury—navy herringbone jacket, plain waistcoat, and striped trousers. Kramer wished he'd worn his Continental Army uniform, with the musket and tricorne. Kettlegorf entered singing, "Let me in, I hear music." On they came, their mood at once intense, festive, and bemused. Lipman rushed into her office, ascertained that nothing had been touched, and rejoined the others in the reception room, telling them that a protest like this was in the best tradition of the First Amendment.

By three to one, the professors in the building now outnumbered the students, whom they ignored. They stood in a huddle and high-fived and hugged one another as Matha took one look at them and frowned.

"We're with you!" shouted Professor Godwin. The professors began to sing "We Shall Overcome," but faltered when they could not remember the lyrics beyond the first words.

"Right on!" said Professor Kramer again, growing bolder.

"We don't want you here," said Matha.

"We don't?" asked Betsy Betsy.

"No, we don't," said Matha. "Look at these people, will you? They're not with us. They're just putting on a show. They're on a nostalgia trip." And before the accuracy of her assessment had begun to sink in for her comrades, she added, "I'm out of here."

She flung open the door of MacArthur and stomped off in a rage, to be followed closely by the others, Jamie Lattice toddling ducklinglike behind her. Now the only occupiers of the building were faculty members. When they saw that the students had exited, they looked to one another, and then they left too, thus bringing to a close the shortest building takeover in the history of American education.

And that might have been that, except for the fact that Beet College property had been invaded and occupied, and a few laws broken. The majority of adults who had remained outside MacArthur as well as those who went in knew something had to be done. Bollovate and thus Huey did as well.

They all gave the matter some thought. And then they came to a decision. They would do what they always did when they did not know what to do. They would call a faculty meeting.

CHAPTER

8

"THE MEETING WILL COME TO ORDER," SAID HUEY. "WE should proceed with a reading of the minutes."

"Forget the minutes," Manning called from his seat. "Let's deal with the so-called radicals."

"Shouldn't we read the minutes?" Huey turned to Bollovate, who shook his head. "Well, then, we won't read the minutes. Should we call the roll?"

"I think we should have an invocation first," said Chaplain Lookatme, who was standing by the door. "This is so important a meeting. Don't you think we need the presence of our Friend?"

"But we've never had an invocation before," said Huey.

"Our Friend won't mind," said Lookatme, with the coy, self-satisfied smile that came upon him when referring to his Friend.

"Should we have an invocation?" Huey asked Bollovate, who said nothing.

A debate ensued as to whether an invocation would be violating the separation of church and state. This gave rise to questioning whether a college was equivalent to the state, and did a chaplain represent a church? After half an hour, the faculty decided to send Lookatme packing. The man was crestfallen, but not so's anyone would notice.

"Our Friend will bless us anyway," he said.

"What a Pal!" said Manning.

Peace sat behind Manning, and maintained a silence that was unusual for him. Not the fact of the silence itself; for four years he'd kept quiet at faculty meetings in the vain hope that they would get on with greater dispatch without a contribution from him. But the silence he kept on this day was more watchful, and in some ways a consequence of his assignment. If he were being asked to resuscitate the college, he had to think about the whole institution more analytically.

The meeting was held, as were they all, in the Faculty Room, an airplane-hangar-like building unto itself on the north side of the Old Pen, which managed to be both muggy and drafty no matter the weather outside. It was among the oldest structures at Beet, its shell dating back to the days of Nathaniel himself, and originally had served as the area for pig auctions—called the volutabrum, or pigsty. When it was converted in the 1830s, someone at the inaugural meeting moved that the name be retained.

Large gilt-framed oil portraits of former Beet presidents covered the four walls, surrounding the rows of chairs and looking down on the gathering like the elders of a church. Each was illuminated by picture lights mounted in shiny brass. There was James Janes (1711–1766), Beet's first president, a drunk and a womanizer who beat the students with the branches of a cherry tree and was known to French-kiss his dog, a beagle named Dr. Brewster. There was Duncan "The Sneaker" Raymond (1758–1820)—the soubriquet did not appear on the legend—whose cherubic grin and chubby red cheeks belied his arrest and conviction for embezzling college funds. A dandy, though a pudgy one, he'd posed wearing a red Glengarry and a Black Watch tartan kilt under which he reportedly had concealed the pilfered stash in Black Watch tartan garters. Directly beneath Raymond hung Nicholas McVitt (1781–1862), with the scrofulous face of one of the late stages of the picture of Dorian Gray, and who seemed to be looking up Raymond's kilt. He was the only known male nurse to serve on both sides in the Civil War, and was tried for desertion by each.

And there were several more rimose faces peeking out from handlebar mustaches and Smith Brothers beards, including that of President Chauncy Dicey (1929–2004), Huey's immediate predecessor, a lepidopterist who committed suicide by shotgun in his office and whose likeness bore the look of someone who had just glanced out his penthouse window as King Kong was strolling by. Dicey had left no explanatory note, only a cassette on which he repeated the name Beet, with increasingly darker emphasis.

Huey had not sat for his own portrait yet, though it was suggested the college might save money if they hanged the subject instead.

"Is there old business?" said Huey.

"The Self-Reinvention Center," said Professor Hoffmann of Public Speaking. He'd proposed this idea at the last faculty meeting. "But I want to withdraw my motion."

"Why's that?" asked Huey.

"I'm not interested in it anymore. I'm a new man these days."

"Can we please get going?"—Manning again.

Peace leaned forward and said, "Cool it. You're turning them off."

"Would that I could."

Huey presided from a heavy, thronelike dark wood chair at the head of the room. To his right sat Joel Bollovate on an identical chair, his belly spilling over his tooled black leather belt, like lava over a cliff. Though it was unusual for a trustee to attend a faculty meeting (no one could recall it happening before), Huey had determined upon "conferring" with Bollovate that an exception to custom was in order. Why Bollovate had asked to attend, no one knew. He merely told Huey he wanted to see how the faculty would respond to the takeover. Matha Polite was there for much the same purpose. The way of her presence, also extraordinary, had been paved by Keelye Smythe, who had persuaded his colleagues (though not much persuasion had been required) that students should be allowed in "since their fate was at issue." And Ferritt Lawrence was there too, as everyone agreed on his indispensability as a representative of the people's right to know.

There being no old business, it was on to what Manning was calling for. The faculty was to decide whether or not the MacArthur Five should be punished, and if so, to what degree. Should they be admonished, placed on probation, expelled for a term or two, or tossed out forever, their names to be expunged from the Beet College records?

The threat of expunction had so shaken Jamie Lattice that he remained hidden in his room in Coldenham under his coverlet awaiting the meeting's outcome. His tiny head was wedged into a history of Elaine's Restaurant, complete with photos of the regulars in grim and belligerent poses indicating they were writers. Betsy Betsy went on a crying jag. Goldvasser called his dad in Nevada and asked if he were like expelled or something, would that like affect his admission to law school and stuff? Bagtoothian, with time on his hands, tortured a frog in the bio lab.

Manning rose again. "May I move that all five of the rebels without a cause be expelled for the spring term?"

"Are we taking motions yet?"—Huey to Bollovate. "I think we should have some discussion first."

A series of speeches followed, each ten to twenty minutes long. In rows and rows sat the professors in tweeds—all one hundred forty-one of them—like woolen dolls, boneless and loose-headed. They flopped in their polished black Beet College chairs with "Deus Libri Porci" at their backs and stared ahead at Huey and Bollovate. The air smelled of flax and varnish, with a hint of pharmacy, and it glistened with dust gilded by window-sunshine and the off-white globes hanging from long wires on the ceiling. Were it not for the substance of the occasion, the scene might have been mistaken for a congregation of philosophers or theologians or friends, even, who had convened to show their mutual affection and respect. But this was a faculty meeting.

"I find Mr. Manning's question to be very insensitive," said Professor Godwin.

"And why is that?"—Manning.

"It fails to take in the fact that the students are alienated."

"Pardon my negativity," said Manning. He seemed to be searching the floor for a spittoon. "Don't you also think they've been marginalized for their otherness?"

Among the lengthy speeches were several that compared both the administration and the student protestors to Nazis; two that compared Matha Polite to Martin Luther King Jr., Gandhi, and Marie de France; two that recalled the Army-McCarthy hearings; one more obscure speech that invoked the Claus von Bülow trial; an oral memoir of a summer spent picking grapes with César Chávez; and a parable involving a prince, a hare, and an apple, which seemed to favor the apple.

Professor Eli of Narratology—a one-person subspecialty of the English and American Literature Department—rose to speak. He said he judged the uproar "more a grapheme than a Grand Guignol. While I do not mean to get lost between the *énoncé* and the *énonciation*, or to apply a diegesis where the extra-diegetic is sufficient, the truth—or what we can determine of it, since none of us seeks to contaminate *différence* with the hierarchical, or to substitute the phonocentric for the logocentric—is that it is what it is. I hope that by so saying, I have not undermined anyone's radical skepticism."

No one thought he had.

Two of the presentations were so off the wall, they elicited responses of terrified silence. The first was delivered one-third in English, one-third in Spanish, one-third in German, by Hermann Lopez of the Film Department, who claimed to have grown up in La Paz, but whose nickname, "Triumph of the Will Lopez," did not come from nowhere. The second was a rant against the obtuseness of the reading public by Jack Umass of Sociology, who hadn't been himself lately. The author of *The 100 Smartest and Most Intellectual People in America*, Jack had fallen into a depression when his book sold only one hundred copies.

"Do you have any Advil?" Peace asked Manning.

"I just swallowed the bottle."

Had one been awarded, the prize for the most discursive speech would have gone to Professor Fannie Quintana, of Women's and Fashion Studies, who spoke in the voice of a sopranino (dogs swooned to it). She began with a recollection of the nuns who taught her in elementary school, then swung into the story of her bitter divorce, digressed to a condemnation of anyone who wore real fur, and wound up with an apostrophe to her mother that so choked her, she could not remember what she had been saying, much less where she was going, and collapsed in a heap of attractively layered clothing.

Upon Quintana's disintegration, Manning stood once more, looked Bollovate in the eye, and said, "Mr. President, may I ask what Mr. Bollovate is doing at a meeting of the faculty?" He did not wish to appear rude, he said, but "trustees have no business being in on faculty deliberations." He turned to Godwin. "Or am I being insensitive again?"

While many of the faculty were weighing whether or not to agree, or disagree, or partly agree and partly disagree, Jacques La Cocque, the college librarian, defended Bollovate's presence. La Cocque wore tattersall vests, and his head appeared to have been sawed off at the back, so that his hair lay flat against it. He said he thought it would be "*très utile* to have Mr. Bollovate's presence." He looked to the trustee for approval of his approval.

Professor Ordas of the Tarzan Institute stood and asked, "Is it because Mr. Bollovate is a man that Professor Manning objects to his presence?" Then Professor Jefferson asked if Bollovate would have been allowed in had he been female.

"Man! I feel like a woman," said Manning. He was about to respond that Bollovate should not be welcome if he were a cross-dresser, a mink, or a tree either, but he merely shrugged and tossed a wave of disgust at the front of the room.

As Professor Jefferson was thanking her colleagues for their too kind but much appreciated remarks on her remarks, Professor Gander of Professional Public Policy and Government Appointments Studies stood to deliver his specialty, the perfectly formed academic speech. Tall and slope-shouldered, he had the mind of a Polaroid snapshot; whenever it evidenced itself, one was at first excited, then depressed. His voice, a cello without music, had undoubtedly saved his life more than once, as anyone who listened attentively to what Gander was saying would be moved to gut him with a hunting knife. But the orator of the perfectly formed academic speech had practical experience to abet his natural gifts. He'd recently returned from a leave of absence as assistant White House press secretary, where for two years he'd explained America's successes in Iraq. He was expert in lulling all within earshot to a demicoma, particularly when he mentioned "governance."

"Now this is an issue that has come before us many times," he began. Half the eyelids in the hall drooped at once. "And, I am certain, it will come before us again." The other half followed. "What we must remember is that we are the faculty of Beet College, which gives us a great deal of power. But with power comes responsibility."

Manning muttered, "Shit," and slumped.

"It is not enough to have rights," said Gander. "One must also do right. Shall we not do right? I do not think so." Peace chuckled. "Mr. Bollovate is not one of us. Yes. But then again, he is. And so, the governance . . ."

Nothing more of his speech was heard until Gander thanked his college colleagues for their collegiality and their kind collegial attention. Then everyone clapped heartily and gratefully, except for Peace, Manning, a few others, and Bollovate himself, who throughout the to-do had sat motionless as a hippo in a swamp, his little round eyes unblinking.

Peace turned toward a high, wide Faculty Room window and saw Bacon Library through the ripples in the glass. The massive facade. The scrolls atop the pillars. Another story came to him— why was he thinking in these terms lately?—of John Grimes, the hero of James Baldwin's *Go Tell It on the Mountain*, at the age of eight or so, standing on Fifth Avenue across from the two stone lions at the New York Public Library. The boy wondered if the lions were there to protect him or keep him out.

Had Peace been able to see farther, beyond the campus and

onto the interstate, he would have caught sight of Livi in her Civic, looking like a million bucks in knockoff Prada sunglasses and a black turtleneck, driving south toward Boston. That morning on the spur of the moment, as her husband had headed off to the faculty meeting, she'd decided to attend the annual convention of the American Society of Surgeons of the Hand taking place at the Ritz. Two main activities occurred at such conventions: lectures and job interviews. Livi was not going for the lectures.

At last the professors took up the business of the student demonstrators. The faculty voted nearly unanimously for no punishment of any kind. Apart from the fact that so many of their own number had joined the occupiers—and *they* certainly were not going to be punished—many expressed the sentiment that the students had been in the right, though no one could say exactly what they had been right about. And they forgot entirely about the demands other than amnesty, but so had the students. Except for Manning, who wanted the one-term expulsion, and a biochemist named Watson, who hated everything about undergraduates no matter the circumstance, and who voiced his opinion that the Mac-Arthur Five should be sent off in shackles to the Supermax prison in Florence, Colorado, the rest of the Beet College faculty, save one other exception, voted to let them off scot-free.

Matha looked pleased by the decision; it taught her what she had wanted to learn. Bollovate, too, for the same reason. Huey, of course, looked pleased as well. Ferritt took notes on their reactions, writing on his little pad: "There was a firestorm of protest."

The only moment worth noting was the point at which Professor Porterfield, that other exception, chose to speak—something he'd never done. That, he recognized, was his mistake when the Free Speech Zone vote came up; he should have expressed free speech. He would do so now. He raised his hand, stood just before the question was called, and said, in approximately twenty-three seconds (a record for faculty meeting speeches that stands to this day):

"Mr. President, I would like to raise two objections to letting the protesters off. One is sort of technical. But I always thought acts of civil disobedience were undertaken to incur punishment, not to avoid it. The second has to do with the message this decision would send. In other words, with teaching. In my judgment, we're doing the students no favor by pretending crimes have no consequences."

Then he sat again as quietly as he had risen, and calmly beheld Huey, who conferred with Bollovate while most other faculty members muttered and mumbled. Manning applauded and tried to whistle. Matha Polite stared at Professor Porterfield with renewed interest. All at once she realized something about this man that had a direct connection to her future. Bollovate realized the same thing about his own future regarding Peace, which meant Huey did too. Ferritt not only realized it, he was composing the "hed" on his piece for the *Pig's Eye*: "Porterfield Betrays Students." Peace's colleagues may have realized it as well, though some were more dimly aware than others. Members of the CCR certainly realized it, and quickly looked to one another across the room for mutual confirmation.

It had not occurred to any of them before. Until that moment, it would have been as removed from anyone's mind at Beet College as anything could be. Beyond remote. Impossible. As distant as the half-life of uranium. As far away as Nairobi. But now, for wholly different sets of reasons, it was there, as plain as the nose on everyone's face: Peace Porterfield had to go.

And sure enough, for the first time in his life—in the misty rivers of the mind where momentous thoughts flash like a carp's head, brown and white, just below the surface—Peace was beginning to realize the very same thing.

freestanding tower, gray and shadowed off to the side. Behind the castle stood a spread of vague blue-gray hills and a sky of lighter blue-gray in which puffy white clouds swung upward in a fuzzy comma. The day looked bright and yet also about to rain. To the left and right of the castle were trees full of leaves of resplendent greens, which grew more distinct the closer one came. Several trees tilted to the right as if pushed by a wind. Three black sheep occupied the middle distance, one grazing, two lying on the sward. And a boy and a girl walked on a path that seemed made of marl or some crumbly material, and ended halfway up a hill. He wore a straw hat and a blue shirt. She wore a red shirt and a white skirt shaped like an inverted egg cup. In the foreground were the brambles of a hedge, over which young Peace would climb while calling out to the boy and girl and telling them to wait up because he had questions to ask them.

That's what he would do as a teacher when looking into a poem or a novel or a story. He would translate himself into the object of his interest, using an instinct that was a boon to his students and a saving grace to himself, especially when he was down or disgruntled or feeling out of place—a time like the present.

It was seven days into November. He had left the faculty meeting on the day of the MacArthur Five decision two days earlier without speaking to his colleagues, who, though they had voted against him, would have spent another hour privately congratulating him on his moral courage. He had gone to be with Livi and the children. And in the days following—whenever he could wrest himself from the interminable and ineffectual CCR meetings, which had grown testier by the day, and bright with savage hauteur—he devoted himself to family and to the classroom.

"May I ask you a sophomore bull session question?" Livi said to him one evening when they stood together scraping the dishes. "What are you looking for in your life, Peace? What do you want— I mean, besides us?"

"To be useful"—without hesitation.

"Useful to whom?"

"To my students, so they'll be able to live in the world more alertly, or interestingly, I guess. I'm not crazy about big lofty pronouncements."

"I know. But the way everything is going, I thought it was a question you might ask yourself." She kissed his cheek. "Just trying to be useful."

In any given year he would teach a wide range of courses in subjects that simply interested him, and because they did, interested his students as well. Max Byrd had followed Peace from course to course, from a lecture course in the Metaphysicals, to seminars in Dr. Johnson, Conrad, and African-American novelists, to a conference group on the Irish Renaissance—a crazy salad, except that these various subjects came alive in the hands of a teacher of the first rank who gave Max and all serious students the goods. This fall, Peace was teaching but one course, since he'd taught three courses last spring, hoping to free time for writing. But the trustees' assignment intervened. His one course—Modern Poetry—had become almost excessively important to him, like a safe house.

A bleak and dank Tuesday began with a lacerating phone call from Bollovate, pushing him about the CCR's progress; a shouting complaint from the curator of the college museum that several pieces of African art were missing, and did Peace know anything about it and what was he going to do about it (as CCR chairperson, Peace had somehow become the catch-all for every college gripe and tantrum); a reading of his notes on yesterday's meeting of the CCR (in which Lipman proposed that the new curriculum be built around "The Great Gray Lady: How the *New York Times* Gives Us the World"), and another corrosive call from Bollovate.

Before heading off to the college, he noticed an old textbook of Livi's lying open on the kitchen table. The page was dog-eared and underlined at a description of a proximal row carpectomy, a procedure to remove three of the eight bones in the wrist, to relieve pain. A so-called salvage procedure, it is usually done to correct a botched surgery. The underlined portions detailed the procedure step by step. He took note of the book and the page as one does of something unusual that may be of importance later, but then slips one's mind. Unconsciously he frowned.

At noon he left his office. He hiked up the collar of his brown woolen sports jacket against the damp cold, traced the flight of a pair of grackles bisecting a long line of gray mist, and walked across the Old Pen from the library to Mallory, where the English Department taught its classes. Mallory was typical of aggressively modern campus buildings—ghastly yet expensive. The cinder-block walls were painted brown and had so gritty a texture that if one brushed exposed skin against them, it came away bloody. Ceiling lights were pinholes. Linoleum was the color of rotted lettuce.

Yet Peace was comfortable there. He closed the classroom door behind him, sat at the greenish table that served as a desk, and looked out upon the faces of twenty-three people with whom he would talk for the following fifty minutes about nothing but the likes of Eliot, Pound, Elizabeth Bishop, Auden, Yeats, Czeslaw Milosz, John Crowe Ransom, Robert Penn Warren, W. D. Snodgrass, Theodore Roethke, Hart Crane, Sylvia Plath, Robert Lowell, and today's subjects, Marianne Moore and Richard Wilbur.

Modern Poetry was conducted as a discussion group, though the class was larger than Peace would have ideally had it. He was a well-known softy, and many more students applied than the limit noted in the course catalog, figuring Professor Porterfield would always make room for one or two extra, or ten. Twice a week they met to give close readings to poems, usually organized around a common theme, but not always. He wanted to teach them how to read a poem, and more, to absorb the language of poetry so that they might learn to generate original language on their own.

"Original language," Peace told them at the first meeting, "is what distinguishes the real writer from the writer."

He quoted Twain's dictum about the difference between the word and the right word being the difference between the lightning bug and the lightning—not to tell them something about the poets they were looking at, but something about themselves. As thinkers, as people, and, for a few perhaps as future writers, they should only aim to be in the lightning business. The right word as opposed to the word. He would show them a quatrain from Eliot's "Sweeney Erect," but with a word omitted—"suds"—what the darkly comic, beer-drinking, lecherous Sweeney wipes around his face as he prepares to shave. What right word did Eliot choose? he asked them. No, not soap; it gives you nothing but the shave. No, not cream; it suggests only the lechery. Same with "foam," yet foam comes closer because it gets to the beer. And maybe to madness. And why is "suds" the right word? Because it contains the comedy, the lechery, the shave, *and* the beer. That's why.

He did not want to turn the students into poets. He wanted to make them see the world the way the poets see it, at least to see it that way some of the time. Because some of the time, the poet's way of seeing the world is clearest.

And this was the point as it applied to Peace himself. His wife and his best friend harassed him for not living in the world as it is—in Bollovate's world, when one came down to it. Yet from Peace's perspective, teaching and learning were as real as the world got. That may have been his problem. But it was also true. This is as good a place as any to note that if Livi was right and he resembled Candide, it was Candide with brains.

"We must learn to imagine what we know," he told his class. "That was Shelley's idea. Do you see it? There is the life of facts and the life of dreams. And they come together in the imagination. Learn what has happened—history, biology, anything. Then imagine what you know and it fills the facts with noise, color, and light. Whatever you saw is the same but different all at once. Because you looked. Only you. You looked."

How often Max Byrd wrote to his folks in Alabama that Professor Porterfield was his reason for staying in college. What he was learning about computers he could pick up anywhere. Were it not for Porterfield, he'd have come home long ago to work for his dad. Max was mired in debt with student loans, and in many ways preferred his parents' life, minus the poverty, to much of the esoterica and the claptrap hurled at him at Beet. Only Professor Porterfield seemed to speak for the value of learning, indeed for the value of growing up. "And he talks like a real person, Dad. You'd like him."

Even the grumpiest and most skeptical adored him. Why would they not? Peace was on their side. He didn't pander to them any more than he pandered to his colleagues, though the students seemed to better intuit his motives. He didn't agree with them automatically, and tell them how wonderful they were. He didn't say everything they wrote was "brilliant, but . . . ," or "splendid, yet . . ." He never called student poems "interesting." And once in a while he accused his classes point-blank of sloppy thinking and "English major bullshit." He didn't do anything overt to win them over. And he could not have cared less about student evaluations given at the end of every course, though his always shot through the roof. As he'd told Livi, all he wanted was for them to be more alert, more aware, more expressive, and generally smarter when he finished with them than when he began.

And in the interests of caring about them, he cared about his subject. He cared so much about literature he worried about it aloud. "Is *Juno and the Paycock* a tragedy? Is *Riders to the Sea*? How could they both be tragedies? Why did Ellison write nothing of value after *Invisible Man*? Did John Donne suffer? What were Conrad's politics? Does a real writer *have* politics? Why would Dr. Johnson never speak of death?" And so forth. The students overheard him, and beheld the imaginative teacher. So deep would he go in his private-public investigations, sometimes he would look up suddenly in class and blink like an awakening baby as if surprised to see anyone else in the room.

"Mr. Porterfield?"

"Yes, Sarah?"

"I didn't get the Marianne Moore poem at all." Others nodded. They were about to take on "The Mind Is an Enchanting Thing."

"Let's try to figure it out," said Peace. "The mind is an enchanting thing. How so, Max?"

"Because it is complicated?" said the boy.

"In what way is the mind complicated?"

"It moves in many ways," said Jenny.

"And it moves quickly. It darts," said Leslie, a music major. " 'Like Gieseking playing Scarlatti,' Moore writes. She means the mind is quick and agile."

"Quick and agile," said Peace, considering their words. "But so what? Everyone knows that the human mind is quick and agile. Why write a poem about it?"

"Why write a poem about anything?" said Jenny, evoking a wave of light laughter.

"Yeah," said Peace. "Why do poets write poems?"

"To give you something to teach," said Lucky, a black kid from Andover, who could be counted on to say things like that.

"Precisely," said Peace, with a smile. "And what do I like to teach, Lucky?"

"Deep meaning," said the boy in a deep, dramatic bass, eliciting another laugh.

"Quick and agile. And deep," Peace said. "What makes a mind worthwhile? The use of a hand can be quick. The eyes can be quick and deep. The voice, too." He imitated Lucky: " 'Deep meaning.' But Marianne Moore is writing about the *mind*, which is the engine of the hands and the eyes and the voice, the center of everything. What makes that organ special to the poet?"

"I can think of another organ that is quick, agile, and deep," said Lucky.

"I'm sure you can," said Peace. "But try this once to stay on the subject." More laughter, then a meditative silence.

"It can change," said Jenny. "The mind can change."

Peace read aloud the last lines of the poem: " 'It's not a Herod's oath that cannot change.' Good for you, Jenny. And what was Herod's oath? Why would it have been better had Herod changed his mind?" Several students offered the correct answer. Peace leaned back, clapped his hands once above his head, and gave them the thumbs-up. "What?" he teased. "You've read the Bible? What heresy is next? The Greeks?"

So the class progressed, from Marianne Moore's poem to Richard Wilbur's "Mind," which was on the same subject but took a different turn. The mind is as blind as a bat, said Wilbur, that flaps about in the dark. Yet once in a glorious while, it can find a new flight path and "correct the cave."

They talked and talked. They looked up, they looked down— heads bent over books. So open, so private. This was the beauty of teaching—under the wheedling and the grappling, the strange loveliness of the enterprise. In their jeans, their baseball caps, even their nose rings and their saucy tattoos, the kids were, to him, breathtaking.

"Professor Porterfield?" asked Jane of the dramatically long blond pigtail. "You're always talking about original language. But I don't really understand."

Peace nodded, acknowledging his use of the term might have been vague. "All these poets we study," he said. "They reached into themselves to find words that were theirs alone. They took the effort to do this, not because they wanted to show off, or to baffle readers with strangeness for its own sake. They wanted to discover who they really were, what they really believed. And their own language would tell them. The words they used—the words we're talking about today—they could have come from no one but Moore and Wilbur."

Jane was still searching. So, evidently, was Max, and if he was not getting this, no one would. On the spot, Peace came up with an exercise deliberately geared toward heartbreak.

"I am going to do something now," he told them. "And when I do it, I want you to write. Don't think about it. No throat-clearing. Go with whatever comes to mind."

With that he stood, walked to the classroom door, opened it, and closed it. Then he looked back at the students looking at him. He opened the door again, and closed it again. The tumblers in the lock were heavy, clear, and loud.

"That is what I'd like you to write about," he said. "The sound of a closing door."

They went right at it. When fifteen minutes had passed and the class time was nearly over, he called upon several students to read aloud what they had put down.

Robyn wrote something that began: "In my father's house there were no doors." She went on to tell that she had grown up on a navy base, and she and her mom lived in a trailer. "No walls," she said. "And no doors."

Lucky, not a joke in him now, wrote of clinging to his father's pants cuffs as the old man was walking out on him and his mother, brothers, and sisters, for good. He had left on a Sunday. After the door had closed forever, the family had sat down to eat blueberry pancakes.

Lucille wrote of having been hauled off to a police station in her hometown in Louisiana when she was twelve; she had heard a jail door close. Prentice wrote of the breakup with his partner, who had told him, "We just don't click." But, "The door clicked."

Peace leaned forward and gave them a hard look. "Original language, you see, has nothing to do with arcane or fancy words," he said. "Most often it is composed of the simplest words. But they come from you, only from you."

At ten to one the class was over, but everyone kept his seat a moment longer. "That's another thing about the mind," said Jenny, gathering her books and talking to no one in particular. "It can make itself sad."

"Yes, it can," said Professor Porterfield.

CHAPTER

10

IN THE WEEK BETWEEN THE INCIDENT AT MACARTHUR HOUSE (in campus folklore the seizure of the building was downgraded to an incident) and the class in Modern Poetry that Professor Porterfield had just taught, a number of things happened regarding Beet College that struck those who observed them as out of the ordinary. There were other events that went unobserved—equally odd, if not plain weird. And they all occurred in a remarkably short span of time.

On one occasion, men and women bearing tripods, theodolites, and miniature blue and orange flags on metal sticks were seen pacing out steps on the campus periphery, where they planted their flags. When asked what they were doing there by reporter Ferritt Lawrence, who tended to ask that question of everyone, they explained they were measuring the shoulders of the college roads in order to dig more trenches for the rainy season. This explanation satisfied Lawrence, who did not think the event worthy of a story for the *Pig's Eye*. But it was considered unusual by others, since the strangers with tripods and tiny flags were doing their work hundreds of yards from any of the campus roads. And in New England all seasons are rainy.

On another occasion, small parties of men in suits and recent haircuts were noticed being led on what appeared to be a walking tour of the campus. Behind them trailed a hard-looking blonde in red tights and a black leather miniskirt, holding a clipboard. The tour guide was President Huey himself. And though no one could hear what he was telling the group, he was clearly happy and over-excited, making the exulting noises of an appliance salesman. He flapped his arms like a gull on a trash bin, and one could even make out a faint yet ecstatic screak.

In autumn on a college campus most everyone is too busy to pay sustained attention to such sporadic irregularities, so while these events might have been mentioned in passing once or twice, more urgent topics were being discussed, such as how clownish Dean Henry Muddler looked on his Moped, whether or not the galootish Dean Smitty Smith was a true albino, was Dean Jenina McGarry a dyke or a wannabe, and wasn't Dean Wee Willy Baedeker a horse's ass. The CCR's progress or lack of it bore deep into every-one's minds, which was why it had become more the subject of brooding than of chatter, though some faculty members, armed with basic survival instincts, made plans to work elsewhere.

And yet there were more extraordinary occurrences.

One day over lunch at the Faculty Club, Keelye Smythe was wondering, in the presence of Professors Lipman, Kettlegorf, Booth, Kramer, and Heilbrun, about a certain matter for which this rump meeting of the CCR had been convened. The Faculty Club had served as an abattoir in the 1880s, and though the structure's walls were taken down and replaced a dozen times in the interim, and were now covered in mauve fabric erupting in hydrangeas, still, every so often someone complained of smelling blood.

What was unusual about this CCR meeting was the absence of the chairperson. And the subject about which Professor Smythe was wondering, since they were running out of time, when all things were considered, when one really faced facts, when one took into account, after due deliberation, the competing pros and cons of the matter, was whether—he was just wondering—Professor Porterfield were the right person to serve as chair.

"He's very amiable, and of course he's a personal friend of mine—why, I believe I was the first to welcome him to the department four years ago. I think it was I who proposed recruiting him from Yale. Yes, I'm sure of it. I might venture to say I am his closest friend in the college. And I really, really truly like him."

Smythe would have gone on like this for a dozen more such sentiments, but the scientist Booth, impatient for the end of the equation, waved him toward a finish.

"I'm simply not certain," said Smythe, "if he's in touch with the times."

"Exactly," said Lipman. "I'm sure he's a fine teacher, and a fine scholar, though you gentlemen, and lady [Kettlegorf beamed], would know more about that than me . . . I." (Lipman's only advanced degree was from the Columbia Graduate School of Journalism, where she had written her master's thesis, "The Media: Is It in Trouble?") "But," she said, "the way he runs our meetings, he's a bit old-fashioned."

"Exactly," said Heilbrun, who was dressed in a Brocton—a gray double-breasted lounge suit and a shirt with a white wing collar.

"Exactly," said Kramer at nearly the same time.

"What our esteemed colleague does not seem to realize," Smythe went on, taking a quick, surreptitious glance around the club to assure himself that the esteemed colleague was not nearby (he need not have bothered; Peace never went near the place), "is that we require a curriculum with some zip to it, pizzazz, something new. Innovation!" He banged the table lightly. "That's the ticket. That's what the trustees are looking for. I mean, Peace is a very nice man—"

"Very nice," said Heilbrun. He dabbed on a touch of lip balm.

"Exceptionally nice," said Kramer.

"But," continued Smythe, "I just don't know. Something is missing."

"Missing," said Kramer.

"I mean, he's very intelligent," said Smythe.

"Very intelligent," said Kramer, whose echolalia had begun to get on the group's nerves three weeks earlier.

"And very nice," said Heilbrun.

Kramer was about to say, "Very nice," but Smythe cut him off. "I just don't know," he said, as if actually contemplating the matter. "Something is different about him. I didn't see it at first."

"A bit standoffish," said Booth.

"A bit standoffish," said Kramer before anyone could stop him.

Before anyone could stop *her*, Kettlegorf made it through the opening bars of "I'm Gonna Wash That Man Right Out of My Hair"—causing people at the other tables to turn their heads in alarm.

The group continued in this vein through the consommé, into the salmon fillet, past the seasonal fruits, and toward the decaf cappuccino. By the time they stood to leave, they had reached no firm conclusion save that Professor Porterfield was a very nice, very amiable, very intelligent fellow, and that they all liked him tremendously.

So there was that unusual event, to be added to the others, if anyone had been doing the adding, that is.

And there was Akim's random numbers-and-letters generator. Like a cyclopean eye, his laptop shone in the dark of the cave. The numbers rolled, the letters rolled. Hour after hour, day after day, the generator kept searching for the Homeland Security Department code without success. That was unusual.

And then there was this event, which occurred off campus during a gray mizzle.

Joel Bollovate and Matha Polite met in town for drinks at the High on the Hog Lounge in the Pigs-in-Blankets Bed 'N Breakfast. Now, this was *very* unusual, both for the fact that the chairman of the board of trustees had invited an undergraduate for a drink, and because no one ever had drinks at the High on the Hog until after ten at night, when the locals showed up for pinball, sang along with "Roxanne" on the jukebox, played with action figures, and compared symptoms of PTSD. Bollovate and Matha had the lounge to themselves, except for one barely visible ectomorphic figure, half draped by shadows, who remained very still in the corner and to whom they paid no attention. They sat under the print of the dogs playing poker and drank cabernets.

"You interest me, Miss Polite," said Bollovate. He grabbed a dozen salted peanuts.

"You interest *me*," said Matha. The two of them had just exclaimed "Cheers!" and were surveying each other, as if for size.

"Why do I interest you?" asked Bollovate.

"You fuhst," she said, hearing herself sliding back into southern.

"Well, for one thing, you're a leader," said Bollovate. "I watched you during the MacArthur House bullshit. The other students listen to you." Matha smiled demurely. "I'm a leader too."

"That's why Ah interest you?" asked Matha.

"That is one of the reasons. I also noticed that you don't care much for Beet College."

"And that appeals to you?"

"Maybe you're wasting your time here," said Bollovate. He signaled for two more cabernets, and scooped up a fistful of pretzel sticks.

"If yuh don't mahnd mah askin', Mr. Bollovate, what are yuh gettin' at?"

Bollovate downed his second wine, ordered a third, and encouraged his guest to do the same. "As you know, Miss Polite, Beet College is in bad shape. It pains me to say so, but there might not *be* a Beet College come spring."

"That would be awful," said Matha. They looked straight at each other, innocent as larks.

"So," Bollovate went on, "you might be faced with the choice of transferring to another institution, or taking employment. Frankly, I must tell you, I think you're ready to go to work right now."

Once again, Matha was torn for two or three seconds. She was a great if underappreciated poet and an important radical feminist, that she knew. But Mr. Bollovate seemed to be offering her a real job.

"Of course, one of your demands was my dismissal." He dug into a dish of oyster crackers.

"Oh, don't pay any mind to that, Mr. Bollovate. We were just funnin'."

"Miss Polite"—taking her hand, which had been left on the table for the taking. "Miss Polite, I would like you to think about something. You don't have to make up your mind right now. But I'm setting up satellite corporations to develop quite a few large properties on the East End of Long Island. Very large properties, I kid you not. Tens of thousands of acres in all, where they used to grow ducks and potatoes. A waste of space, if you ask me. The plantings I have in mind will have three-car garages and cost from four to ten million apiece, each occupying a plot under an acre. You do the math. The point is, we will be needing people to sell those houses, smart people, born leaders who know what side is up, if you get my drift."

Matha studied the entirety of Joel Bollovate, mentally weighing him from nape to base. "Real estate," she said at last. "You know, Mr. Bollovate, back home mah daddy's in real estate. And mah sister Kathy has a thrivin' real estate business in the very location you're interested in."

"Perhaps it's in the blood, Miss Polite," he said, giving her hand a squeeze, to feel the blood.

"Well, Ah certainly *will* think about it!" Now it was her turn to order up the drinks.

In a short while the two of them wobbled out of the bar. They did not need to find a place to wobble to, since Bollovate had taken the liberty of reserving a room at the inn. So they went upstairs to continue taking liberties. Matha, who knew what side was up, insisted on being on top.

These disparate events—the people with the flags, the tour party, the CCR secret lunch, the coming together of Matha Polite and Joel Bollovate, as well as the missing African artworks that the museum director had called Peace about—oh yes, and a vanished Calder stabile that had stood on the lawn outside the History Department—all of them, viewed independently, might have remained isolated incidents. Taken together, however, they added up to a definite change in the emotional weather at Beet College, one that had come on fast, and noticeably different from the usual collegiate mass neurosis. It was hard to put one's finger on it. It was not yet a full-fledged nervous breakdown, but it showed promise.

Five additional contributing occurrences deserve mention. They also were disparate, yet connected, directly or indirectly, to the personage of Chairman Bollovate.

Late one afternoon, the November gloom was relieved by the sight of a mobile unit of Chuck E. Cheese's that had set up shop smack in the middle of the visitors' parking lot. The trailer played a little Chuck E. Cheese's tune of enticement with bells, and at once the students ran toward it. It seemed—as Ferritt Lawrence learned after some crack investigative work—the college trustees had decided to lease a portion of the lot to the fast food chain to improve cash flow. The kids loved it, at least at first sight. Many found the games more challenging than their courses. And even the faculty, though there had been some reflexive grumbling in the beginning, seemed to take to it too. They seemed especially impressed with the robotic mouse. Speaking for Fine Arts, Professor Kettlegorf gave the franchise her blessing. "I just adore the yellow!" she told one of her classes. Then she sang "Yellow bird, up high in banana tree."

The second was a correspondence among several parties best presented verbatim:

November 3
Dear Mr. Bollovate:

The Registry of Deeds would be pleased to have you visit us in pursuit of the questions raised in your letter of November 1. But I am afraid we cannot send you the document in which you are interested, and we cannot send you a copy of same. Any papers as old as the one you require are very fragile, as you must imagine, and are kept sealed under Plexiglas. The Registry does not permit the making of facsimiles, but guests are free to come in and take notes. You would be most welcome here. We have quite a few historical exhibits in the main hall, supported by private donations by philanthropists such as yourself.

Very truly yours,
Norton Richards, Registrar
Essex County, Massachusetts

November 4
Dear Mr. Bollovate:

May I say how grateful we at the Registry are to have received your generous contribution of $5,000 for our historical exhibits. Please find the tax deduction form enclosed. Also enclosed find two Xerox copies of the land grant you requested. I would greatly appreciate it if you kept this transaction between us.

Very truly yours,
Norton

November 5
Dear Joel:

The document you messengered over is fairly straightforward, yet it creates a problem. The land was originally transferred under a charitable trust that stipulated any current or future use for educational purposes only. That is, the Beet property was given to establish a school, and if it is transferred again, even after three hundred years, the new owner also must set up an educational institution. The Probate Court of Massachusetts oversees charitable trusts, and it is there—if you so instruct me—I shall argue that the original deed contains precatory language, not legally enforceable. In that case, should you wish to change the terms of the trust, you would need to sue the heir to the land, if you can find one living. As your attorney, I'd be happy to handle that for you. Or you could always simply buy him or her out. Of course, you know, Joel, as a trustee you would be forbidden to buy the property yourself, or to develop it or make any profit from it.

All the best,
Sam

November 6
Dear Mr. Bollovate:

Great news! I have found Nathaniel Beet's heir, and he is the only one! What do you think of that! He is Beet's great-great-great-grandson's nephew twice removed, and his name is Francis April. He doesn't work, as far as I can tell, and he spent all the family dough on expensive wines and Joe Namath memorabilia, if you can believe that. I think he's a fag, if you'll pardon my French. Anyway, he's hard up for cash! What do you think of that! Lives in Provincetown with a schnauzer named Nathaniel. Hope this is what you need. Invoice to follow.

Your pal,
Gus Tribieux
Private Operator to the Stars

November 7
Dear Mr. April:

I wonder if I might see you on a matter of business. I have a financial proposition which I believe will be of interest to you.

Yours,
Joel Bollovate
Chairman and CEO
Bollocorps

Then one morning, Mrs. Whiting upped and quit. She walked away from a position she had held with quiet distinction for three decades, without a word to anyone but Professor Porterfield. him she simply left a note of gratitude and wished him wel

The fourth extraordinary event involved Professo himself who never lost his temper, but in this ins middle of a class, when Peace was working his way through *Hugh Selwyn Mauberley,* Bollovate threw open the door and asked Professor Porterfield to see him, now. Peace told him he'd meet with the developer after the hour, but Bollovate said he was a very busy man. Peace did not wish to participate in a scene in front of the students. He excused himself and went to stand with his intruder in the hall, as students crowded round the closed door.

"Don't do that ever again, Mr. Bollovate," he said as the two men faced each other.

"Time is money, Professor Porterfield. We are just about to hold a board meeting. The trustees need to know if you're getting this job done or not. There's talk that you're not."

"They don't need to know right now"—looking down at the developer.

"Yes or no?"

"Yes," said Peace. "The committee will provide the sort of plan the board is looking for. You have my word." He did not know how this would happen, but he meant what he said. "Just don't interrupt a class of mine again."

"You're an employee here," said Bollovate, his nostrils dilating, his cheeks puffing to a purple soufflé, and one jagged tooth showing just above his lower lip, which (yes, it did) trembled.

"No, sir. The students and faculty are the college. You're the employee." And he went back to teach.

In many ways, this exchange stood out as the most unusual incident among the unusual incidents, because it represented a first for both men. It was the first time Peace had felt the urge to pop anyone since his St. Paul's baseball coach called the opposing catcher a "dumb nigger," and it was the first time Joel Bollovate had quivered with rage and humiliation since his high school's yearbook editors had voted him the man most likely to be fat.

Speaking of which: the three-foot-high alabaster pig that made up the acroterion above the cornice on the Temple? That was missing too.

Finally, there was an event that occurred outside the college purview, involving the rest of America, and thus went unnoted at Beet. While the story of the imminent closing of the college had trotted along—prompting editorials saying on the one hand that it was unimaginable, and on the other, it was not—a poll was taken by ABC and the *Washington Post*. It simply asked a large sampling of citizens whether they would care if all the nation's four-year liberal arts colleges closed forever.

The answer was, 71 percent "could not give a rat's ass" if the institutions vanished from the face of the earth, just as Manning had thought. So while the results of the poll prompted editorials of their own—on the one hand, the American people didn't realize the consequences of what they were saying, and on the other, they did—the businessmen of America got interested.

"You know," Bollovate told his fellow trustee developers at the board meeting following his contretemps with Peace, "this may be a sign of things to come. I mean, look, pro basketball players don't go to college anymore. The best prospects don't. Why should they? They become millionaires right out of high school. And the NBA nabs them while they're young, before they can be injured playing college ball. Major League baseball players don't go to college, most of them. It's only a matter of time till pro football catches on and gives in." His fellow trustees were rapt, eyes googly. This was their kind of talk. "You see what I'm saying? There's nothing four years of liberal arts gives them but [chuckling] Plotinus!" The others chuckled too, without knowing why. "After four years of history and the Greeks, four years of Shakespeare, how can they possibly fit into the country? How can they help themselves? Help us?

"Tell me"—as he was unwittingly about to paraphrase Virginia Woolf—"would the world be any worse off if Shakespeare hadn't existed?"

"We could teach them all they need to know in six months," said Giles Rogaine, a developer of tract houses outside Framingham.

"Six months!" said Bollovate. "Damn straight! Instead of paying tuition—for what?—they learn to earn! They *make* money. And

CHAPTER

9

THE BETTER TEACHERS AT ANY LEVEL POSSESS INVENTION AND imagination. These powers are not the same and are not equal. An imaginative teacher is always inventive, but an inventive teacher is not necessarily imaginative. Between the two, invention is a comparative cinch. It's a three-eared camel or a farting Sri Lankan ambassador or a three-eared Sri Lankan camel schooled in international diplomacy who farts out of one of his three ears. That's all it is.

But imagination? Ah. Imagination is enthralled only by the camel, the ordinary humpy, durable, malleable-mouthed, diva-eyed, superior camel. Wow. The imaginative teacher walks around the animal, dreams into it, worries about it aloud in front of a classroom. The students overhear him as he worries. What's so fascinating, Professor? Professor? Can you hear us? Professor?

The imaginative teacher is thought itself. And to come upon one such person in a lifetime is to find, well, gold.

Peace Porterfield was an imaginative teacher. As a boy, he would dream into a painting in his parents' house—a nineteenth-century English landscape his father had picked up in a junk shop to cover a wall over a mantelpiece. In the center of a green valley stood a whitish castle that included several towers, and another they make it sooner. Everybody wins." He leaned forward. "Do you know what the average four-year college costs these days? The average? Thirty thousand bucks! That's what!"

"Your crapper costs more than that, Joel." All laughed.

"And it's *worth* more," said Bollovate. All laughed again.

Bollovate remembered the Department of Homeland Security. "That's the model," he said. "Six months of courses like Homeland Security. Trade schools, boys! There's our future. Online trade schools. Am I right?"

"You're right, Joel."

"Online trade schools. Great for youth. Great for business. Great for America."

"Joel"—the consensus—"you're a genius!"

CHAPTER

11

THAT YEAR, PARENTS WEEKEND WAS COINCIDENT WITH VET-
erans Day, November 11, which meant one less holiday for the college
and less wasted time for the CCR. But considering the nonprogress
the committee had made so far, the combining of events was of little
help to Peace. And he'd lost November 8 to Sensitivity Day, when
he'd decided to stay working in his office and be sensitive to his assignment. Sensitivity Day went without a hitch, save for an incident
when a midlife-crisis motorist took so long to read the revised Slow
Children sign, he wrapped his red Corvette around a mailbox. In
an effort to get with the esprit of the college, Chuck E. Cheese's
served a Sensitivity Meal, but they had difficulty coming up with
components. Since no product involving a living thing could be
included—eliminating burgers, salads, cheeses, and shakes—the
Sensitivity Meal consisted of a Coke, a gift certificate for double
burgers with fries, and a Chuck E. Cheese's bobble-head.

Parents Weekend and Veterans Day created two pockets of fes-
tivities at the college and in town, separated by the dark woods.
That is how one would have viewed the scene from above, say from
a helicopter—a typical New England landscape in which the tea-
black darkness is occasionally relieved by small and desperate
flickers of light.

In town, the event had all the fun of a Thanksgiving Day Parade, with people on television remarking on the fun. Beet had no living World War I veterans available to march, and only two from the Japanese theater of World War II (one of whom refused to admit the war was over, and yelled "Kraut" and "Gerry" at the plastic models of sashimi in the window of the Soo Piggy Soo Soo Sushi restaurant). The vets from Vietnam and Iraq numbered twenty-six, thirteen from each conflict. But the two groups hated each other so openly that one refused to march anywhere near the other, with the Iraq vets wearing combat fatigues, their faces painted green and yellow, and the boys from Vietnam dressed in sombreros, flak jackets, and fuchsia Speedos. Manning marched with his buddies from the Marines, who provided the parade with its only dignity. He had fought in no war, but took the day seriously, and never missed a year.

A couple of hundred Beet citizens lined Main Street, looking strikingly related to one another, and swaying more from the November wind than from their singing, which was made up of clashing patriotic anthems belted out simultaneously. The Beet High School marching band, the Porkers, tried to play "Hail to the Chief" for some reason, but wound up in an offbeat rendition of "Sentimental Me." The children of Beet, standing at their parents' knees, gave miniature American flags a desultory wave, then grew tired and dropped them to the sidewalk. Beth Porterfield attempted to push her little brother in front of a slow-moving Army Jeep, but thanks to her mother's grip on the boy, as well as the pace of the Jeep, failed.

"Here's Professor Manning!" Livi shouted to the kids.

Marching in parade dress, Manning turned and winked.

Over at Beet College, the parents didn't know what to expect of the weekend. Of course, they'd kept up on the situation with the trustees and the CCR, which by now was reported regularly in cities like San Francisco, Miami, Houston, Chicago, New York, and, it goes without saying, Boston. The story was described as "a wakeup call" for colleges all over America. Dean Baedeker had offered himself to the PBS *NewsHour* to analyze the matter but was turned down in favor of Professor Manning, who served the topic more ably, since he saw it as unrelated to his own career. Manning presented his bottom-line theory. He was opposed by Donald Trump himself, who had just come from another television appearance where he had forgiven Miss USA for partying and sullying her title. Trump asked the PBS audience, "What's wrong with making a buck?"

Manning countered, "Nothing. Unless that's all you make."

By now, Beet had become a big national story, no doubt about it. With nothing to opine on but Iraq and gay marriage, columnists—some of them alumni—produced emotions recollected in tranquillity, lamenting the passage of *les neiges d'antan*. News stories focused on the finances, the keener reporters noticing how many colleges were closing because of money, how many administrators were caught with their hands in the till, how much plain mismanagement was hurling institutions into bankruptcy. That poll showing Americans willing to see four-year liberal arts colleges disappear was repeated, producing the same results.

America speculated:

Can you imagine New England without colleges? Take colleges out of Massachusetts and what would be left? Chowder. That's what.

Hell, can you imagine the whole country without colleges? American culture would be cut in half. What would happen to plays and movies no longer able to include the drunk, stubble-chinned, chain-smoking, self-loathing, brutal but deep down kind and inspirational professor? Where would one behold the undergraduate who finds love, loses it, yet learns the lesson of a lifetime and faces the future with clear eyes?

What would become of the college essay, and those revelatory moments when one realizes that one's parents are people too, or that life consists of something bigger than oneself?

What would happen to phrases like "the press of work"? Who would "concur"? Who would "demur"? Who would "recuse" or "adumbrate" or find things "cathartic" or "emblematic"? What would happen to letters of recommendation and "without hesitation"?

What would happen to secondary education? Schools like Groton, Exeter, Andover, and Peace's own St. Paul's would be the first to bite the dust. Why go through all that fancy-schmancy preparation if one is merely aiming to work for Bollovate? On the other hand, public education might get a boost because without the brass ring of attending a top college, the private schools would be deprived of their competitive advantage. At long last, there would be an equal playing field in American education. Say! Did Bollovate have something after all?

"You see?" said Manning to Peace after returning to the campus. He was still in uniform. "Colleges are thought of as any old business, so they're available to the same standards. Thirty years ago, did you ever hear of anyone talking about colleges as money-makers? You bet your ass you didn't. Look at these parents. Don't you think half of them are thinking about money right now? Is the school worth it? Are their kids better off working at IBM?"

Whatever their thoughts, most parents had come for the weekend simply to be with their kids. Matha Polite's mama and daddy drove the metallic bronze Range Rover up from Virginia in spite of their daughter's e-mailing them that Parents Weekend had been canceled due to a blizzard. All she needed was for one of them to call out her three names, with that slow southern emphasis. As it was, Luelle wondered why people kept referring to her daughter as Matha, but concluded it was a Yankee mispronunciation.

The weekend was kicked off by a welcome speech from President Huey in Lapham Auditorium. There sat the parents like obedient children, looking up at a man on whom most of them would have looked down in any situation other than a college—if they noticed him at all. Huey was in his glory. He had no significant talent, save a nose for his superiors, but he possessed an old-fashioned West Virginia senator's gift for speechifyin', and though his public talks contained no more wit or wisdom, or information for that matter, than his private ones, many were pleased to listen to them, the way people are pleased by the soothing repetitive rhythms of a train. Students, however, being less tolerant of their leader, greeted his appearance with a razzing parodic chorus of "I Did It Their Way."

Huey stood at the podium, cleared his throat for effect, and told the convocation he knew these were "stormy days," and the "winds of change" might be blowing "the great old ship" of Beet College "to and fro and hither and yon." Yet he for one was convinced that "smooth seas lay ahead" and "the albatross or the sharks, whatever, would soon give way to the doldrums and the scallops." He also asked the parents to donate what they could, each according to his ability. Ferritt Lawrence took down the speech word for word, noting that though Huey "sent shock waves through the community," he was "no stranger to controversy."

Outside Lapham after the talk, students and their families collected in huddles. Mothers and fathers of freshmen in particular confronted Huey, their noses inches from his, asking, What did he think the college was doing, admitting students to a school they planned to shut down?

"You'll pay us back every cent, you fraud," shouted a DuPont executive from Delaware.

Huey, who was so adept at tergiversation one could barely recall the subjects he evaded, took the assault with a frozen smile. Showing the bouncy self-confidence of a fencing instructor and backpedaling toward his office, he told the man, "You know, I've always been interested in the DuPont Corporation."

Matha Polite was "pissed" to see her parents standing next to Akim's, making chitchat. For one day only the radical poet was distracted from her campus mischief, though the Bacon takeover remained on schedule five weeks hence. She wanted to get Daddy alone. Lately she had experienced an irresistible desire to learn all there was to know about real estate. And Akim had never known so strong a wish to be near his parents, to the point of broaching the subject of chess with the rabbi. (He'd decided not to tell them about the cave or the TATP.) Matha approached anyway, said a breezy "Hi" to Akim, which sent him reeling with puppy love, and collared her old man. She needed a spoon-fed lesson in his trade before her upcoming business conference with Joel Bollovate at Sow's Motel, down the road from the campus.

With Huey's remarks consigned to legend, the rest of Saturday was to be spent by the students ushering their parents to activities meant to highlight the college. In the late afternoon there would be a football game on Beet Field with the cheerleaders jumping up and down, assembling into injury-threatening pyramids, shaking their pompoms, and yelling "Piggy Piggy Piggy Piggy, Oink Oink Oink!"—a traditional cheer that always deflated opposing teams, which had been preparing those very words as a taunt.

In the evening there would be concerts in the Old Pen by twenty-four of the college's a cappella groups (the other sixteen were on tour), each singing "Old Black Joe," "Camptown Races," and "Nobody Know Da Trouble I Seen." This medley was followed by a lecture by Professor Godwin, "Who Speaks for the Halt?" The day would end as did most days at Beet and other colleges—after the parents had gone back to their hotels—with binge drinking and casual sex, and most of the students simply headed for sleep.

For now, they guided their parents to selected classes. Those who attended Professor Smythe's class, Analepses and Anaphora in the Oeuvre of Dan Brown, could barely make out a word he said, while those who went to Professor Kramer's class left frightened. Kramer decided to do a one-man reenactment of the Battle of Blenheim, striding up and down in front of the room in full battle dress and wielding a two-handed sword. And no one went to Booth's class because it was chemistry. The students in Peace's Modern Poetry class actually wanted to show off their teacher. But more than a few in other classes were visibly anxious about exposing their folks to what they had been paying for. When the eerily quiet visitors finally emerged from Professor Lipman's much-sought-after seminar, three parents vowed to cancel their subscriptions to the *New York Times*, and two inquired as to the procedures involved in withdrawing their children from the college immediately, with a refund or without.

After his show class, Peace headed home for a rare lunch when the whole family could be together. On the way out he saw Manning walking toward Lapham. "And how are you pleasing the parents today, Captain?" he asked the Marine.

"Believe it or not, I'm on a faculty panel about diversity."

"They invited *you*?"

"I volunteered. I wanted to ask my fellow panelists if they thought that holding a different opinion constituted diversity."

The town parade was long over (having taken but twenty minutes from start to finish), and Robert was sitting on the hall staircase when Peace came in. Head in hands, he was counting to one hundred, very softly and seriously.

"What are you doing, Bobby?" asked his father.

"I'm giving myself a time-out."

"Why? Did you do something wrong?"

"No. But I'm going to."

"And he means it," said Livi, greeting her husband with a kiss and asking, "How goes it at the House of Wax?"

"Never better."

She took his hand and led him into the kitchen. They sat together at the corner of the long pine table, where they could be close. Livi had laid out two chicken salad sandwiches.

"Well, I've got some news that will make you even happier." Peace tried not to look apprehensive. "I've been offered a job in hand surgery."

"Where?"

"In New York," said Livi, with too broad a smile suggesting her own anxieties. "What do you think?"

"And you learned of this when?" His lips were tight.

"Of the opening? Ten days ago. They interviewed me in Boston. I should have told you, I know. But they just called with the offer today, when the children and I got home." She looked him in the eye. "It really is a wonderful chance. What do you think?"

"What do you think I think? Why are you doing this?"

"Doing this? Oh, you mean my life. I didn't invent the job, Peace. But here it is."

"But you timed the move deliberately, didn't you? To get me to quit *my* job?"

"Yes, I'll admit, it was in my mind. Not the first thing, but yes. Did you think I was kidding when I said the college isn't worthy of you?"

"That's for me to decide, Liv. Not you or anyone else. So now your solution to my problem is to break up our family."

"We're not breaking up. Lots of families have split locations. One parent works one place, the other—"

"And that's your idea of a family? A jerry-rigged commuter marriage?"

They weren't raising their voices, but they had never spoken to each other in grimmer tones.

Livi studied the planks of the kitchen floor. "Look, I'm sorry if you think I engineered this offer just to push you around. You have to know I wouldn't do that."

"That's good, 'cause I'm not pushable. If I leave Beet College, it will only be after I've tried to do what they've asked of me. And it's not because I'm the good boy doing what he's told—though that's probably what you think. It's because trying to help the college is right. The place deserves to be saved."

"Do you honestly think you'll do that? Even if those clowns on your committee come up with the most wonderful plan ever devised, a real rainmaker, would Beet College ever be safe with people like Bollovate in charge? Manning's right. Once money alone drives these institutions, they're goners."

"So what do you do? Run, hide, and go work for GM? If you can't fight 'em, join 'em? Do you really believe those people who say let the liberal arts colleges go under know what they're doing? They're not thinking. And Manning is only half right. The theory is fine, but he's not acting on it. Sure, he has a point about the bottom line. But that doesn't say there's no recourse. He had a liberal arts education, you had one, I had one. What's it for, if not to enable us to beat back people whose only values are dollars?"

"The liberal arts are dead, sweetheart."

"The hell they are. They're just playing dead." He stood to leave. "You're a smart lady, Livi. Brilliant, sharp, all that. But this is something you don't get. You like to say 'when pigs fly,' because you think they don't fly. But I make them fly. All humanists make them fly. That's what a liberal arts college is about—making pigs fly. And the fact that pigs don't really fly makes our work the more satisfying."

She sat very still. They weren't arguing about pigs.

After a minute of silence—"I've got to get back." They hadn't touched their sandwiches.

"Peace, this is a good job for me, a rare chance. Of course, I want you to come with us and get out of this sinkhole. It's what I've wanted for years. Shoot me. But I want you more than anything. If you stay here, we'll make the new arrangement work. I swear to God. And if it isn't working, I'll quit." She stood in front of him and took his hand in both of hers as if examining it for damage.

"I hate this," was all he said. Their lips brushed in what passed for a kiss.

Heavyhearted, Peace returned to the campus to participate in his own faculty panel discussion, "How Many Cultures in Multicultural? How Far to Go?" But as he drove the Accord past Gregory—who had deteriorated in the past months and was now so out of it that without stopping a single car, and motioning like a bullfighter with a cape, he waved everyone past the gates—Peace decided the hell with it. He made a U-ey at the top of the entrance driveway and exited, to another flourish from Gregory. He bagged the panel—something he would not have thought of doing a mere three weeks ago—and drove home.

"Did you come back to ask for a divorce?" asked Livi, with genuine fear, when she saw her husband at the door.

"Nope," said Peace, giving her a squeeze. "It's Parents Weekend. Let's be parents!"

So the anger fled and the working couple did what working couples do if they want to be a family once in a while; they stole time. They thought they would steal it at Crane Beach in Ipswich, which would be blustery and empty in November, and perfect for the four of them to run about in the swales of the dunes. Not much to report about the rest of their afternoon, really. Mother, father, son, and daughter did nothing more interesting than to play tag and toss around a dog-chewed yellow tennis ball on the hard flat sand at the edge of the ocean. The sky was blue. The water gray. The sand was brown, or maybe tan. The children were so happy with this uninteresting situation, they hugged each other, albeit just once, and though the hug ended with them shoving each other away, they were sufficiently embarrassed by the act to tickle their parents.

Nothing more was said between Peace and Livi about her new job or the New York move. Nothing was mentioned of Beet College, or was thought about it, either—a personal best for Professor Porterfield, who had ingested the college whole since mid-October and often felt he had become what he'd eaten. He did not even recognize the fact that for those few hours the institution and its woes had vanished from his system, though anyone observing him, Livi definitely, could see the burdens lifted from his face. He was thirty-six, for chrissake. Today he looked thirty-six.

After the beach, the Porterfield family moved on to the Lobster Shack, where they chomped on lobster rolls made the way lobster rolls are supposed to be made, with huge chunks of meat and the rolls toasted and submerged in artery-clogging butter. The parents drank beer, the kids root beer. Robert raised his glass toward the others, but then said nothing.

"Do you want to make a toast?" his mother asked the seven-year-old.

"No," said the boy. "I just wanted to raise my glass. They do it on TV."

And so they did it in the Lobster Shack as well. Peace raised his glass, Livi and Beth theirs. And the guy behind the counter, too. And two more guys at the bar. And a woman with a rugulose face and slathered makeup, she raised her glass. And a plump older woman in jeans and a Sox cap worn backward, she did also. And two fishermen in their fifties, with red scars like lightning on their forearms, and buried eyes. Outside the window, the sun dug into the sea. And they all raised their glasses, saying not a word.

In the evening back at the house, Livi said the kids could stay up and watch a DVD. Beth picked out *Horse Feathers*. From early on their parents had taught them not to fear black-and-white movies, and introduced them to the Marx Brothers, with whose anarchies the children eagerly identified.

"Yeah! *Horse Feathers!*" shouted Robert.

They sat in the corner of the living room they called the den, all four bundled together on the couch, laughing from the moment the movie began. Soon came the part where Groucho is standing in front of a classroom and Chico and Harpo are heaving chalk and erasers at him. Livi and the kids laughed even harder, but none as much as Peace, who was so taken with the scene he clicked back the DVD to watch it again. Noting the force of his hilarity, Beth and Robert were sort of frightened. Livi, too. But Peace just laughed, in deep and heavy gales.

CHAPTER

12

"WE'VE GOT IT!" PROFESSOR HEILBRUN ANNOUNCED. FOL-
lowed by Professor Kramer, he leaped up the wooden staircase,
wearing a scarlet Inverness cape wrapped about him like a cloak,
and an Oswestry—an ivory brocade Edwardian jacket, striped
waistcoat, and black dress trousers with a chamois codpiece. "A
touch of whimsy," he explained. The two men celebrated their
own entrance like strippers geysering from a cake.

The date was November 20. This meeting in Bacon represented the twenty-fifth in the CCR's brief yet enervating history,
and the other committee members, Chairperson Porterfield included, sat around the refectory table, stunned with fatigue. Meeting after meeting had produced nothing but a series of crackpot
ideas interrupted by spasms of gossip, and as Thanksgiving approached and the curriculum report was due in three weeks,
Peace was wondering if Livi had put a curse on the project, and if
Beet College might close its doors after all.

Peace had tried several tacks in the interest of equal participation. He asked the committee members to define the meaning of
a liberal arts education personally. Then he asked them to come
up with a common definition as a group. He studied the more successful curricula in colleges similar to Beet in size and traditions.

He e-mailed professors in other places who had experience in this sort of project. He asked his six colleagues to do likewise. He moved disciplines around like modular furniture. He made a good-faith effort to get the committee to consider atypical combinations, even though he was pretty sure that such inquiries would result in the usual multi-this-or-that sausage. He tried a host of different centerpieces for a new curriculum—programs of study organized like the spokes of a wheel around a hub of government or history, literature or philosophy, the social sciences, even math and physics—with the thought that one area would be made to lead creatively to another, and expose the entire realm of learning to students as a rational construct. Hope had flared briefly with an offshoot of such an idea—a proposed curriculum divided among studies of discrete epochs such as the Dark Ages, the Renaissance, the Enlightenment, the periods of Romanticism and Modernism. But in the end that plan crumpled as well, as did so many other ideas, when concrete practice was envisioned.

Naturally, Peace blamed himself for the committee's failures, and his fellow committee members agreed; they blamed him too. But to be fair to them all, the task simply might have been too enormous and too much to ask. Perhaps no solution could do all that was expected—to satisfy the highest intellectual standards, to be intrinsically interesting, and to have mass and commercial appeal to boot. In any event, time was certainly running out. And the last few meetings, including the one of the present afternoon, had opened with a drowned, world-weary silence; that is, until Heilbrun and Kramer burst upon the scene.

"What have you got?" asked Smythe listlessly.

"The answer!" said Heilbrun. "We—Kramer and I—have solved the problem of the new curriculum!" The two men plonked themselves down in their seats, flushed with anticipation. Peace, hopeful to the last, gestured for Heilbrun to continue.

"Well, we were asking ourselves—Kramer and I [Kramer nodded rapidly]—what is the one thing truly fundamental to Beet College? What lies at the heart of the meaning of the school? Its deep-seated intentions, its essential purpose, its—how shall I say—raison d'être?"

"Why not say raison d'être," yawned Smythe. Heilbrun ignored him.

"Well?" said Booth, who'd had it up to here with the babble of humanists. "What is it?"

Heilbrun looked to Kramer, who looked to Heilbrun. They spoke in unison. "Pigs!" they said. Then Heilbrun said it alone. "Pigs!" Then Kramer. "Pigs!"

Peace tried very hard not to look as if someone had rabbit-chopped him in the back of his neck. The table hunched forward, seemingly aware that it was about to be treated to yet another demonstration of insanity. Someone asked the obligatory, "What are you talking about?"

"Until now," Heilbrun continued, "we have been approaching this matter of a curriculum as if it pertained solely to the mind, unconnected to more basic aspects of life." Kramer nodded more rapidly, and continued to nod nonstop during Heilbrun's presentation. "But last night, as I was dozing over a terribly boring history of Croatian mime theater, an old song came into my head—'Come on people now / Smile on your brother . . .'" He repeated the lyrics, this time singing.

Kettlegorf leaped at the chance to sing along with him. Then Lipman and Booth and the rest, except for Peace and Smythe, all singing together: ". . . 'right now!'"

The blood drained from Peace's face—that being one of two songs his parents sang mercilessly to him when he was still in the crib. The other—and he stiffened at its recollection as well—was . . . but Heilbrun suddenly sailed into that one too: "'This land is your land, this land . . .'"

"Are you getting at something?" Peace asked.

"It's the land," said Heilbrun. "Your land, my land—"

"*Our* land?" asked Smythe, with a snigger.

"Our land, yes," said Heilbrun. The group seemed happy, if bewildered. "You see, the song brought me back to the consideration of original purposes, of the consciousness Charles Reich talked about in *The Greening of America*. [Again Peace paled.] What was Beet College in its origins?" asked Heilbrun. "Two simple things, if you don't count God. A pig farm and a library. And for many years it thrived as a single entity composed of books and attention to the soil."

"The pigs soiled, all right," said Smythe. "Anyone seen Latin?" He tended toward jealousy as well as a desire to fit in, lending him a leer that was both with it and without it.

"So I came up with a thought," Heilbrun went on, "and phoned Professor Kramer at once [Kramer confirmed this with jackhammer nods]. Why not create a curriculum by going back to the land, and establishing a pig farm?"

"You're not serious," said Smythe.

"Quite serious," said Heilbrun. "You see, the students, our students, have been educated in a vacuum. They have no connection to the life of the earth. They have no kinship with the land. And yet, this land is their land, this land is our—"

"Please!" said Peace.

"The sad truth is that none of us has any connection to the land either," said Heilbrun, looking sad. "We have forgotten our roots. And the students have forgotten theirs. Most of all, they have forgotten how to work with their hands. So [he smiled to Kramer, who smiled back] here's the plan: We create a wholly new course of study that has our students take classes and do farmwork. They could build the sheds for the pigs, and the sties. They could repair the fences and lay the roads. In short, do all the work of the farm. A curriculum of hand and mind!"

"Pigs!" said Kettlegorf, as if goosed by an electric prod. "The students could study the pig as a being, a cultural figure. I don't know, but there must be a great deal of literature on the pig."

"The etymology is Anglo-Saxon," said Smythe, appearing interested for the first time, since the turn in the conversation afforded him an opportunity for erudition. "The Anglo-Saxon *pecga* and the Low German *bigge*, both meaning pig. Then there's the medieval Dutch, and finally the Middle English *pigge*." Everyone save Peace seemed impressed, mesmerized actually, so he continued. "'And whether pigs have wings,'" he quoted. "Does anyone know where that comes from?"

"*Alice in Wonderland*," all but Lipman said at once, plunging Smythe into a momentary gloom. He soldiered on nonetheless. "And there's *Charlotte's Web*. And Dylan Thomas—'Pigs grunt in a wet wallow-bath and smile as they snort and dream.'"

"Snort and dream!" said Kettlegorf.

"And there's Beatrix Potter," said Booth, suddenly enthused. "*Little Pig Robinson*."

"And Samuel Butler," said Smythe. "'Besides 'tis known he could speak Greek as naturally as pigs squeak.'" Kramer tittered.

"And A. A. Milne," Kettlegorf chimed in. "Piglet. And Edward Lear."

Smythe: "'Dear Pig, are you willing to sell for one shilling your ring?'"

Back to Kettlegorf: "'Said the piggy, I will!'" She sighed. "I will! Just like that! The piggy is asked to part with his ring, out of nowhere, mind you, and he simply says I will! Is there a more generous figure in all of literature? I think not."

"And Miss Piggy!" said Lipman, who did not know as many literary references as the others but wanted in on the discussion. She also mentioned the movie *Babe*.

"Don't forget *Animal Farm*," said Booth. "Which reminds me. We're not only talking about pig literature. There must be a very extensive pig history. I mean, all the pig farms in Europe and America."

"The Allies slaughtered pigs in France," offered Kramer. "Chopped their heads off with bayonets." He pursed his lips knowingly.

"And biology," said Heilbrun. "Why study crustaceans when we could do the same thing with pigs?"

"And economics," said Smythe, who now was clearly aboard. "A pig farm is a business. I am sure that basic economic principles apply. Industrial farms. Conglomerates driving out the smaller operations. Consolidation versus independents. That sort of thing."

Having not a whit of information on the subject, the others vigor-
ously agreed.

"And languages!" said Kramer. An amateur linguist as well as a
militarist, he rattled off the words for pig in different languages:
"French—*cochon*, German—*schwein*, Czech—*vepr*, Finnish—*sika*,
Afrikaans—*vark*, Croatian—*svinja* . . ." The others attempted to stop
him, but he was supercharged with excitement. "Danish—*svin*!
Bulgarian—*svinia*! Polish—*prosiak*!" He had delivered the Sanskrit
(*varaaha*) and was approaching the Maltese (*qazquz*) when Heilbrun
put his finger to his lips, and Kramer finally calmed down.

"You've made your point, dear boy," Heilbrun told his colleague, who was sweating like a *kwiskwis,* pig in Mingo, which he
whispered to himself.

"And songs!" exulted Professor Lipman, who fancied herself
an expert on contemporary groups. She cited Eminem's "Chokin'
This Pig," Dave Matthews's "Pig," and Nine Inch Nails's "March of
the Pig," as the others wondered what she was talking about.

Though they knew it was coming, they could do nothing to
stop it. Kettlegorf launched into "Piggies" from the Beatles's *White
Album:* " 'Have you seen the little piggies / Crawling in the dirt . . .' "
She made it two-thirds of the way through.

Faster and faster the committee members talked, with Professor Booth, the lone scientist on the committee, seizing the floor to
get down to brass tacks. "You know, if this is to be a real working
farm, we need to decide on what breeds to raise."

"How many breeds are there?" asked Kettlegorf.

Now it was Booth's turn to show off. "There are weaners," he
said, searching the air for more specifics. "There are Stock Boars
and Tamworths and Iron Age Pigs, which are a cross between the
Tamworth and the wild boar. There are the Large Whites, of
course, like Latin . . ." He paused, considering what an entire farm
of Latins would do to the plant life. "And the British Saddlebacks.
Pietrains and Landraces—you've seen them, with their lop ears
that cover most of their faces." No one had, but they all nodded.
"And there's the Duroc, which I like very much, that reddish brown
color. I nearly forgot the New Zealand Kunekune."

"Kunekune!" said Kettlegorf. She clapped in ecstasy.

"But who will tend to the farrowing?" said Booth, who saw that the others did not know what he was referring to. Everyone but Peace was rapt. "When the little pigs begin to appear," he said coyly.

"The students!" said Heilbrun again. Kramer, too.

"And the feeding?" said Booth, who was becoming a sort of evangelist to the group. "Who will grow the clover, the alfalfa, the chicory and turnips?"

"The students!" Lipman and Kettlegorf cried as one.

"And what about the business of the farm?" said Booth. "It's very important that the enterprise be more than self-sustaining. It's got to make a profit. The college endowment is all gone, you know. I've been paying attention to Mr. Bollovate—reading what he tells the papers. And if I understand him aright, the days of the nonprofit college are long over. Every tub on its own bottom. That's the way Mr. Bollovate describes it."

"And he's the tub to know," said Smythe. All laughed, except Peace.

"So the pig farm has to pay for itself and then some," Booth went on.

"You know?" said Kramer, about to come up with his first original thought, "this may have been Nathaniel Beet's plan all along. *Deus Libri Porci*. God leads to learning. Learning leads to money." How Peace wished Manning could have heard that.

"But who'll run the business?" said Kettlegorf.

"The students!"—everyone but Peace.

"And the slaughter of the pigs for ham and bacon and sausage?"

"The students!"

"And who will package the meat?"

"The students!"

"And manage the sales and the accounts?"

"The stu . . ."

There was no stopping them. Peace wandered into two lines of thought. The first was that soon, he knew, the now hepped-up committee members would hit a snag and run out of gas and grow surly and destructively witty, as they'd been doing for the past five weeks, and yet another meeting would come to nothing. The second was, Livi had been right about one thing. He sank deeper into his chair and vowed to go home and draw up the new curriculum himself.

"You know," said Booth. "Most of the little male pigs will have to be castrated."

"The students can do it!" said Heilbrun. And all except Peace agreed the students could castrate the pigs.

CHAPTER

13

BUT TO RETURN TO FERRITT LAWRENCE: HE HAD BEEN HAVING another bad day—the one-thousand-and-fourth such day in his career as a junior journalist. This one had preceded the Veterans Day/Parents Weekend holiday. Ferritt had been spending the afternoon in his room in Coldenham, preparing his answer to a take-home quiz, "Should the media police itself?" He was brooding and depressed that his chosen profession might have been misdirected, after all, and his parents may have been right when they tried to steer him toward a career in air conditioner repair. With the sky over Beet College going black and the clouds crushing the sun into a saffron line, his spirits had not sunk so low since last winter's German measles prevented him from attending an invitation-only dinner in the Communications Arts private dining room for columnist Bobo de Pleasure, "the conservative's liberal and the liberal's conservative." De Pleasure was speaking about his new book, *How to Become a Columnist,* the sequel to his two very popular previous books, *Is There Anyone in America I Don't Agree With?* And *I Could Not Agree More!*

Ferritt had been getting nowhere, absolutely nowhere, in his pursuit of the story of the closing of the college, the story of a lifetime. The CCR members with whom he continued to hold off-the-record conversations were on their own kicks and were telling him that if he wanted a story "of lasting significance" he ought to write about *them*, their remarkable successes and their hidden gifts.

Professor Kettlegorf prodded him to detail her early potential as a ballerina, a prodigy if she said so herself, and how she had sacrificed certain stardom for the greater good of teaching "our nation's future." She also mentioned her heartbreaking experience with the ship's captain in Kansas, but when pressed by Ferritt said she could not go on. She did start to sing "Red Sails in the Sunset," but by that time Ferritt was out the door.

Professor Smythe was deep into his ninth year on his seminal, comprehensive, and definitive study of the difference between the concepts of the egotistical sublime and negative capability. When, in a rare burst of innocent curiosity, the boy asked the professor if those ideas weren't just elaborate terms for self-concern and self-lessness, Smythe chuckled bitterly and accused him of misprision, which silenced him for once.

Professor Booth tried to persuade the young reporter to do a six-part series entitled "Booth: A Life in Chemistry." And Professor Kramer agreed it would be an excellent idea, or perhaps another idea would also be excellent.

Professor Heilbrun, who was wearing a Ruckley (navy single-breasted lounge suit), had meager experience with journalism or its standards and thought Ferritt might wish to write about his treatise on Charles Pisherwold, a dim-witted thirteenth-century serf who was born without the sense of taste and wrote passion plays to be performed by cows. When the reporter seemed uninterested, Heilbrun asked whether he wished to hear him sing the entire score from *Two By Two*. He believed he was the only man living, including the former Broadway cast, who could do that.

Since Professor Lipman was Ferritt's instructor in the *New York Times* course, he decided in the end to do her bidding, and had produced but one piece of writing in all those weeks, other than his piece attacking Professor Porterfield at the faculty meeting. It was Professor Lipman's own story, "To Publicize or Criticize: A Celebrity Editor's Dilemma."

"The question is . . . ," said Lipman.

"Is what?" said Ferritt.

"No, that's what you write. The question is . . ."

"The question is?"

"Yes. When you've written the preliminary material and are about to state the problem, you write, 'The question is . . .'"

"Do I always do that?"

"Yes. Or sometimes, if you are dealing with the past, you write, 'The question was . . .' But here you write 'The question is . . .'"

What was worse, his editor on the *Pig's Eye*, Jacob McMinus III, grandson of the notorious Drunk Thief of Wall Street, had taken to downing Ecstasy with Tab every morning. By late afternoon, when the paper was closing, he sat slumped over in his swivel chair, spinning himself faster and faster and muttering limericks about girls from Cape Cod.

Am I the only honest, responsible, sober professional in this outfit? Ferritt asked himself. The question was: Did every great journalist suffer this way?

And then, on the day of his deepest despair, he got lucky, because on that rock-bottom afternoon, he'd decided to do what all the great journalists had done before him, when they too questioned the validity of their calling: he determined to get shit-faced. And so he slipped into the safari jacket that had briefly belonged to Diane Sawyer (purchased on eBay for a song), climbed upon his mountain bike, rode to town, and parked himself in the darkest corner of the High on the Hog Lounge at the Pigs-in-Blankets Bed 'N Breakfast, not five minutes before Matha Polite and Joel Bollovate had sat down at the onset of their partnership.

Ferritt had been the figure barely visible to anyone, and quite invisible to Matha and Joel as they had moved closer together with each glass of wine. He'd watched them with dark and narrow eyes. "Knowledge is power," he said to himself, and so he would not forget, he wrote it down.

From that day in the bar, during which he had taken care to remain undetected, to the present, this week before Thanksgiving,

Ferritt followed Matha wherever she went. He would have liked to follow Bollovate as well, but since the trustee's main mode of transportation was an Apache Longbow attack helicopter minus the missiles and customized for his private use, the reporter was discouraged. Matha would do as a quarry because she frequently led him to Bollovate anyway. The chairman would pick her up outside the college gates, and they'd drive off to their business conferences. What was the story in their trysts? Something connected with the fate of the college? If not, at least a scandal, which Ferritt hoped would be "juicy."

So he followed the two of them to Sow's Motel, and he believed he was becoming a first-rate tracker, though he trailed the couple at such close range—his mountain bike grinding its gears behind Bollovate's black Escalade at a distance no greater than sixty feet— they could have spotted him every time. Fortunately for Ferritt, the pair were so absorbed, not in each other but rather in themselves individually, he could have lain in bed between them without being noticed. He didn't need to; he could listen in with his cassette recorder outside their window.

Their pillow talk—Joel's and Matha's—had lately shifted subjects from Matha's limitless future in Long Island real estate to Professor Porterfield's limited future at Beet. At least, limited was the way both of them wanted it. Matha was more forthcoming.

"I'm mystified, Mr. Bollovate," she said one afternoon in their special Room 207. Supine in the king-size bed, they appeared a lower-case i beside a capital O. She sipped from a bottle of Johnny Walker from the mini-bar, he from a miniature Chivas Regal. "I know why I want to get rid of Professor Porterfield. He's too goody-goody and too smart, and he might actually save the college. But you, Mr. Bollovate. I don't get why you want the same thing."

She continued to call him Mr. Bollovate in spite of their intimacies. The formal address seemed to heighten her excitement in bed, or rather the excitement she expressed, at the peak of which she would often cry out, "Oh! Mr. Bollovate!"

"I want him out because he's not doing his job."

"But you can't dump him—can you?" asked Matha, craning

her neck back to behold the print of Don Quixote over the head-board. "He has tenure. He's protected. And he may not be doing his job, but no one could do better. If you get rid of Porterfield, you'll get rid of the college."

"Tenure!" Bollovate sat up in the bed and swiped at the air. "How I hate that word! Tenure! Where else on Planet Earth is there a thing called tenure? In a dildo factory? Oh, yeah. A dildo maker is awarded a job for life because he's just so good at his work? Give me a break."

Matha slid deeper under the bedcovers. She'd hit a nerve. Mr. Bollovate seemed to have so many nerves.

"And if the dildo maker begins to get sloppy? Goes berserk? Produces whoopee cushions instead of dildos? He's fired! That's what happens. But not a college professor. Once a college professor gets tenure, he can fuck up all he wants or go to sleep for the next twenty years. He's got fucking tenure!"

"So," Matha asked in a soft and careful voice, "how could you get rid of Professor Porterfield?"

"Does he screw around?" asked Bollovate. "Nah. That wouldn't do it. All those professors screw around." It came to him where he was.

"Actually," said Matha, "he may be one of the few professors at Beet who doesn't screw around."

That was so. Other than Professor Porterfield, Keelye Smythe was the lone member of the English Department who had never had an affair with an undergraduate—though not for lack of trying. Once, in pursuit of a plump exchange student named Lufthansa, he'd written her a love letter suggesting that the passion they could share would rank among those of the exalted lovers of history and mythology, like Troilus and Cressida, Hero and Leander, Daphnis and Chloe, Venus and Adonis, and Edward, Prince of Wales and Wallis Simpson. Smythe's twelve-page letter was a philosophical-cum-philological argument that included blank spaces in the text. When he gave it to Mrs. Whiting for typing, he put the spaces in brackets and instructed, "insert endearments here." Mrs. Whiting handed back the untyped letter without comment.

"What about the antifeminist bullshit?" asked Bollovate. "I wonder if we could get him on that."

Matha said nothing, but she knew the "antifeminist bullshit" was a more usable charge than murder if they wanted Porterfield out. She recalled a recent incident at Columbia. It involved a professor caught chewing his Salisbury steak too demonstratively in the faculty cafeteria. A young woman complained that the offender had behaved inappropriately, and he was brought up for "lewd chewing." The fellow tried to explain that he was merely masticating, but that only made matters worse.

"We can get around tenure," said Bollovate. "He could be thrown out for cause. He's supposed to be serving the college's needs, and he's fucking up."

Matha regarded him sideways, like a puzzle that required a different approach if one were to solve it. "Well, I can't see why you're telling me all this. What could I possibly do to get rid of Professor Porterfield?"

Bollovate had thought of what. "For one thing, you and your band of misfits could storm the CCR meetings, make it impossible for them to meet."

"What good would that do? They're not getting anywhere anyway."

"I want a change in public opinion," said Bollovate, who purchased that very thing often enough to know what he was talking about. "I want the students to think that Porterfield, by failing in his job, is doing them in."

Matha understood what he meant, if not his motives. If the majority of students were opposed to Porterfield, the faculty would turn on him too, because there was nothing they valued more than the collective opinions of people in their late teens. Yet again she was torn. If keeping Porterfield resulted in rescuing the college, her own mission would be thwarted. But if dumping him had the same consequence, that is, if he were replaced by someone who could do what the trustees had asked, what difference did it make? On the other hand, she had begun to see her future lay in real estate more than in poetry. And she might very soon overtake that bitch Kathy in her very own trade. Also, the disruption of the CCR would bring one more time-wasting annoyance to the college.

"The trouble is," she said, "Professor Porterfield really *can* do the job. You'd be better off letting him alone." She gave him the fish eye. "Unless, for some reason, you don't want him to succeed."

"Save those smarts for when you're working for me," said Bollovate. He pulled on his pants and left her in the motel room. "I go. You stay." She would have to make her return trip to the college on her own, which annoyed her practically, not emotionally.

But who was this standing in the wavering light of the motel parking lot, notebook in hand, looking, he hoped, like Hemingway in riding boots astride a hill in war-torn Spain? Ferritt Lawrence greeted her cheerily to cover his guilt, stuffed some items into his backpack, and offered to leave his bike at the motel and pay for a taxi for them both.

"What do you think of Professor Porterfield?" she asked him on the way back to Beet. Few people ever asked Ferritt his opinion of anything, not even driving directions, so he responded at great length. Professor Porterfield was just the sort of faculty member he despised, he told Matha. "He keeps to himself. He teaches, talks to his students in office hours, and goes home. He doesn't gossip. He doesn't tell me a thing, you can bet on that. He ignores the press. Can you believe it? Treats me like a pest."

"What if I told you the MacArthur Five was about to rise again? At least two more times," said Matha.

"That would be a story," said the aroused Ferritt.

"Well, very soon, and I'll tell you when, we're going to raid a CCR meeting, bring the committee to a halt."

"A grinding halt?" Ferritt asked.

"And something a lot bigger," said Matha, as Gregory gave their taxi the toreador defense at the gates. They rode past Bacon. "A takeover to end all takeovers. I'll let you know. You'll have an exclusive."

Ferritt had not been this excited since he was given a one-day press pass to sit in on a session of the Council on Foreign Relations.

At last here was the payoff for all the fallow weeks, and for all the crafty maneuvers involved in following Matha and Bollovate. Then he blundered. "And what does Mr. Bollovate think of the committee?"

"How would I know what Mr. Bollovate is thinking of anything?" she asked, her voice a block of ice.

"Oh," said Ferritt in an awkward attempt to sound casual, "I happened to see Mr. Bollovate leave the motel shortly before you did. I thought perhaps you had run into him."

Matha spoke ruminatively. "Of course, I could always phone all the local papers too. Maybe stories as big as the ones I'm contemplating should not be restricted to one news outlet. A college paper at that. Maybe it isn't fair."

"I don't know a thing," said Ferritt at once.

"See that you keep it that way." But she did not trust him and vowed to screw him, figuratively, at the first opportunity. In his own preprofessional way, he made the same vow, and wondered if there were anything else Matha Polite had to hide.

Deposited at Chillingworth, she left him without a thanks or good-bye and climbed the stairs to her room to summon her Gang of Four. Ferritt remained in the taxi, reviewing the pictures he had taken with his cell phone. He also played his cassette recorder, whose reception was muffled and staticky. Still, he could make out much of the conversation, and the words "Oh! Mr. Bollovate!" came through loud and clear, which gave him hope of getting his story after all.

In fact, the day concluded with several of the principals more hopeful than they'd had when it started—making it an unusual day in New England. Bollovate, still smarting from his face-off with Peace outside the classroom, was hopeful that he'd engineered the professor's eventual dismissal for incompetence or neglect of duty. While it was unlikely that charges would ever become formal, the mere accusation might be sufficiently discomfiting to force Porterfield to quit. Even so, students would have to turn against him as well as the faculty and administration, a circumstance that seemed unlikely, but—given Bollovate's determination and Matha's new assignment—not out of the question. If that should happen, Porterfield would feel as though he had let down the people he had been charged to help, and he'd walk.

So that was Bollovate's hope. And consequently it became President Huey's hope, and it was Matha's hope, and Ferritt Lawrence's. It was also the hope of Peace's fellow committee members. And, had he been in on any of the multiple schemes aborning, it would have been Akim Ben Laden's too (though he liked Professor Porterfield and felt he owed him his life for the incident with Latin the Pig), since the failure of the CCR would mean the destruction of the Satan college.

But these days Akim harbored other hopes, such as that the Homeland Security Department might disappear, but not before it appeared. The permutations for the codes had reached the high millions. It was near Thanksgiving. Would the search ever yield an answer?

And Akim held a more immediate hope. He had just emerged from the bathroom on the top floor of Fordyce, and he very much hoped that on the long walk back to his cave he would not drop the soup bowl he had just filled with his first batch of TATP.

CHAPTER

14

DID PEACE HAVE FRIENDS OTHER THAN DEREK MANNING? HE
had a few from prep school, and a few more from college with
whom he communicated episodically, in the way that most men
prefer to maintain their friendships. And he corresponded with
some of the kids he'd taught in Sunset Park. With five or six faculty colleagues, too, he had cordial relationships if not full-blown
friendships, marked by the occasional drinks or the occasional
lunch, or the very occasional dinner party. Peace and Livi ab-
horred dinner parties, particularly faculty dinner parties, and
they often said they produced Beth and Robert as excuses to de-
cline invitations. In their four years at Beet they had thrown only
one obligatory dinner party for the English and American Literature Department, at the end of which Livi had asked her husband
if buying a flame thrower required a waiting period.

As it was, though, Manning constituted most of Peace's social
life. And much of that occurred on the gym floor. In previous
years, before the Day of the Bollovate, the two men had met twice
a week for one-on-one basketball games, which they played to the
death. Now, in late November, they were going at each other in
their first game of the term.

It was the Monday before Thanksgiving. Peace had invited

Manning to play in part to work up a real sweat, as compared to the purposeless games of the CCR, and to spill his many woes to his friend.

"You know what's wrong with you," said Manning, after listening to the litany. Peace had kept it short, his sentences fragmented, and he was so uncomfortable in talking about himself, much less his difficulties, that anyone other than Manning might have thought he was recounting a lucky streak. Manning, who had legs like pilings and a vertical leap of three feet, sailed over his taller opponent and slammed the ball down with a whoosh. "What's wrong with you is that you're not PC. You're not P, and you have no sense of C."

"And you do?"

"I don't need to be PC. I'm Jewish." They were playing losers-outs. "And that's a perfect example," Manning said. "If you had an ounce of common sense, or a sense of self-preservation, you'd hang with black guys on the faculty, or Chinese guys, or gays in wheelchairs. But no. You hang with a Jew! So wrong, my friend. So yesterday."

"How do you do that?" asked Peace as his opponent again drifted over him and stuffed the ball in the basket, this time double-handed.

"Jewish legs," said Manning. He stole the ball off Peace's dribble. "Are you going to play, by the way, or bellyache?"

"Bellyache," said Peace. The ball echoed in the empty gym, the late autumn light streaming through the wire mesh on the high windows and making whorly patterns on the court. Manning knew not to pick up on the subject of Livi and the children going to New York. That was too raw. So he pretended the most important thing was how to devise a curriculum that would save the college, rid Peace of the sight of Bollovate, and set him free of his dreadful committee. As a government professor he fancied his lot superior to the English professor's, but he was experienced enough to recognize that a committee made up of his own types would have behaved no better, only with fewer verbal flourishes.

"That's why you'll never find me on a committee, unless it's to write obits for the faculty meeting. I like doing that."

"Thanks for your help," said Peace, as he stood flat-footed and watched his friend nail a long jumper. "You've been practicing."

"For *you?*" Manning smiled.

"Okay. No more Mr. Nice Guy." Peace took the ball. "Let's change to winners-outs." He hit seven straight shots from all over the court, and "Game." Manning took it as well as could be expected. They sat side by side with their knees up and their backs to the wall, like two kids on a playground in summer.

"Are you asking me something or just venting?" said Manning.

"Here's my problem. I mean, apart from figuring out how to have a family life without a family." He stared briefly at the floor. "We're up against it. We have to produce something. If I make up a plan on my own, I don't think I'll have trouble selling it to the rest of the group. They really aren't as foolish as they've been acting."

"And Wagner's music isn't as bad as it sounds," said Manning. "Or did Twain say that?"

"But when they hear something that works, they'll know it and jump aboard, I'm fairly sure, if I can come up with a decent idea."

"If you do," said Manning, "you'll be doing everyone a service way beyond bringing dollars into the college. Nobody knows what to do with higher education these days. There's so much horseshit in the curriculum as it is."

"Between deadheaded tradition and the current nonsense," said Peace, "there has to be a clean, clear education designed to help young people find useful lives, to help them live in the world. I mean, that's it, isn't it? To learn how to live in the world? And you know, Derek, no matter how much they mess up, I believe most of the faculty believes that too."

"And I believe that deep down, Miss Frank, everyone is good. Why don't you seek help in Bliss House?"

"No, I mean it."

"I know you do. And in my happier moments, all three of them, I see it your way. A hundred forty-one overeducated people can't be wrong all the time. But the kind of curriculum you're suggesting would be hard enough to put in place in a matter of years, much less weeks. You're talking about a reeducation of the educators. I think the trustees snookered you."

"Not if I do what they asked."

"You want to know the trouble with this place—fundamentally, I mean?"

"I do," said Peace. "But no bottom-line lectures."

"It's a different bottom line. Our colleagues are lazy, morally and intellectually lazy. Nobody cares about the students these days—a fact I find grimly hilarious because that's all anyone claims to care about. They spend so much time and energy trying to come up with what they think the students want. But our colleagues are gutless, because rather than concentrating on difficult, complicated material, and teaching that—worthwhile material that, by the way, they perfectly well know and were taught themselves—they offer pap. Instead of playing offense, they are always backing up the way we play D on the court here, countermoving according to the moves of people barely out of childhood. The joke is, nobody is on offense but them. The faculty is playing against themselves and getting creamed. What the students want, what they crave, is inequality. They want to rely on people who know more than they do, and they want to come out of Beet College a little smarter than when they went in.

"And you think the kids don't know what's going on? They go through the motions of sitting in classes they laugh at—Native American Crafts and Casino Studies?—and spend half their time partying, out of boredom, and the other half in a stupor, dreaming about becoming The Donald's latest apprentice or the next American Idol. This is what popular culture hath wrought. Have I not seen the best minds of their generation competing to be on *Survivor*? They dream the big preposterous dreams because they don't want to earn the small ones. And that's because we so-called teachers don't give them the small dreams anymore. No wonder Ms. Polite and the Four Stooges want to close the place down. The college has become a Green Room—without a show to go with it."

"You're saying it's attitude more than substance?"

"One drives the other." Manning thought about it. "You know, you might not be talking about new courses as much as a new way to see the array of courses we have. Maybe you could trick our colleagues into taking an interest in what they teach, make them good students again by coming up with something they want to learn. Between you and me, I think most of the race and gender stuff is bunk, and you know what I think of the professors of newspapers. But even with those folks, it's the way they see things, not the material itself, that sinks them, the dumbass idea that the purpose of education is to make people proud of who they are instead of what they might become.

"Oops! I better keep my mouth shut. I'm not standing in the Free Speech Zone."

He turned to Peace. "You know, pal, all this *tsuris* might not be bad for you. You've led a pretty charmed life. You've earned it insofar as anyone can. But life ain't charmed. So this may be your initiation into the club. Welcome. I wish the club didn't exist." A sigh and a quick recovery. "But don't despair. We're coming up on How to Prepare for the Holidays Day! I'm thinking strychnine. How about you?"

They went quiet. "Livi said I was happiest in Sunset Park."

"That's the kind of neighborhood I grew up in. I don't recall too many ecstatic moments."

"She didn't mean that. She meant the quality of the kids. They were raw and rough, but—I don't know—they had a lovely sort of innocence. When I read them stories or told them stories. Anything, really. Stories from Shakespeare, or stories of ballplayers, it made no difference. You could see their faces unfrown, open up."

"They were off-guard."

"In a way. At any rate, they were transported out of Sunset Park for a while."

Manning studied him. "You're an aristocrat," he said.

"Hardly."

"I'm talking about E. M. Forster's definition of an aristocrat. A good, decent person who does the right thing and doesn't show off about it. No wonder you're unfit for human company."

"Got one more game in you?" Peace stood and flipped Manning

the ball. They went at it again. "Where do you think you fit in all this, Derek?"

"Meaning?"

"Well"—hitting a long jumper from the corner—"you've been here a fair number of years. Why don't you do something about it?"

"'Cause I think it's hopeless, if you must know"—missing a chippie. Peace took back the ball.

"So if it's hopeless, what do you do with the rest of your life? You've got twenty years before retirement, whether it's here or somewhere else." Peace spun around him and floated it in for a basket.

"I can look after myself." Manning gave Peace a what-are-you-getting-at squint, and missed another easy shot. "I'll leave the rescue of civilization to you."

"That's just another wisecrack."

"Are you baiting me?"

"If you had the guts you find missing in our colleagues, you'd help fix this mess yourself." Peace was ahead six to nothing. Manning was missing by more with each shot. His hair stood straight as quills.

"You're trying to tick me off, aren't you?"

"Maybe." Now it was seven-zip, eight, nine.

"It's been a while since I've been called gutless."

"It's been a while since Margaret died."

Pop! Manning shot a left so fast, Peace was on his ass in half a second. He reached up to his nose and examined the blood in his hand. Manning knelt next to him and wiped away more blood with his own hand.

"Hey! Peace!"—tears in his eyes.

"I went over the line. I was trying to get your goat."

"It worked." He took off his T-shirt and gave it to Peace, to stanch the bleeding, and helped him to his feet. "Is it broken?"

"Nope." He slapped Manning's shoulder. "Not enough behind it."

Manning was holding the ball on his hip. "You think I crawled into a shell after Margaret, don't you?"

"I wouldn't blame you if you had. But I don't think you're the man you're becoming. A good-hearted wiseass who lives on the sidelines." Peace held up his fists, pretending to fend off another punch.

"Say, wasn't this conversation supposed to be about you?" Manning said. "Between your troubles and mine, I like it better when it's yours. You can keep the shirt."

"Derek? My remark about Margaret? It wasn't aristocratic."

"I don't know. Maybe it was." Manning noted the clock on the scoreboard. "Gotta go."

"Derek . . . ?"

"Not another word. We're square."

"Shalom?" said Peace.

"Peace," said Manning.

That night after supper, as Livi sat reading in the one soft living room chair, Peace took the kids on the couch with him to tell them a story. He had not done that for a while. They sat on either side of him as he told them about the celebrated jumping frog of Calaveras County, and Rip van Winkle, and a story of Chekhov's that he made clear and simple. He found they were happier when he cast the old stories in his own way, rather than reading from books where he had to explain some of the words. It was the story they wanted, none so much as a story from Peace's own life. So, when he was done with the masters, he dredged up—he did not know why—a story told him by his father, whose father had told it to him, about a boy in a boat sailing down the path of the moon. As he finished the two children fell asleep, leaning against him like books on a shelf.

15

THE THOUGHT OF DISRUPTING A CCR MEETING STRUCK
Matha as both redundant and an unnecessary sidestep for the
MacArthur Five, which had recently been reduced to the MacArthur Four. Jamie Lattice e-mailed Betsy Betsy that he had contracted mono and had no strength for anything but lying in bed
and reading stories about the Algonquin Round Table. Bagtoothian volunteered to go to Lattice's sickbed and "snap his
scrawny neck." But Matha said they all should concentrate on the
task at hand, the "subtext" of which, she informed her comrades,
was to make Professor Porterfield appear antistudent.

"What good will that do?" asked Goldvasser the night they met
in Matha's room. "I thought we weren't like supposed to attack
Porterfield."

"I changed my mind. If Porterfield fails, the school fails," she
said, as if she believed it.

Pumped, as they put it, by their success at MacArthur House,
the group agreed to storm the CCR meeting scheduled for the following day, which was the Wednesday before Thanksgiving, and
afforded an excellent opportunity to leave the campus in turmoil
before the holiday break. They stayed up all night working out
their tactics and rehearsing the spontaneous things they would

yell in unison. Bagtoothian, Goldvasser, and Betsy Betsy also realized that since the CCR meetings were held in Bacon, their attack offered them an opportunity for a twofer.

"As long as we'll be in the library anyway, why not just stay and take it tomorrow?"

There were five reasons not to, Matha told them. They had to occupy Bacon at night, when no one would be around. They had to break in to add drama. For maximum effect, the Bacon takeover had to come on the eve of the faculty meeting at which the new curriculum would be presented, that is, the night of December 18. Thanksgiving was coming up, and she had plans. And finally, she said so.

"Do I have to do all the thinking around here?" She glowered at her retinue. They smiled sheepishly. "For fuck's sake," she said, leaving them sitting on the floor as she parked herself at her laptop.

Bagtoothian went over to a corner of the room and set small paper fires on which he squirted loops of lighter fluid.

"Will you stop that!" Matha yelled at him. He looked up at her like a dog, not understanding what he'd done wrong.

She had been in a foul mood all day. As the others chatted conspiratorially, she wrote a furious letter to the editor of *Beet* magazine, the alumni publication, for rejecting one of her poems. Besides student poetry, the magazine published articles by professors about why they liked being at Beet; affectionate memoirs by Beet alumni; crossword puzzles the solutions to which were data from Beet's history; the Riddle of the Month, to which the answer was always "Beet"; a droll essay by the editor on how things had changed since he was a student—for the better, and yet for the worse too, and yet not at all; and an editorial expressing the hopes that one day the publication might be recognized as a real magazine. Matha's poem was the first piece they'd ever rejected, and they had no form letter to send her saying her work was not for them, or that it did not meet their needs at present, so they just sent back the poem scribbled with the words "no good." In her note she called the editor a "fuck-shit."

By dawn the students were exhausted, yet managed to form a

ragged line on the Chillingworth staircase and proceed to Chuck E. Cheese's, whose hours had been expanded to 24/7. By now, Chuck E. Cheese's had company in the visitors' parking lot. So successful was one fast food outlet that Bollovate and the trustees, with Huey's concurrence, decided to add a Denny's franchise as well, and then a Pizza Hut and a Popeye's. The parking lot was growing into a fast-food megalopolis, the trailers flashing their lights day and night like an Atlantic City slot machine. To all this success an objection was voiced by the college nutritionist, who for thirty-two years had labored to make the campus cafeterias the New England college model for healthy eating. But her protest was brief, since she was fired.

In fact, though the fast-food joints were raking it in, many students complained of recurrent tummy aches. Faculty cracked that the parking lot was just as honky-tonk as the strip mall outside town. But that was no longer true. The strip mall had been denuded by its college competitors.

In town itself, eateries were suffering, and a few went out of business altogether. The This Little Piggy Muncheonette could not stay open without student customers, who now did not need to leave campus to do their munching. The building was boarded up and abandoned, leaving its totemic pink fiberglass pig forlorn and stranded on the roof.

Peace awakened about the same time as Matha and her cohorts were chowing down Breakfast Pizza Meat Patties with Double Ham Sausage and Triple Cheese Sauce, and coffee shakes. For the first time since mid-October, he felt something interesting begin to form in his mind as he approached the day—a constructive thought regarding his task with the curriculum. It was an ice blink of an idea that flashed on the horizon, came and went, and came again and stayed. For once, he did not drag himself to the breakfast table. Beth and Robert ate docilely, apparently having agreed upon an armistice—a sign, he knew, of their unhappiness at the prospect of the move to New York and their parents living in separate places. But he had stood shoulder to shoulder with their mother, assuring them that the new arrangement, however uneasy it made them at the outset, would work. On this morning, after some hours of genuine deliberation rather than self-recrimination, Peace was beginning to believe that himself.

He took a few notes, trying to recall the ideas or half-ideas that had come to him during his wakeful hours. He slipped the material into a manila folder, which he labeled "CCR," and then went off to meet with the committee. He would have e-mailed his notes to Mrs. Whiting's replacement in the English Department, but there wasn't any. Three other departments, History, Economics, and Physics, had lost their assistants at the same time, under circumstances similar to Mrs. Whiting's, and were without clerical help. Huey had sent around a memo explaining this as a temporary measure. "A bit of belt-tightening," he said.

Livi waved Peace a lingering good-bye. Though she and the children would wait till Thanksgiving weekend to head for New York, she had begun to pack some things, books mainly. She had secured a furnished apartment and a school for Beth and Robert. She told Boston North she would be leaving at the end of the month. Her fellow ER doctors threw her a surprise party in which the overplayed joke was to give their cherished colleague of four years a great big hand.

Off Peace went for the nine o'clock meeting. Off went the MacArthur Four for the same destination. All arrived at the door of the Bacon conference room at once—the seven committee members and the four revolutionaries—as nine bells rang from the Temple. Confronting one another, both groups hesitated. Smythe, not sure what was happening, went around shaking everyone's hand. Kramer did likewise. On the way in, Matha stifled the urge to wind roses around the balusters.

"What are you doing here?" Peace asked the students.

"We're stopping this illegitimate committee," Matha answered, striding into the conference room ahead of the others.

"And why are you doing that?" asked Peace.

"Because it's illegitimate," Matha said. She sat in Peace's place at the head of the oak table and gestured for her comrades to join her at the other seats. The committee members collected in a corner. Peace remained standing in the doorway.

"Why do you say it's illegitimate?" he said, calm as toast.

Matha made a plaguey frown. Her voice was beginning to soar to Dixie again. "Because the committee is against the students!"

Bagtoothian said, "Yeah!"

Goldvasser started to say "Yeah!" but reconsidered.

"So legitimacy is determined by whether or not something is good for the students?" asked Peace.

"That's right!" said Matha.

"Do the students want Beet College to survive?" asked Peace, and before Matha could shut Bagtoothian up, he hollered, "Yeah!"

Peace looked over the four revolutionaries and decided to talk to them like real people. "Look," he said. "We ought to be in this together. The trustees aren't kidding about closing the college, and they don't seem to care that your lives and ours [he indicated his colleagues] will be turned upside down. Look around you. Look around, Matha. This magnificent library houses all anyone would need to lead an informed and moral life. Now the library and the college could go down in a matter of weeks. And nobody will ever get them back. And we'll all go away as if we were never here. And why? Because the people in control of us say so. Because we're not making enough money. Does that make sense to you? You, Matha? Go back to your rooms and let us do our work. We'll save this place if you'll let us."

Smythe, Booth, Heilbrun, Lipman, Kettlegorf, and Kramer stared at him as if they were seeing their colleague for the first time. They were on the verge of believing what he said, and they were not at all persuaded they liked the faint affection they were feeling. Was it affection? Or collegiality—perhaps it was that? Or magnanimity? Or the simple desire to help? Whatever its source, the sensation was short-lived, and when it faded, they were themselves again. One thing for sure: they had not felt anything like it before.

But Matha was certain of her feelings. And she was particularly nettled by Peace's reverence for Bacon. Unmoved, she began to shout, "The CCR is illegitimate! You're illegitimate! Beet College is illegitimate!" She pounded on the conference table. The other three joined her. At this point a young woman librarian rushed in to remind them severely that this was a library, and to cut it out or she'd call the campus police.

"Don't do that," said Goldvasser.

"Fuck off," said Matha. But by then a crowd of students who had been in the Reading Room had congregated at the conference room door beside Professor Porterfield. The group included Max Byrd, who told the MacArthur Four that a few people were actually in the library to get some work done.

"You fuck off too, kiss shit, ass kick, kick shit!" Matha yelled at Max, who looked at the spoiled southern girl and exploded in a laugh. So did the librarian. So did the students gathered in the doorway, and however cautiously, so did the members of the CCR—all but Peace, who regarded Matha as one would any child out of control. She caught the look, and was livid.

At the reverberation of the laughter, Matha turned a shade of crimson that Peace had not seen since his college days. Bagtoothian wanted to punch someone, but found to his discomfort that he was laughing too, as was Goldvasser, as was Betsy Betsy, who was alternately tittering and apologizing for it. Now all but one of the MacArthur Four were laughing, and the other students and the CCR members were laughing even harder, and this went on for half a minute, producing a noise more alarming than joyful.

Peace was not laughing. Matha was not laughing. She stood as though frozen, caught like a shoplifter in the act, and then she fled, brushing past Peace and flashing him a glare of hatred colored by humiliation. Back to Chillingworth she ran, up the stairs and into her room. She wanted nothing to do with her comrades, who tried to follow her, but whom she dismissed with a disgusted flutter of the hands. She wanted nothing to do with anyone again, because this was the worst—absolutely the worst—moment of her life. Believe it or not, so far it was.

It occurred to Peace to go after her. Whatever nonsense she spouted, she was a student and therefore someone in his charge. And clearly the girl was troubled far beyond things political. It wasn't that he thought all people redeemable, whatever their ages. And he really did not know Matha; she might remain this unattractive forever. He simply felt sorry for her, sorry for her vexation and shame, sorry for anyone who suffered ridicule for something so small and meaningless. He promised himself to seek her out later and try to help her, which was his job.

Lying on her side in bed, the sounds of merry derision still playing in her memory, Matha wept great globular tears, and when she was all wept out, she slept.

She dreamed she was standing naked on the stage of the Ninety-second Street Y in New York to read her poems, and yet there was a Century 21 sign dangling on chains over her head. She began to read her internationally acclaimed work, "My Phone Was Ringing Off the Hook," but discovered that the lines had been changed to include phrases like "priced to sell" and "location location." The meter had been altered—a jumble of iambs, choriambs, and a duple foot—but when she tried to explain the changes to the audience, they shouted, "The meter is running."

And then, as the gods occasionally spring from mechanical devices, her cell phone rang, and Matha was awakened by the opening bars of "The Internationale" and by the voice of Ferritt Lawrence.

"You said you'd tell me when you were going to take the CCR," whined the journalist.

"I forgot." She had not. She wanted to remind him she held the upper hand, and that he'd better keep his mouth shut about her trustee lover. But things were different now. "I have a better story for you," she said, having hit upon her means of revenge in the sudden alarm of her ringing cell phone.

"It better be good," said Ferritt, struggling to regain the advantage.

"What would you say," said Matha, "if I told you that Professor Porterfield—dear, beloved, much-admired Professor Peace

Porterfield—had done something so awful, so unacceptable, so inappropriate, so hurtful"—she paused to listen to Ferritt's panting—"that no student at Beet College, certainly no woman, would ever see him in the same way again? What would you say if I told you that for the offense he committed he could lose his position, and never work in any college or university?" She thought she heard Ferritt sweating. "And what would you say if I told you I know exactly what he did, because he did it to me?"

Ferritt could barely form the words. "I would say," he inhaled, "what did he do?"

Now Matha inhaled. Ferritt was certain she was choking down a sob. "He . . ." She had regained her composure. "He called me a hysterical female," she said.

"A hysterical female?" said Ferritt. "He said that? He really said that?"

"Or *an* hysterical female. I'm not sure," said Matha, because she was not.

HOW QUICKLY, HASTILY, IT ALL HAPPENED. PACKING GAVE
way to moving men with massive upper bodies stuffed into girdles,
and the sudden appearance of a moving van like a whale washed
up at their door, and the hundred or so boxes of books, and Livi's
dresses and sweats and scrubs and the Nikes and the pumps, and
the chest of drawers they had picked up in Brattleboro for seven
dollars, and the ampoules, tubes, and bottles and the loofah brush
from the bathroom, and the bunny bath mat and the squishy yellow ducks and more toys, games held together by rubber bands,
Monopoly and Stratego, a basketball, a nerf football, a baseball
glove with Bobby written all over it in ballpoint pen, and Skunkie
and Care Bear—all boxed and stacked like the houses of the
Pueblos in the back of the van, which grunted, exhaled, then re-
ceded down the road, away. And Livi and the children tottering in
the doorway as though they were about to enter the house rather
than leave it. And stoic Peace, hauling the duffel bag on his shoulder in the fireman's carry, and lugging two battered blue Sam-
sonite suitcases to Livi's Civic. And the kisses and embraces and
the tears, and the worst of it—the driveway empty, the road empty,
and the roaring silence of the house.

He had wanted to drive them to New York, and see them safe

in the sort-of-furnished apartment in Murray Hill that Livi had rented online. Online, too, she'd enrolled the kids in the Dalton School, which happened to have two vacancies due to its out-of-state quota. (Because of the kids' ERB scores, the school waived interviews, for which their parents thanked their lucky stars.) He'd wanted to see them settled and then take a train home. But Livi assured him she could make it on her own. And he was exhausted. Besides, she said, it would be harder to see him pull away from her. He poured himself a beer and flopped down in front of the TV, which he failed to switch on.

What was Livi wearing? He pictured her. Keds, jeans, one of his sweaters—the blue cardigan—and for no good reason, a red beret.

Not to worry. It was Saturday. He would drive down to New York next weekend, and a week would hardly be unbearable. If only he'd ever practiced and spent one day without them before.

He would take a walk. Yes. There was so much to see. There was nothing to see. The flowers at the side of the road were gray buttons on sticks. The stones on the road, gray. The road itself, hard as an anthill. The skeleton trees, shorn and brittle. Dry, dry. Past the cord of wood and the stack of kindling beside the house. A shot of wind cut through his Pendleton and his chinos. A crow complained. Past a broken wheelbarrow. Past a shed scorched in a fire and covered in creosote. Over the frozen puddles. Past the defunct Esso station with the rusted pumps and cement porch.

Know what he'd miss most? Besides the children's brawls and never-ending whys and the sight of them sleeping? He would miss Livi's toes touching him in bed—she asleep, he not quite. He would be lying awake, worrying. And then she would twitch and her toes would graze his legs between the ankle and the knee. He would never turn away. He would hold his leg very still and absorb the casual presence of his wife.

He was aware he was thinking like an exile—a state of mind that made him uncomfortable, because it was larded with self-pity and self-aggrandizement of the worst sort, the moral. Yet he could not help feeling as though he were standing in the stern of a ship with the land disappearing behind him and none ahead. That's where the exile came in, the word meaning not so much what one is as what one no longer has. Peace no longer had Beet College, or vice versa. No matter what transpired before Christmas, that was indisputable. But to have nothing in its stead . . . Even Archimedes needed a place to stand on, or the lever was useless. And Peace's aspirations were no way near as grand as moving the world; he just wanted his family.

Only an hour did he walk. Tired of playing Heathcliff, he returned home and to the task before him, taking notes longhand, thinking, then writing some more. The strangest thing had happened at the last CCR meeting, after Matha and her crew had been dispensed with. The committee sat and met as they always did, and as they always did, accomplished nothing. But he was not listening to them. Their mouths opened and closed and their arms moved up and down like a belly dancer's, and they made every sign of speaking, even passionately. But they were underwater; he heard them not. When the meeting concluded, he did not even acknowledge them. He stood and walked out. The others, not knowing what to make of his barbaric indifference, steamed off in a huff.

But now he worked. For the rest of that bleak Saturday he worked—his thoughts flapping around like Wilbur's bat, bumping into this or that and redirecting their course, little by little blundering toward something worthwhile—in his terms, useful. Everything was available to correction, Peace believed, even Beet College. The place was a mess, but it wasn't such a mess as all that. Nothing is. Life wasn't all fog, and it wasn't all cant. Some things always remain clear and true. How to live in the world? Play fair, do good, harm as little as possible, trust in human capability, help the helpless, laugh when you can, find a few to love. How to teach? Settle on the valuable things, and dream into them. Learn to imagine what you know. What was so goddamn hard about that?

So that was Peace on that Saturday afternoon. And, as he worked on his project, others worked on theirs.

Akim, for one, was wandering the campus, attempting to pick his spot. He had decided not to go home to Scarsdale for

Thanksgiving, though his mother wrote that his father was becoming a changed man, and this "stupid chess mishegas" might at last be over. Akim loved his mother, but thought her note might be a trap, so he stayed put. In any event, he was on a mission, and the campus emptiness and quiet over the holiday worked in his favor.

He must find the best place to blow himself up. The explosion had to do maximum damage, not merely to Beet, but symbolically to America, to the West. That course he'd taken with Professor Porterfield on Conrad: he recalled *The Secret Agent*, where the anarchists' target was the Greenwich clock. Brilliant, no? To strike at the heart of the West's source of time? It was the sort of target he was looking for—a site of equal magnitude, the obliteration of which would announce to the corrupt, depraved Western world and more locally, to Beet College, who Akim Ben Laden is, or was. He envisioned the *Times* subhead: "Device Was Work of Straight-A Student." But the bomb in *The Secret Agent* went off too soon, which caused an even greater disaster. None of that for Akim. He checked his watch.

Gregory eyed him warily from the gates. He was about to call the campus guard till he realized he was the campus guard. He called him anyway. As much as he enjoyed his conversations with Akim, there was something different about the boy. "Grynthe," he called out. Akim waved but had no time for small talk.

He was down to cases. His explosive act had to occur in the coming three weeks, before Christmas, Hanukkah, and—he was pretty sure—Ramadan. If the college closed after that, even if he succeeded, who would know what he did? he asked himself, phrasing it: "If a suicide bomber blows himself up in the forest . . ." Should he blast off in the forest?

It would be especially nice and fitting if he could do the deed on December 18, which was Osama's birthday, at least he thought it was, and Kiefer Sutherland's and Ty Cobb's.

Bacon Library was big. That could be a good target. MacArthur House was where Professor Lipman had her office. That could be better than good. What would the college do without

Communications Arts? He could always stand at the center of the Old Pen and make a crater of himself. They would notice that. But no harm would be done to the school. Lapham Auditorium? Perhaps. Bliss House? Nathaniel's Tomb? The man was dead anyway. The Faculty Club? The Faculty Room? The *Pig's Eye*? Homeland Security? Sure, if he could find it.

And that was another thing that needed doing. The random search for the Homeland Security Department code rolled on, numbers and letters appearing and disappearing, ACCESS DENIED popping up on his screen, mocking his effort. ACCESS DENIED. The story of his life. All afternoon he spent in his peregrinations. The answer would come to him. He had faith. Only one thing bothered him as he scanned the campus: the Passover song "Dayaynu." He could not get the chorus out of his head.

"Akim!" It was Chaplain Lookatme, who was so happy to have found a position at Beet, he never left the campus night or day. "You look as if you're searching for God. Our Friend is with you in your search. Will you remember that?"

Akim said he would.

Then toward evening, an amazing thing happened to the boy. Someone said, "Hi." It was Max, who didn't have the money to go home over the holidays, and was out for a walk. So he walked with Akim, who could not remember the last time anyone did that voluntarily. Seemingly oblivious to his companion's idiosyncratic appearance and behavior, Max chatted on about his courses, his folks, how outrageous it was that the college was going under. Though Akim held opposite views of Beet, he found himself listening appreciatively, even nodding in agreement from time to time; in short, behaving normally. The experience was rattling yet not terrible. Under the kaffiyeh and the robes, did little Arthur Horowitz still breathe? He invited Max back to his cave to watch the random searches, which might not be the most entertaining thing Max ever saw, yet had its hypnotic appeal.

"How do you manage it?"—referring to the cave.

"I just did it. If a cave is good enough for Osama—"

"Isn't that horseshit?" Max said, patting Akim on the back. "I mean, who would model his life after bin Laden? You're joking, right?"

For the first time, Akim allowed that he could be joking. The thought had not occurred until Max had presented it so bluntly. "Well, I like the beard," he said.

"The beard! The beard's ridiculous! Makes him look like a hooch dealer, if you ask me."

Akim allowed how that was true, and changed the subject. He seemed to have found a friend in Max, so he kept talking. He would not mention the suicide bombing in his plans, of course, though he brought up Matha, how she spurned his affections.

"Matha Polite's a jerk," said Max.

And Akim had to allow some truth to that as well. This was a brand-new experience—straight talk. He found he liked it. "What do you think of the Homeland Security Department?" he asked.

"Sounds worthless to me."

And Akim felt a pain in his face. The muscles ached. He hadn't used them in years. He was smiling.

"But you say it's protected by a security code?" asked Max. The computer geek was intrigued.

As for Matha: after her malicious gesture against Peace, she determined to take Thanksgiving weekend with her sister Kathy, for whom she expressed a sudden conversion of feelings. She only hoped Kathy would do the same. They had been at each other's throats too long. "Don't you think so, sister?" What would Kathy say to their spending the holiday together, just the two girls, who, after all, had so much to be thankful for?

"And it shames me that Ah've never laid eyes on the East End of Long Island, or should Ah say, your empire?"

Kathy smiled as she put down the phone, and continued smiling throughout the weekend. She met Matha at the Hampton Jitney—"Jitney! I swan! Such an elegant name for a bus!"—that stopped in the center of Quogue, where Kathy lived and worked. Her house was a postmodern postcolonial, with a gambrel roof and a view to die for, just steps from the ocean; that is how she would have described it had it been on the market. Her office was another "gem" on Jessup Avenue, where she reigned as queen of real estate, not only in Quogue and nearby Westhampton but throughout the East End. Her special form of advertising—skinny-dipping off her boat in plain sight of would-be buyers—worked like a dream.

"And this office is precious!" said Matha as she flitted from desk to unoccupied desk, pausing at every one and patting it like a dog. "So this is where all the people who work for mah big sister sell the houses! Mah oh mah! It's thrillin'! That's what it is. Thrillin'!"

Kathy hunkered down behind her own desk in the back, hands supporting chin, still smiling in every feature but her eyes.

"This work interests you, dear? Why, Ah thought you were a poet!"

"Ah am! Ah am a poet!" said Matha. "But woman cannot live on poetry alone."

"Ain't that the truth. Would you like to see some of the places Ah'm sellin' right now?"

Would she! Matha beat her sister to the cream-colored Mercedes and fidgeted with whoop-de-do excitement in the death seat. Kathy drove her from property to property, including the monstrous 36,000-square-foot home ("Oh, it's yummy!") belonging to a multimillionaire named Lapham, the great grandson of the man for whom the Beet auditorium was named. She also showed her the writer Harry March's old island, which had been lost to a fire last summer and lay like a long blackened log in the creek.

"What was he like?"

"Harry March? He was nuts but high-minded. Nothing underhanded about him. Nothing sneaky, if you know what Ah mean."

Matha said she did.

Kathy answered all her sister's many questions about interest rates, fixed and adjustable, and about when a jumbo mortgage should be recommended and how to talk to buyers when they first approached and how to check up on their net worth. Lots of questions like that. Kathy responded to all in ample detail, often tossing in an endearing anecdote to emphasize a point. She also fielded questions about how she liked her work, and did she think she'd be doing it forever.

In the late afternoon, while back at Beet College Peace was working on the curriculum, and Akim and Max were in the cave staring at the rolling numbers and letters, Matha sat with her sister on a dock on the canal in Hampton Bays near the entrance to Peconic Bay, their legs dangling. Gulls patrolled the pilings. The sun flamed in its descent. The sisters sipped Tanqueray gin.

"Kathy, what's a dummy corporation?"

"Why do you ask?"

"Ah overheard a friend of mine talking to a business associate. He said something about setting one up—a dummy corporation. Why does one do that?"

Kathy wondered whom her sister was keeping company with. "Well, the usual reason is a kind of sleight-of-hand. If a fellow wants to buy somethin' he's not supposed to, he has a dummy corporation do the buyin' for him, so there's no paper trail. Happens in real estate all the time."

"Is it illegal?"

"Not if you don't get caught. But it's a bad idea, Martha."

Hearing her real name jolted her. "It's so good to be with you," Matha said after a while.

"And it's so good to be with *you*." They put their arms around each other's shoulders, squeezed, and sat real close.

And Ferritt's Saturday? His folks, both periodontists, lived in Buffalo, and Ferritt spent the weekend in his room, as most people did who lived in Buffalo. He banged out his sensational story about how Professor Porterfield had insulted Matha and the nation's women, and hit Send, shooting off a blind copy to Professor Lipman. He told her the story was embargoed till Monday morning, which gave her but one day to tell everyone in the college, especially her fellow CCR members. Ferritt lay on his bed, gazing at the photograph of Cokie Roberts that he had fixed to the ceiling with airplane glue. He knew he must be feeling "over the moon," so he was.

And Joel Bollovate's Saturday? It began in his townhouse in

Louisburg Square, with his usual hearty breakfast of hash browns, home fries, sausages, steak, yogurt, Bananas Foster, biscuits with blueberry jam, eggs over easy, a slice of spinach quiche, an over-size mug of Sheila's cocoa, and his favorite, succotash.

"Isn't the succotash just the way you like it, dear?" asked his wife, who looked concerned. She was seated twenty-six feet away at the far end of their tortoiseshell table, in the center of which stood the three-foot alabaster pig Bollovate had "borrowed" from the roof of the Temple to see what price it might fetch. The Bollovates had to peek around either side of the pig to see each other.

"It is perfect, as always," said Bollovate, wiping the skin of a lima bean from the waxy film below his eyes.

Protruding from the four walls of the dining room were heads of animals—mammals, birds, and fish—killed or ordered killed by Bollovate on safaris in Kenya and Tanzania, as well as excursions elsewhere: an antelope, two moose, a dugong, an eland, an emu, a howler monkey, and a dachshund belonging to a neighbor. (The pup had crawled under the backyard fence. Bollovate claimed he mistook it for a rat.) There was also a Tasmanian devil, a South African quagga, a wombat, a narwhal, a snapping turtle, and a beige wolverine looking so alive it might have crashed through the wall on which it hung as far as the neck, its body stuck on the other side—all looking down upon Sheila and Joel. The most compli-cated trophy was the head of a warthog with a heron in its mouth, with a perch in *its* mouth. Bollovate sat under the dikdik.

"I was hoping we might spend the day with the children," said Sheila.

"That would be nice. Do they plan to get up?"

"Oh, Joel. I know they're teenagers on the outside, but they're just babies."

"Babes on meth," said Bollovate.

"Oh, Joel."

"Anyway," said her husband, "I have a business appointment this morning. At least, I hope I do." Gus Tribeaux, his investigator to the stars, was arranging a meeting with Francis April, America's last living Beet. Bollovate calculated it would take fifteen minutes and a hundred thousand dollars, make that seventy-five, to cheat April out of his inheritance. He also had something he wanted to bring up with that creep librarian La Cocque.

"You spend so little time with us these days," sighed his wife. "So much to do. Eh?" Sheila was as fat as her husband, but not the same shape. Her body was zaftig down to the waist, at which point it spread out its territory, giving her the appearance of a record-setting yam.

"You want to maintain your life style, don't you?" said Bollovate.

"Yes, I do. Which reminds me. I think we should go out to dinner again soon. It's been so long. I hear Sow's Motel in Beet has a nifty new dining room."

Bollovate searched her expression for danger, but it was flat as a lake. His belly churned acid to the point of crapulence. He let the moment pass. He might not have been so confident had he known Sheila had employed a private op of her own, and contacted her own attorney, who happened to be Bollovate's accountant. The couple sat in silence like Botero inspirations, over the expanse of the table, assessing each other as they would a wedge of strawberry cheesecake.

And Derek Manning? In the evening he called upon his friend to make sure he was okay. They did not say much. A few sentences about tomorrow's Patriots game, a few more about the weather, one or two *pro forma* complaints about overeating on the holiday. Oh, yes. And were Livi and the kids okay? When Manning rose to go home, the phone rang.

"We made it. The movers are doing their thing. We're fine."

"I miss you."

"I miss *you*."

"Do you have food for dinner?"

"We'll order Chinese. Or Japanese. Or pizza. Or Thai. This is New York, honey!" He was saddened by her excitement. "Hurry and come to us next weekend."

"I'll drive down Friday morning."

"I love you, Peace. Oh, wait. Children!" The sound of scuffling.

They were both at the phone. "Hi, Dad! Hi, Dad! My room is great! My room is greater! Love ya, Dad!" Livi reclaimed the receiver. "Please take care of yourself. Eat. Sleep. That sort of thing. Oh, Jesus! Children!"

"We'll talk tomorrow," said Peace. And the house was quiet again.

It would be all right, he would see to it. Livi was up to whatever lay ahead, and he would be too. He sat in the time-soiled leather chair with the ineradicable Coke stains and the horizontal streak Robert had etched with a butter knife. He looked out the window at the pine boughs and the smudges of clouds. He looked for a long time, and did not move in his chair until ten o'clock, when he climbed the stairs and headed for bed. Monday, he would have some terrible surprises flung at him. And that Saturday hadn't exactly been a dandy either—except for this: at the end of it, Professor Porterfield knew definitely what new curriculum he would propose to the students and faculty of Beet College.

CHAPTER

17

BY NOW THE BEET STORY HAD BECOME A STAPLE OF THE news. Television crews moved onto the campus over the weekend to ask the professors and students how they felt about the prospect of the college closing. "How do you feel?" they would ask them. And also, "How does it feel?"

And there were stories of other imminent college closings as well. The subject, originally addressed as an intellectual calamity, was increasingly discussed as an element of the marketplace. Those colleges with fat endowments, or those able to make money on their own, were the ones that swam. The others were bound to sink. So versed had the public become in these matters that the fates of the colleges were generally lumped under "business news," though there also were references on *Entertainment Tonight* and similar programs, which featured prominent Beet graduates.

Among the college's alumni were three U.S. senators, two congressmen, one cabinet member (Interior), one Supreme Court justice, the CEOs of six Fortune 500 companies, the CFOs of four, an Episcopal bishop, forty-eight writers for Comedy Central, and the booker on *Ellen*.

The story was featured on *Dateline, Frontline,* and *Nightline,* also on *60 Minutes* and *48 Hours. All Things Considered* considered it. In a caterwauling session on the *Chris Matthews Show*, a writer for the *Wall Street Journal* shrieked at a writer for the *Nation* that Beet College wouldn't be in this fix if more criminals were given the chair and that the Rosenbergs got what they deserved.

If some were resigned to the prospect of a world without Beet, that was not true of the Massachusetts State legislature. The Commonwealth had a longstanding interest in Beet College. The Board of Education had been certifying it annually for over two centuries under the provisions of a charter dating back to 1755, when Beet was a quasi-public institution. The certification was a formality, but it linked the college to state government—a connection symbolized by the presence of the governor at commencements, where Huey marched at his side, asking what it was like to be governor. Then too, the state's attorney general had jurisdiction over nonprofits. Why was the college closing? asked the legislators, who were so relieved to be focusing on something other than charges against themselves for bribery or indecent exposure, they asked the question louder and with greater frequency.

And what was all this about Beet selling off valuable property? More had disappeared besides the Henry Moore, the Calder, and the African art. A 1916 Steinway middle grand (one of only twenty of a discontinued model) was missing from the Music Department, as were several semiprecious stones from the Geology Department, as were two fourth-century amphora lifted from the Classics Department and said to be worth $300,000 apiece, and a twelfth-century hauberk and other knightly apparel worth God-knows-what, a jorum dating to King David, and assorted items such as an oxbow, a boot jack, and a watercolor of a collie that belonged to Teddy Roosevelt (the collie, not the painting). The librarian who had chastised Matha reported first editions missing, including *Uncle Tom's Cabin, Typee, Huckleberry Finn,* and *Leaves of Grass.* She told Jacques La Cocque, who told her that Mr. Bollovate took the editions for appraisal by Bauman Rare Books in New York, and to mind her own business. "*Taisez-vous* or you're fired," he said.

Rumor had it, too, that pieces of furniture, including a George

III armoire, were missing from the president's house, and that Huey had tried to sell the house itself, until he was reminded he didn't own it.

And where the hell was the pig on the temple?

Joel Bollovate's influence in Springfield derived from property deals he had made for lawmakers over the years, and he had been able to keep political noses out of his transactions and out of Beet's affairs—at least until recently. Akin to Daniel Webster only in this, Bollovate fended off the state as Webster had in 1819, when New Hampshire sought to take control of Dartmouth College. In his defense before the Supreme Court, Webster called the school "small, and yet there are those who love it." Bollovate, employing his own brand of eloquence, informed the legislators of the multiple copies he kept of canceled checks made out to cash.

But then old-money Massachusetts got into the act—names like Cabot, Wigglesworth, and Lamont, which by their mere appearance petrified Massachusetts pols, whose grandparents had been employed by the old guard as chauffeurs, cooks, butlers, and maids whom they chased upstairs, and caught. When that breed did not go to Harvard, they went to Beet. Tradition meant something to such people, even if little else did.

Of course, the state of Beet's fortunes meant most to the students and faculty. Over Thanksgiving break the faculty worked themselves into a stew. Ordinarily their view of the world outside their province was like Jane Austen's: it did not exist. The world was there to comment upon wryly—elections, taxes, upper-class murders, that sort of thing. It gained reality only in the light of faculty opinion. If there were ever the slightest doubt about this, there was television to back them up. For, when the outer world was heaving under the throes of this or that, who would it call upon to explain its travails? Why, professors, that's who.

But these days, thanks to the crunch created by the trustees, the faculty had become part of the outer world themselves. They were included in the macrocosm. And, as clearly as they could see little stories within Beet—which colleagues were nitwits and dolts, which departments were utterly worthless, which promotions were going to be denied, and so forth—they had trouble recognizing themselves as part of the bigger picture. Their powers of observations seemed diminished, their intelligence useless, and they'd lost corrosive wit—the surest mark of their superiority.

What was worse, they were made privy to what the rest of the world lived with day to day—a humiliating sense of insecurity born of being at the mercy of others. And the others were the bean counters, the easy targets of their contempt. Could it be that the bean counters were winning? Should they have learned to count beans too?

All the cockiness (subdued and refined so as to pass for manners) was knocked out of them like a kick to the breadbasket. *Ooof!* Where did that come from? The Great Houdini struts his belly to the crowd and a Yalie sucker-punches the wind out of him forever. So this was how the other 99 percent lived—awakening in dread, dining in anxiety, sleepless with terror. Why hadn't someone given them a course in reality training, to prepare them for this experience? Their confidence, born of nothing more than circumstance, was slapped and mugged, dragged into dark alleys and beaten silly. What were they to do?

Students being students, they were the last to become agitated at the situation, but over the long weekend it was all their parents asked them about. It was all their friends from other colleges asked them about. It was all the people at the cleaners, the grocer's, the butcher's, the bars, and other hangouts asked them about. "Is Beet Beat?" asked the *New York Post*. And *Time*: "Does the Beet Go On?" and *Newsweek*: "Does the Beet Go On?" By the time the holidays were over their talk was perfervid, their nerves frayed, and even those born with heads on their shoulders were beginning to lose them.

That may have been why, on the Monday morning of their return to College, when they picked up their copies of the *Pig's Eye* and read Ferrit Lawrence's story, "A Hysterical Female, or An Hysterical Female—What Professor Porterfield Thinks of the Women of Beet"—they threw a fit.

Ordinarily they never would have reacted that way, and they

didn't sincerely feel the fit they threw. Most who knew Matha Polite kept their distance from her, the way one does with any dangerous relation with whom one still has to live. They didn't like her poetry either. And they didn't trust what she said, ever. And they didn't believe Professor Porterfield said what she said he said. And they didn't even care all that much about it, whether he said it or not. But such was their state of mind—what with the college's closing imminent and final exams more imminent. And what would become of them? And where would they go? And when it came down to it, they were only kids, and all this was a shitload of trouble for kids to bear. They overreacted to the story, and though most of them acknowledged what they were doing, they did it anyway.

One may only imagine what the Monday morning meeting of the CCR was like. Before Peace had settled in his chair, Professor Kettlegorf, blushing and sputtering, asked him: "Do you have any idea what you've done? You've set us back irreparably! Irreparably!" No song came to her mind. She was *that* exasperated.

Booth: "It's a very serious matter. Very serious."

Heilbrun: "A disgrace, sir. Nothing short of a disgrace." For this grave occasion, he'd decided on a Newport—a black frock coat, plain gray waistcoat, gray striped trousers.

Lipman: "Frankly, I don't know that I want to serve on a committee with anyone who holds such views!"

But a moment like this was Smythe's meat. "Peace," he said, his voice a bite of marzipan. "No one understands better than I how one can say some damaging, even reprehensible, things under pressure. And you certainly have been under a lot of pressure. Not one of us—not I certainly—would blame you if you cracked. Not one iota. So I understand perfectly how this debacle could have occurred." He patted Peace's arm. "But of course it can't be tolerated. You simply must resign. I shall be happy, I should say unhappy, to serve in your stead . . ." He looked at the others for approval, which was proffered. "And the first thing I shall do as chairperson—you can count on this—will be to tell the entire faculty and administration what a splendid job you did. Truly splendid. But for the sake of our work, I really feel it would be best—"

"Don't be stupid, Keelye," said Peace. "I didn't say those things. And I wouldn't resign if I did."

That offered the group an opportunity for one of their tizzies. If their chairperson did not call Matha Polite "a" or "an" hysterical female, the point was moot. But if he *could* have said such a thing, what then? And if it were possible that he could say such a thing, yet still not step down, well, would it make a difference if he had said it or not? It was too much to deal with.

Having nearly been called "stupid," Keelye mounted his highest horse. "Well, naturally, we'll take your word you didn't say it. But why didn't you deny it for the reporter?"

"Yes. Why?" from Heilbrun, and, of course, Kramer.

"Because he never asked me," said Peace.

"The paper says you were unavailable for comment," said Lipman. "In journalism, that means you refused to speak to the press because you had something to hide." The others were glad to receive the insider's skinny.

"I wasn't available because he never tried to reach me," said Peace, still not grasping how this nonstory was about to, as Lipman would say, develop. "Now, shall we get down to the business of discussing the curriculum?" But the others were too shaken to go on. "All right. Tomorrow then. But let's come prepared. Okay? I'm sure I don't need to remind you, we have twelve days to come up with something and less than a week after that to persuade our colleagues to approve it. At the faculty meeting on the nineteenth, it's do or die."

The others crept away burdened not by their inability to complete their assignment, but rather by the saddening probability that Professor Porterfield had done nothing wrong.

Was Peace what Livi had called him—a babe in the woods? Or what? The poor fellow walked out of the committee meeting actually thinking that his colleagues would straighten themselves out, the matter would blow over in half a day, if it had not already done so, and now, with a free couple of hours at his disposal, he could get an oil change for the Accord for his trip to New York, Livi, and the children on Friday.

But one hardly needs to be told that by the time Peace descended the steps of Bacon, the story of—what was it exactly? His insult to women? His contempt for students? His rape and disembowelment of Matha Polite?—was spreading like a fast-moving cancer. And the trouble with a fast-moving cancer is that it grows like an embryo—two cells, four, eight, sixteen, and oh my! You're as good as dead before you know it. So was Peace. Any professor would have been, because trouble for a professor grows faster than a fast-moving cancer, doubling and redoubling, often because the professor himself makes matters worse by speaking up, or (rarely) by attacking the idiocy of the accusation, which Peace was considering.

And Peace Porterfield was not just any professor. He was virtuous in general and blameless in this instance. Who would not wish him every calamity? His colleagues in the English Department were so excited at the prospect of verbally tearing him limb from limb, they sputtered and stammered. The department members, the students, the dither of deans—they must condemn him. Shun him. Destroy him. What choice did they have?

Max Byrd did not join in the romp, needless to say. Neither did his new friend Akim. Gregory waved to Peace and shouted, "Phyppo," as a salute of support. And that was about it, save for some few of the 141 faculty members who, while clucking isn't it awful and isn't it sad, knew the scandal was ridiculous, but said nothing to dispel it.

Chief among the few was Derek Manning, who decided to make real use of the Free Speech Zone. He stood an hour in the cold and spoke of Professor Porterfield as the finest man he knew. He said that this Matha Polite business was the stupidest moment in the college's history—"in some stiff competition." He was so hoarse by the end of it, no one could hear him promise to resign if anything were done to Professor Porterfield—"the best goddamn teacher in this goddamn place."

All this had happened and was happening as Peace descended the library steps and stood in the sights of the television cameras and crews collected in brightly colored knots on the lawn of the Old Pen. The college was starting to look grimly festive, like a street fair in a seedy neighborhood, what with the fast-food joints in the visitors' parking lot and the whirligig of American media camped on the green. They had been sent to cover Beet's likely closing, but now they heard this thing some professor had said, which was so much "sexier." The story could lead the news that evening. The professor who hated women chaired the committee charged with saving the college. So how about this? "Anti-Feminist Professor Brings Down College." No, to be even-handed, let's phrase it as a question: "Can One Bigoted Professor Bring Down One of America's Premier Colleges?"

"Will you speak with us, Professor Pottersham?"

"Porterfield. Sure."

"Did you say all women are hysterical?"

"No."

"Did you say *some* women were hysterical?"

"No."

"Do you think women are hysterical?"

"No."

"Are women equal to men?"

"Yes."

"Why did you say those inflammatory things in the student newspaper?"

"I didn't."

They were getting nowhere with this guy. But there, coming out of College Hall, were President Huey and Chairman Bollovate.

"I must tell you. I'm shocked," said Huey, who added a good deal more, but it all came down to his being shocked.

And Bollovate? "I'm very sorry to say this. But it looks like we picked the wrong man."

"Will you have to close the college then, Mr. Bollovate?"

With a sigh and a shrug: "I hope not."

Catching sight of the scrum of reporters, Ferritt Lawrence tried to join up with them. He introduced himself as the author of the Porterfield scoop, and was disappointed when the grown-up journalists did not hoist him to their shoulders. He spied Peace disappearing from the Old Pen, and he ran to him.

"Professor Porterfield?" He was breathing hard. "Any comment on my story?"

Peace kept walking. "What story is that, Mr. Lawrence?" He could not resist.

"About what you called Matha Polite."

"I never called her anything."

"She says you did." Now they were at the Accord. "Where are you going, Professor?"

"To change the oil."

Classes were supposed to be going on, but students and faculty milled about the Pens. Chants erupted from time to time. "Down with Male Chauvinists!" "Down with Porterfield!" One young woman wearing a sign that read GIVE PEACE A CHANCE was hissed till she fled. Another was more successful when she delivered an impromptu speech citing the plight of the American Indians, the plight of the Palestinians, the plight of the Tibetans, and the plight of HIV sufferers, but lost the crowd when she came to the plight of the Holocaust.

Some danced alone to music on their iPods. Some did not. Some sent text messages. Some did not. Some stood on their hands. Some thumb-wrestled. Some played Sudoku. Some did not. Some, including Dean Baedeker, positioned themselves to be interviewed by the TV people, and when that didn't happen, repositioned themselves. No one knew what to do or where to be, but this is what panic looked like in a college—an expressionistic play, and a bad one. It wasn't a mob scene. It wasn't a march. It was a swirl—without purpose or destination, scumbled over by a vague if anachronistic sense of decorum. This was a place of learning, after all. People came here for a gentler life.

Yet those amassed there were not harmless either, and like any crowd, no matter how privileged, this one could do damage, especially if led by someone who did have a purpose and a destination.

She looked down upon the spectacle from the steps of the

Temple. She had climbed the hill to survey the world she'd brought to life. And make no mistake: Matha had brought it to life. Years from now, when historians spoke of the last days of Beet College—the end of an institution older than the nation itself—her name would be linked to the monumental event. And who was this Matha Polite? Only a student. A student and a poet. And yet a student and poet with the heart of a lion. And where is she now, this Matha Polite? Why, all you need do is drive out to the East End of Long Island and behold the billboards every five miles: "Polite for the Elite, Realtors." Did you know that her older sister, the needy one—Kathy or Connie or something—works in her office, too? Matha gave her a job. Just like her to do that.

Too bad that like all students and poets who are also charismatic political leaders, Matha had in her one super-duper lollapalooza of a blunder; she was still planning to take Bacon Library on December 18. Poised on the Temple steps, she hit upon a decorative way to do it. She could not help herself. She thought of it as a good thing.

Livi phoned as soon as she saw her husband's sweet stunned face on television. The Beet story did lead the evening news after all. She told him what she always told him about getting out of there, but this time with fear in her voice. Suddenly the idea that snakes could kill did not seem merely idiomatic. That was her husband—the best and most decent man in the world—they were talking about. People not fit to speak *to* him were talking *of* him. She would rend them with her teeth.

Less volatile was Peace's own reaction. To all who called his home that night, and there were many, he repeated with patience that the quotation was false, the accusation absurd. No, he did not plan to step down from the CCR. Yes, he did think he could continue in the chair effectively—questions and replies looping ad infinitum, or pretty close. He heard them all out. He hung up on none of them. He did not raise his voice in anger or lower it in shame. Good old predictable Peace. What should one do with such a man?

Yet he was plain disgusted—with the others and with himself.

More with himself. Why was he at the mercy of people like this? He was trapped. He couldn't go anywhere in public because he'd be stared at. He couldn't go down to New York as planned because the reporters might follow him. He wasn't as worried for his family as for the journalists. If Livi got hold of them, murder would be added to the charges.

He went out for a midnight run, took a header, and lay on his belly with his forehead bleeding.

So the Monday after Thanksgiving weekend ended with the students and faculty in panic mode, and in gossip mode, and Livi and Manning in fury mode, and Matha in clover, and Peace on his face. Bollovate, who sent a congratulatory note to Matha, was never better; Huey, of course, the same. And six of the members of the CCR agreed to meet in secret in Keelye Smythe's house (Ada served souvlaki, which her husband called "boring"), and decided to follow Smythe's suggestion that they attend no more meetings with Professor Porterfield "until this whole unfortunate business can be resolved." The TV crews waited and watched, expecting more trouble and loaded for bear. Ferritt handed each of them his card, FERRITT LAWRENCE, JOURNALIST. Jamie Lattice, feeling oh so much better, emailed the MacArthur Four that number five was back. Akim and Max continued to watch the letters and numbers dance on the screen.

In the quiet of the middle of the night, the college seemed to contravene the pathetic fallacy. Every pocket of darkness appeared shades darker—the buildings, the pathways, the trees, even the sky, which was never really dark at night, on this one seemed to have shut the hatch on itself. No moon or stars. No winking jetliner. No shopping mall searchlight projecting a hazy flare. It was as if Beet College were doing to itself what some others wanted to happen to it—die. And it was showing them and everyone else what it would look like dead.

Affrighted, interdicted, astonished, all bloody, all panting, Peace said to himself, "If this is the best . . ." One knows the rest.

CHAPTER

18

BRICOLAGE—THAT'S ALL IT WAS. THE NEW CURRICULUM
Peace had devised was a construction achieved by using things
already at hand. Bricolage, yet workable.

He walked from the parking lot toward his department to deliver the graded papers for his Modern Poetry class. It was Tuesday
of finals week, December 17. Between the Monday after Thanksgiving and the present, he had become all that anyone was speaking of. L'Affaire Porterfield. That horrid Porterfield business. He
did not mind his status as a pariah as much as simply being the
center of attention.

Professor Jefferson opened the I Am Woman Center twenty-
four hours a day to everyone except Professor Porterfield, and
played a medley of Mariah Carey songs over the loudspeaker.

Professor Dalmatian announced that Bliss House was available
for anyone who had difficulty with anything, except Professor Porterfield, who had "forfeited his right to bliss."

Even the Robert Bly Man's Manliness Society condemned
Peace on the grounds that insulting women wasn't manly.

And the CCR met daily, sans chair, mainly to discuss whether
or not Professor Porterfield had been telling the truth, and
whether or not they liked Professor Porterfield, and what was

Professor Porterfield doing at this moment, do you suppose? Professor Lipman wondered if she should go to him in private, since it was rumored his wife had left him—a rumor of which she was aware because she'd started it. The committee also spent half a day debating if they were in violation of the spirit, if not the letter, of the student strike by holding their meetings indoors.

Oh, yes, the student strike. On account of Peace, a collegewide strike was called. It was Matha's idea. At least it was her idea to look back to the 1960s again, and use someone else's idea. In the spring of 1969, she learned, Harvard students went on strike, and the long-term results were so delicious—personal relationships ruined, managers replacing leaders, politicians in the trees, and so much more—the thought was irresistible.

The student strike had begun on December 7. Matha liked that date because she knew something important had happened on it, somewhere. The MacArthur Five had T-shirts made up showing a pink-and-white clenched fist thrusting into the air. They tried a computer-generated picture of Latin on strike, but the raised hoof looked awkward. They tried to take a real picture of Latin wearing the striped T-shirt, but what he raised wasn't a hoof.

Matha had become more than a leader now; she was a martyr-leader, the most attractive kind. The CCR was as good as dead. Curricular reform was as good as dead. "Strike for women! Strike for the women of Beet! Strike for women everywhere!" That's what she shouted in public, where she spent much of her time.

"But explain something to me," said Betsy Betsy one night in Matha's room, which had become part headquarters, part shrine. "How can we go on strike? We're not workers. We don't belong to a union. What are we striking *for*—I mean, besides women everywhere?"

Matha said she'd slap Betsy's face if she ever asked such a dumb-shit question again, and Betsy wept. "We're not striking *for* anything, Miss Shitnose. We're striking *against* the college. We want to close it down, remember?"

Striking meant boycotting their classes. That left many hours of the day vacant, which were filled with talking about the strike.

"What about finals?" asked Lattice and Goldvasser.

"I don't know," Matha said. "I guess taking finals would be okay. They don't come up till the last week of term. We can kill a lot of time until then."

"Yet still get into law school?" said Goldvasser.

"And not get into too much trouble?" said Lattice.

Betsy Betsy was hoping she could do some media reporting on the college. She would ask the reporters what it felt like to be reporting.

Matha concentrated on her new and inspired and, if she said so herself, simply yummy plan for occupying the library. She had not let Bollovate in on her surprise—a happy one, she was certain, because over the course of their business conferences, he'd given every indication he wanted Beet shut down, no matter what he told others to the contrary. After his note to her on the Porterfield story, she'd written back, "When the college closes, what are you going to do with the property?" He did not reply.

Meanwhile, faculty members had watched from safe insessorial locations on the sidelines. Like Betsy, many were uncertain as to the common sense of students on strike, but they participated zealously nonetheless. Under strike rules, faculty could not hold classes whether or not students appeared. A few like Smythe came up with an alternative plan that would allow them to teach, and yet also to side with the students in their grievances. They would hold class, but not in the classrooms. They would teach out of doors, sitting on the ground. "Like the Greeks," said Smythe, not accounting for the climatic difference between a New England and a Greek December.

Naturally Peace had continued to teach in his classroom. Most of his students showed up. Some stayed in their dorms because they really weren't sure about Professor Porterfield, though experience and their better judgment, combined with their knowledge of Matha, ought to have taught them to be on his side. More stayed away simply because they were too upset about the college and their futures to know what they should do or where they should be.

Only once did Peace allude to the goings-on, when he quoted Marianne Moore's "In Distrust of Merits"—"We devour ourselves." But he did not look around to see if anyone caught its application to the current situation. The temper of the group was not such that they would be alert even to matters at hand. These days, they did not come to class to learn more about the modern poets so much as to feel safe. Whatever they thought of the college at the moment, it was a comforting place to be—a classroom.

In any event, the strike had lasted only three days, with students too concerned about their own fates to get worked up about condemning Professor Porterfield.

Otherwise, not much had happened during the two weeks of Peace's disgrace and ostracism. The TV crews came and went and came again. The faculty had gone beyond frazzled to a state of numbness undergirded by desperation. Hoping to appear attractive to other institutions, professors hurried to finish books they'd been working on for decades. Phyllis Loo completed her *Bowdler Bowdlerized*, the only known study of Dr. Thomas Bowdler's letters, in which Loo had expurgated references to indecent passages. Damenial Krento, who called himself a dwarf but was two inches over the limit, polished off the footnotes for his *Brief History of the Epigram*. Professor Holton of the Film Department was a chapter shy of completing his definitive *Van Heflin: Brute in a Suit*. And the Benson brothers, both from Biology, put the final touches on their joint autobiography as the only tenured former Siamese twins in academia. They would have used the euphemism "conjoined," but they happened to be born to missionaries in Thailand. Writing the book was easy for them because, as they boasted, they could complete each other's sentences. Unfortunately, the sentences, once complete, conveyed little.

Akim, actually, did accomplish something during this period. It started with his trying to discover if his Homeland Security courses were giving finals. They would be online too, he supposed. But the department answered all his many inquiries with TRY AGAIN LATER. When he informed them, whoever and wherever they were, that there was no later—either the department gave finals during finals week or not at all—the reply he received was THANK YOU.

He was sure the administration of Homeland Security operated at the same level of intelligence as the courses. Pinto, the one department member, probably did not know if there were finals. He probably did not know there was such a thing as finals. Akim tried to imagine what a Homeland Security final exam would be like: "Is it safer to live in New York City or on Baffin Island? Discuss"; "True or false: The World Trade Center tragedy can happen again and we must be prepared."

Since being befriended by Max Byrd, Akim had found himself thinking more and more like an ordinary student, and less like a suicide bomber. He'd discarded his kaffiyeh and robes and now wore the standard undergraduate mufti of jeans, running shoes, baseball hat worn backward, and a sweatshirt bearing the name of any college but one's own. He'd shaved.

He'd also moved back to his dorm and had nearly forgotten the two milk cartons of TATP that remained on a ledge in his cave. Blowing himself to pieces no longer seemed as appealing as it once did. He wondered how to dispose of his explosive soup.

And that's what was occupying his mind on the morning Peace walked across campus to hand in his papers. Akim's attention was diverted from his laptop, so initially he failed to notice that the numbers and letters on the alphanumeric generator had disappeared. Just like that. On the screen, pretty as you please, was HOMELAND SECURITY HOME PAGE, as if it had been there all along.

He was in. It had taken a random search of over seven weeks and sixteen million permutations to break what turned out to be three hundred levels of codes, but he was in. Akim almost had to remind himself what he'd been looking for in the first place. The department. That was it. And the faculty member, Professor Billy Pinto. Less prone to obsessiveness these days, he clicked on to the hot links as if he were absentmindedly fiddling with the mouse. And what he saw in front of him was so mundane, he regretted having devoted all that time and effort to the task.

It was a menu, like that of any department home page in the college. There were lists of courses, which Akim knew too well. There was a list of professors consisting of one, and his Web site. There was a brief explanation of the department and its aims—"To make America safer for you and me." There was even a street address, which Akim did not recognize, and so assumed it was off campus. The menu consisted of all the information one would need in searching out any department. Why the ultrasecure password?

Well, in for a nickel, he told himself. He would try the hot link for Billy Pinto. What the hell. He stifled a yawn.

What the hell, indeed. He must have put the hot link in incorrectly, because information on Billy Pinto did not appear. What did appear upon his screen caused him to stare for a full minute without a blink, much as he might stare at his father entering his room, greeting him with open arms and swearing off chess forever. It was then, in this state of astonishment, that he phoned his friend Max.

"Get over here. Now!"

"Waddup?"

"Work for a computer geek."

Bollovate and Huey did not know of Akim's existence, much less of his discovery. At the time Akim was calling Max, the two men had business in Huey's office before the trustees' meeting that afternoon. The sole purpose of the meeting was to dump Peace as chair of the CCR. They would have liked to revoke his tenure and kick him out of the college that very day. But Bollovate, no dope when it came to tactics, knew that would be pushing things. The faculty would stifle its ordinary tendencies toward treachery, and figure that if one professor were dumped, so could they all be; they would protect their own and turn on Joel Bollovate. Yet he had enough to say to the "college mushheads" to make Peace their outcast forever. He would draw up the charges himself. He thought it a nice touch. He could announce Professor Porterfield's ouster at the same time as his own little surprise about the college—known only to himself and Huey—at the faculty meeting day after tomorrow. His day. Joel's day. One would have had to search the campus, indeed the universe, to find two happier fellows. Huey was happy when Bollovate was happy, and Bollovate was happy as a cake.

"But we can't get cocky," he said, taking Huey's chair.

"That would be bad," said Huey, taking the chair reserved for visitors.

"I can't tell you how many sweetheart deals have fallen through at the last minute because of cockiness."

"People get cocky."

"That's right. They take their eyes off the ball. They lose sight of details. It's the end game, Lewis. The end game separates the sheep from the goats."

"The sheep from the goats." Huey squirmed because he was about to say something that came from his own brain. "Joel, I hope you won't mind my bringing this up. But we've never really spoken about what I'll be doing after."

"You'll be taken care of. You can bet on that."

"Yes, but my job. What will it be? I mean, exactly. The title."

Bollovate frowned philosophically, as if he really were considering the question. "How about president?" He beamed.

"Could I still be president?" Huey beamed more.

"Of course, Lewis. We'll always need a president. No matter the situation people are in, everyone wants to know there's a president." He reached across the desk and patted Huey's hands, which were folded and damp.

Huey was teary with gratitude. "That's great, Joel. Wonderful to hear. I'm relieved, I don't mind telling you. It would be hard to start over, at my age."

"Well, you don't need to worry about that . . . Mr. President."

On that Tuesday morning too, three women pursued separate though related quests.

Sheila Bollovate was driving her maroon Lexus to her lawyer's, where she would sign an intention to divorce in the presence of a notary. The document contained 108 pages of property listings. As she drove, she chewed on a Mallomar.

Kathy Polite was leaving her home on Long Island. She was on her way to pay a surprise call on her sister, about whom, frankly, she was worried. Martha had never been a charmer. But over Thanksgiving, she'd seemed less charming than usual, and definitely involved in something over her head. I don't like her, thought Kathy. Who does? But blood is blood. And it was Christmas. Was it not? It was.

It was! With all else going on, it seemed hard to remember. But it was Christmastime. And Christmas in New England carries a greater burden than elsewhere because the region drops into its deepest emotional pit, requiring desperate measures of jubilation.

In the town of Beet, merchants hung large wreaths with red velvet bows on the lampposts. "Rockin' Round the Christmas Tree" crackled over the defective PA system in the firehouse. The Pen and Oink displayed a 1951 copy of *A Christmas Carol* in the window. The Bring Home the Bacon grocers lathed red and green icing on the cupcakes. Marty's Swine & Cheese set up a three-foot Santa made of cheddar, and a Stilton in the shape of a dreidel. In that spirit, the debate on whether or not to place an aluminum menorah in the crèche on the village green had settled on a separate-but-equal arrangement. The menorah was placed beside the crèche, and a sign in front covered in tinsel, read: HAPPY AND MERRY WHATEVER YOU CELEBRATE OR DO NOT IN YOUR OWN WAY.

The first big snowstorm was forecast. Everyone spoke of it and of other big snowstorms in years past, which were always worse than the modern snowstorms. Everyone spoke of hot chocolate. Gregory wished all who passed through the gates a "Mango Isthmas."

Only the recently defunct This Little Piggy Muncheonette failed to rejoice in the season. It appeared in mourning, as did the great pink fiberglass pig on its roof.

But the third woman worth noting was suffused with Christmas cheer that morning. Her husband would be home with her soon and forever, she hoped. She strode along midtown Third Avenue, looking to buy him a present.

"What would you like?" She'd called him on her cell.

"Nothing. Just you."

"Then that's what you'll get. Nothing and me." She walked past the shops until she came to Victoria's Secret.

"Children," she told them at dinner. "Tomorrow I'm going up to be with your father." She wasn't on call for the following two days. Why not? "I'll get a nice policeman to stay with you."

To tell Peace her plan, or make it a surprise? That night she would pack. The next day, the eighteenth, she would drive to Beet after seeing her patients. She could be at the house when he was just about to go to bed. Bed. Looking in the mirror, she brushed her red hair and sang along with Norah Jones.

FOR HIS PART DURING THOSE TWO WEEKS, PEACE HAD SIMply continued to work. Now he proceeded to his office, his papers tucked under his arm. In the midst of all the collegiate mummery, he had in fact come up with something.

Bricolage. Peace's idea did not entail an upheaval of the existing curriculum. All it involved was one course, the planning and implementation of a single course of study to be superimposed on the existis curriculum, and required of all entering students. It would be taught by professors in every department, either by team teaching— an English professor with a biologist, an economist with a member of the Art Department, like that—or by individual lectures combined with small discussion groups.

Yet it would be neither multicultural nor interdisciplinary. If one had to give it a label, it could be called extradisciplinary, since the professors would need to go outside their disciplines to see them from a new vantage point. The course would run the entire freshman year, and if upperclassmen desired, they could take it again as auditors to remind themselves of its applicability to whatever they concentrated in. A new way to see learning, that's what Peace hoped it would be.

"Professor Porterfield?"

"Yes, Jenny?"—from his Modern Poetry class.

"May I speak with you?"

"Sure."

"I wanted to say I never believed any of that stuff about you. I don't know anyone who did."

"Thanks, Jen. I appreciate your saying so."

"Professor Porterfield? Will you be able to save the college?"

"I don't know. We'll try."

All right. What was the course? Storytelling. It would be a course in storytelling. The idea had come to Peace little by little after his one-on-one with Manning—what his friend had said about finding a way to make educators interested in education again, and about finding a different way to see what the college already had, rather than trying to invent something out of whole cloth.

And there was Peace's recollection of the children in Sunset Park and of telling stories there—the kids gathered round him, as though he were a bonfire, rapt in the ceremony of listening. Why does a child say, "Tell me a story"? Because he expects it to be wonderful.

"Professor Porterfield?"

"Hi, Lucky."

"I just want to say hey."

"Hey, Lucky."

As thoughts tend to build on themselves, this one grew for Peace. His mind was his house. First the front door flung open, then the back, then the windows one at a time, and a couple of things dropped through the chimney (bang!) into the fireplace, and more breezed in through the cracks in the walls. What do you know? The idea filled the house. It had size. Stories were everywhere: In the law, where a prosecutor tells one story and the defense tells another, and the jury decides which it prefers. In medicine, where a patient tells a doctor the story of his ailment, how he felt on this day or that, and the doctor tells the patient the story of the therapy, how he will feel this day and that, until, one hopes, the story will have a happy ending. Politics? He who tells the best story wins, be it Pol Pot or FDR. And the myths of businesses, the foundations of religions—the "greatest story ever told."

Every intellectual discipline, every college department was a story in progress. All one needed was to see it that way. Look at his own discipline. Literature was a story. Fiction most obviously, but essays and poems, too. An essay was the story of an idea; a poem the story of a feeling.

The subject had heft and stamina. It could go the distance. It might not rescue civilization, might not even rescue Beet College, but it had something. Peace was sure of that, as he was fairly sure his colleagues would take to it, because the stories of the disciplines always changed, and tellers of the stories changed. Teaching located them within their own stories. They could account for changes as sequels and new chapters. They could be responsible for them—storytellers at work. They might even enjoy them.

"Professor Porterfield?"

"Morning, Jim"—an instructor in History he had hardly ever spoken to.

"I hope you know a lot of us think you're getting a raw deal."

"Thank you."

"We're scared, scared for the place and for our own skins. That's why we haven't rallied behind you."

"I'm scared too."

"Well, I just had to tell you."

"Take care, Jim."

And it was readily understandable because it was basic to human nature, like fellow feeling, if they gave it a chance. Storytelling was almost a biological fact, an inborn insistence. The Jews in the last days of the Warsaw Ghetto: They knew what was going to happen to them, had seen their mothers and neighbors hauled off to the extermination camps, and were themselves dying of diphtheria and hunger. And yet—and yet!—they had the strength and the will to take scraps of paper on which they wrote poems, fragments of autobiography, political tracts, journal entries. And they rolled those scraps into small scrolls and slipped the scrolls into the crevices of the ghetto walls. Why? Why did they bother? With no news of the outer world available to them, they assumed the Master Race had inherited the earth. If their scraps of paper were discovered, the victors would laugh at them, read and laugh, and tear them up. So why expose their writing, their souls, to derision?

Because they had to do it. They had a story to tell. They had to tell a story.

That man in France, Jean-Dominique Bauby, the editor of *Elle* who suffered so massive a stroke the only part of his body he could move was his left eyelid. Yet with that eyelid, he signaled the alphabet. And with that alphabet, he wrote an autobiography. He too had to do it. It was in him, in everyone.

We like to distinguish ourselves from other animals by saying we're a rational species. Are you kidding? But a narrative species? That, Peace was convinced, one could prove.

Who knows? Such a course might eventually expel the nonsense courses in the New Pen, or at least distill the nonsense from them, and leave a residue of something sensible to study, divorced from the promotion of self-adulation. If everything were seen as a story with all the elements of a good story discerned, a Gresham's law of narrative might take hold. Good stories would drive out bad. Faculty and students would start making discriminations. Wouldn't that be something? And even if everything in the college remained exactly as it was—Homeland Security and Communications Arts untouched, God help us—people still would recognize that there are minor stories and major stories. And what do you think of that?

"Professor Porterfield?"

"Hi, Max."

"There's something strange happening at the college."

"You're telling me."

"No, sir. I mean, stranger than you think. We may need your help."

"We?"

"I'm on my way to see Akim. May I call you later?"

"Sure."

The particulars of the course—the components and how they would work with one another—would need to be fleshed out. But even Peace's cursory survey of materials suggested there was plenty to use and to build on. The neuroscience alone was fascinating— the brain's neurons firing to instruct by storytelling, a billion stories in endless competition to deliver information. The psychology:

Peace read that babies learn language to tell the stories already in them. The psychiatry: how schizophrenics have their stories broken. And language itself, its beauty, and its hilarity when someone misspeaks, tells the wrong story. To say nothing of the terror of silence when there is no story to tell. Maybe we Cro-Magnons knocked off the Neanderthals because we could not bear their silence.

If mystery could be taught, there was the mystery of the whole enterprise. Why is it no one ever tells a story the same way twice? Not even the uncle who has told one anecdote over and over at every family gathering for decades—not even he tells it the same way twice. Why is it that when you read a sentence you have written yourself, you still don't know where it's going? Because you want to pretend the adventure is new, even when it was you who created it.

Art as story. Philosophy as story. Linguistics. Math. Scientific research, with its bulky collaborations, as a story. Science itself— evolution originally referring to the unrolling of a scroll. And Darwin, whom Peace thought the most imaginative person in history, seeing the consequences of the leaps without seeing the leaps. The story of one's own life. Self-esteem? If you want self-esteem, Peace said to himself, think big. Our DNA indicates we are all stories waiting to be told. But what are the stories we were meant to tell?

"Professor Porterfield?"

"Yes?"

"I'm from Mr. Bollovate's office. He asked me to let you know there's an emergency meeting of the trustees in the Temple this afternoon. They would like you to be there."

"Sorry. I'm busy."

"Is that what you want me to tell them?"

"Tell them what you please."

He took a breath before entering his department building. What was the story Peace was meant to tell? He'd always thought it was a teacher's story. Now he wasn't so sure. Funny. You go along doing what you do until one day you find yourself seeing your life through a stranger's eyes. And you are that stranger.

What Peace would be asking of his colleagues, he was doing

himself, introducing his mind to itself. Evolution? You could say that again. He was unrolling like a piece of writing. The ink was wet.

But the course was possible, he was certain, ready for teaching. All it needed was someone to pull it together, get the others to take part and figure out the stories they'd been telling all their lives. Bricolage. They would cobble together the subject as they cobbled together the curriculum, as they remade the college.

And it did not need to be airtight, this subject. God, who would want it airtight? Just make it interesting enough, imaginative enough to sustain itself and provocative enough to challenge itself. One person playing point, that's all it would take, Peace knew, just as he knew he would not be that person.

"Professor Porterfield?"

He looked around, but no one was there.

CHAPTER

19

IF A DECEMBER DAWN IN NEW ENGLAND WERE DISTINGUISH-able from the dead of night, one would have said it was dawn that brought the flabbergasting sight greeting all who entered the Old Pen. "What *is* that? Can you make it out?" Partly obscured in mist and darkness on the green, it looked spectral, like a vague elephant, and painted with a mucid glaze. It glowed pink. Big and glowing and pink. Could anyone tell what it was yet? "Why, shit! It's the pig from the roof of the Muncheonette. Goddamn! It looks awesome!"

It was, and it did. The pig, restored to its former prominence, stood majestic as ever at the south end of the green, its curlicue tail aimed at Bacon Library. Students and professors circumnavigated the thing, walking clockwise and counterclockwise, noting its bright blue hooves tucked beneath its ample body, and its bright blue eyes. Such eyes! Such ears! Such a snout! When it had resided on the roof of the eatery, no one could properly appreciate what a work of art was this pig. But here where one could see it up close, its full magnitude declared it the mother of all pigs, more than a totem, a god.

"It's the Trojan Pig!" said Archie Acephalous of Archaeology, who boasted he knew more classics than the Classics Department. He had no idea how right he was.

Occupying the hollow of the great pink animal, the MacArthur Five—four of them present—sat in their prearranged positions. They had entered through the snout, which opened and closed on hinges. The reason only four of the students were inside had to do with weight capacity. Though it was impossible to detect from the outside, the pig rested on a platform atop a scissor-link vertical lift, which in turn rested on four trailer-size tires. The lift was folded flat, and it and the platform were concealed in the lower portion of the pig's belly. Only the wheels showed. The platform could hold a five-hundred-pound level load; that's what the man who rented the vehicle told the revolutionaries. Betsy Betsy weighed 110; Goldvasser and Lattice, 160 and 137; Matha 106. Bagtoothian weighed in at 214, so it was he who remained outside.

But he had a key assignment. When late night approached, someone had to pull the pig to the library, at which point its occupants would employ the hand pump of the hydraulic lift, the scissor would rise, and the happy elevated animal would deposit the little army of revolutionaries at the second-story window. Once in, they would go downstairs and admit Bagtoothian. The plan was a beauty, thought Matha the moment she'd conceived of it.

So far, so perfect. The four had brought pillows and blankets for comfort, and books and magazines to pass the time. They had to wait a whole day. If their presence were to go undetected, talking must be held to a minimum, which was harder on Betsy Betsy than the others. Air aplenty was provided by the pig's nostrils. And it was surprisingly warm in there, given that the pig was never intended to carry passengers. Jamie and Goldvasser peeked out of the nostrils from time to time, Betsy read, and Matha distributed some of the hundred or so oatmeal and chocolate chip cookies she'd baked the night before. She had also put together decorative picnic baskets for the group, festooned with pink excelsior and tied at the handles with white velour ribbons. The others wondered at the meticulous care she had taken with this domestic project, but were glad of it and made no comments other than those of appreciation.

"They're delicious!" said Jamie.

"And the baskets—so pretty!" said Betsy.

Matha smiled demurely before telling them to eat shit.

By late morning it could be said that every student and most of the faculty in Beet College had ogled and circled the pig at least once, making the appropriate remarks of amazement and inquiry—except for Max Byrd and Arthur Horowitz, who had more urgent things on their minds.

Akim's reversion was now complete. He was astonished how smoothly it had happened, as well as how eager he was to cast off the terrorist paraphernalia along with his nom de guerre. He'd even phoned his father—in part to initiate a rapprochement, which the repentant rabbi welcomed, saying, "You made me a better Jew by becoming an Arab than I would have been if I were an Arab and you were a Jew," or something like that. Arthur also needed to ask him about what he'd discovered on his computer screen.

That was the previous evening. Max had been with him, and he too called his dad. Both young men knew they'd stumbled upon an area of knowledge and activity way beyond their experience. They'd stay up all night because of what was on that screen. Max's dad's information abetted the rabbi's, and both combined with Max's own "cyberfreak" expertise. His ability to see the nothing that was not there had proved indispensable. It was then, that morning, the boys decided to consult the professor they most trusted.

Peace phoned Livi at her Manhattan office. "I'm not sure what to do," he said.

"You're sure, all right. But you don't know when."

"The faculty meeting, I guess. But it seems a little cheap to air all that in public."

"Only you would worry about the niceties, sweetheart. If you don't do it in front of the others, you'll lose the advantage. You don't want to give a man like that an inch."

"Are you amazed by all this, or what?"

"I am."

"Do I love you?"

"You do."

"Will I see you soon?"

"You have no idea."

As anyone could guess, the day would turn out to be quite busy for the crowd at Beet, what with finals nearly over and Christmas around the corner. Life was especially frantic for members of the CCR. Professor Kramer took this opportunity to apply to Gonzaga University, the last on his list of possibilities, for an assistant professorship, or if not that an instructorship. It seemed his attempts—and Heilbrun's and Booth's as well—to make lateral moves and win tenure at other institutions of higher learning had been unsuccessful, so now they were willing to take anything. Kettlegorf had no luck either, and neither did Lipman. Lipman had tried so hard to become a recognizable professor. She'd jarred jams, cross-country skied, and bought a chocolate Lab that she named Pinch. Nothing worked. So, rather than apply to colleges, she wrote her old boss at the *New York Times*, noting that there was no job too trivial for her, including writing the column on arts news. Her former employer replied that she should remain in academia, where she would do the paper more good by continuing to spread word of its excellence.

His future protected by Ada's Lacoste money, Keelye Smythe did not apply for a new position elsewhere. He was getting on, after all, and he wondered if this weren't a good time to try something new that would suit his social gifts and talents. Foundation work might do. Or the presidency of the College Board. Or an institute of some sort. Perhaps the government. Any place where he could deny people what they wanted and deserved, but with sincere regret. No rush. He'd look around.

None of them informed the others of their efforts. It might appear to show a lack of faith in their ability to save Beet College. But they were bundles—bales—of nerves. What would happen tomorrow at the faculty meeting, when they were called upon to present the new curriculum? Kettlegorf could not help but think they might have been a bit hasty when they refused to let Professor Porterfield continue as their leader. But when she gave it some thought, perhaps it was more gratifying to attempt to discomfit a colleague than to allow him the chance to save their necks.

Content as he was otherwise, Bollovate, too, had spent a nervous Tuesday night. Sheila had kicked him out of the Louisburg Square house, and got an injunction forbidding him entrance to the Wellfleet house, the Newport house, the East Hampton house, and even the 25,000-square-foot log cabin on the Snake River in Jackson Hole. The settlement demanded in Sheila's divorce papers had so upset him, he wondered if he were suffering congestive heart failure instead of his chronic acid reflux. He had tried to get hold of Matha for a business conference in the Charles Hotel in Cambridge, where he wound up spending the night. But Matha was unreachable, even to him. So he turned on the TV, searched the movie menu, and selected *Dripping Wet Asians* and *Young Thai Pie.*

Come Wednesday he felt chipper again, and in the evening, after checking on a number of hidden bank accounts to ascertain that they remained hidden from Sheila, and checking in on the Potemkin real estate company he'd set up on Long Island, he drove toward Beet College. He would arrive by eleven, just about the time the MacArthur Five would enter the library and Livi Porterfield would get home to surprise her husband. One important errand lay ahead for him, and one more at tomorrow's faculty meeting, and he would be king of the hill. As he steered the Escalade onto the Mass Pike and hooked north, never dimming his brights, he contemplated life without Sheila and the children. The dead trees stood at attention.

It did not take much to figure out what he'd had in mind when he engineered the closing of the college. Oh, he'd engineered it, all right. He'd appointed Porterfield because the young professor was wet behind the ears and likely to fail. He reveled in Professor Porterfield's humiliation, especially after Porterfield had faced him down. But it would have made no difference to Bollovate or his fellow developers on the board if Peace and the CCR had come up with the most dazzling curriculum ever devised. He and his cronies were bound to close the place under any circumstance because the land was a hell of a lot more valuable ("Are you kidding?") with the deep thinkers off it. It didn't take much to figure that out either.

And it might have taken a little more, but not so very much, to figure out that the trustee developers were going to wind up owning the property, which is why they were happy as little overfed pigs themselves at their momentous meeting in the Temple two months earlier when good old Joel came up with his new curriculum scam, which was merely a stalling tactic, until the purchase could be arranged. Now, thanks to the hapless Francis April's need for ready cash (Bollovate wound up paying him $60 thousand plus the promise of a personal introduction to Joe Namath), the deal was as good as done. All that remained to play out were the coup de grâce on Professor Porterfield's disgrace; the anger-cum-melancholy of the milquetoast faculty; the brief if noisy outcry of the parents, and of the old-money alumni; and that would be that. Massachusetts State officials? Don't make Joel Bollovate laugh. The dummy corporation, which had so intrigued Matha Polite and concerned her sister, would front the money, and the man with the iron belly would add to his infinitely expanding territory two hundred and ten acres of prime real estate "in the heart of American history."

All this chicanery had been in plain view from the start, had anyone wanted to take a look. But Beet being a college, populated by people who populated colleges, it occurred to no one to notice anything other than themselves. And so what was not difficult to figure out was left unfigured out.

Yet there were two additional items of pettifoggery known only to Bollovate and Lewis Huey. Not even the other trustees were in on them. And no one would have figured out the far worse of these two things had not Akim Ben Laden, as then he was known, been dissatisfied with his concentration. That the concentration was Homeland Security, as one would soon see, presented a minor irony of its own.

"Laissez les bon temps rouler!" cried Matha exactly at eleven, an hour after Bacon had closed for the night. No one remained in the Old Pen, the novelty of the Trojan Pig having eroded, leaving the campus to darkness and to the MacArthur Five. Bagtoothian was responsible for making les bon temps rouler. He looked around furtively, hand shading eyes like a comic book spy, reached beneath the pig's pink fiberglass tail, disengaged the pole, and pulled.

Matha felt the pig roll and come to a stop. "Are we here?" she shouted a whisper to Bagtoothian.

"Yes, sir," he said.

"Where are we, exactly? And call me sir again, and you're toast."

"Under the second floor, like you said. What do I do now?"

"Kill yourself."

The rental man had shown Matha what button to push to raise the vertical lift. Two chrome-plated cylinders moved upward away from the tractor chassis, and the pig rose a few inches at a time, the scissor link unfolding into three steel diamonds one atop the other and finally reaching its lift capacity of twenty-six feet. It stopped parallel to the library's second-story window, and about four feet away to allow room to open the snout-door. Bagtoothian pushed the structure forward, bringing the elevated pig flush with the building. Matha reached out, raised the window, and crawled through with the others behind her.

"Go let in brains-for-shit," she told Lattice, who trotted downstairs.

The students took their stations and waited, looking about the great domed room, casting shadows in the dark and against the walls of books. Matha congratulated them on their achievement. They were about to desecrate the warehouse of learning they'd targeted on the Day of the Bollovate, two months earlier. And if their occupation of the building would not effect the great work stoppage of the mind they'd envisioned, at least they could serve their community as they always had—as giant pains in the ass. Here they stood, with all that was best thought and felt surrounding them. And it was theirs to abuse. Compared to this, thought Matha, MacArthur House was a piece of cake, which reminded her: "Did you bring in the baskets of cookies?" she asked Betsy, who, lucky for her, had.

"Do you think we can eat all these cookies?" Bagtoothian asked.

"They're not for us, they're for the crowd. It's cold out there. They'll enjoy a snack." Matha was talking strangely, but the others were too afraid of her to point it out.

Since he'd been following Matha, as was his practice, Ferritt Lawrence had seen everything—from the previous night's gentle lowering of the pink pig from the roof of the Muncheonette to its placement on the platform and the wheels. On his mountain bike he'd trailed the pig on its long nocturnal journey, as the Mac-Arthur Five had rolled it into the Old Pen just before dawn. He'd watched it all day, and into the night, when its occupants vacated it for the library. He noted all that, just as he noted that Matha had promised she would let him know when she would pull off the next big radical event. And he noted that once again she'd failed to keep her word. So he stood out of sight and watched some more, knowing exactly what he'd do when Matha emerged from the building.

At their stations in Max's room (Arthur had abandoned his cave permanently), the two students called Professor Porterfield. They'd uncovered the last piece of the puzzle. Peace said he'd come to them. He threw on his navy sweats, opened his front door, and said, "Hey!" Before him stood the most beautiful redhead he had ever seen.

"M. Candide?" she asked.

"The same."

It was close to midnight, the hour the MacArthur Five had determined they would announce their conquest of Bacon. Matha knew the students and faculty were still shaky and frightened, and she would play on their mood. There was no point to a prolonged occupation of the library now. Tonight's act was more symbolic. Since the college was about to shut down anyway, let the students do the shutting. She for whom speech was a perlocutionary act knew she could mislead a crowd one more time. The aesthetic logic of the occupation would appeal to everyone. And the pig, as the instrument of the Beet College finale, was simply scrumptuous.

But as the five were about to descend the stairs, they heard voices. "Oh, my God," said Lattice. "I'm ruined."

"Shut up, you wuss." Matha hesitated on the landing and listened. She knew one of those voices too well.

Bollovate and La Cocque mounted the steps side by side. The kids hid behind the balustrade.

"You've killed the alarm?"

"Oui."

"You understand. I only want to see what it will bring on the open market. I have no plans to keep it. Do you understand?"

"Yes."

"You're sure it's in good shape? It won't crumple in my hands?"

"Oui."

"Is there a reason you speak half in French?"

"No. *Non.*"

The students watched the two men enter the Main Hall and approach the Mayflower Compact lying in the dimly lit cabinet. La Cocque lifted the top of the case, like a waiter presenting flaming food. He reached in, took the document, and handed it to Bollovate, whose appetence for profit made his teeth glow in the dark. He slid the treasure into the large envelope he'd been holding. The students felt heartsick, but did not know why.

Jesus! Matha said to herself. Was Bollovate stealing the Mayflower Compact? Shit! Was she ever out of her league! They would wait till the two men's backs were turned, and go ahead with what they'd planned. But she knew from that moment she was but one of Bollovate's seductions, probably the least of the lot. There was Louie Huey, there was the freakazoid La Cocque, there were his fellow developers on the board, and there was this twenty-year-old girl, herself. How had she come to this pass? Something stirred briefly in Matha Polite. Was it fear? Self-awareness? Shame? The chocolate chips?

Avoiding detection by Bollovate and La Cocque, they crept downstairs and collected at the library door. "Ready?" said their leader.

"Fuckin' A," said Bagtoothian, yet even he was feeling uneasy. They opened the door and stood on the threshold facing the green.

"Brothers and sisters of Beet College," Matha called out. She had no need for a bullhorn; her words reverberated off the library wall. "Brothers and sisters of Beet! Rejoice with us! We've seized the library! Come and take one last stand before Beet College is no more!"

At first there was scant response to her beckoning. Then five or six students wearing parkas over their pajamas emerged from the darkness bearing flashlights. Then ten or twelve. Then many. Faculty, too—until the Old Pen was full of people again, though this time they seemed part of a processional more than a rally. Everyone was bone-tired, hangdog, and wrapped in an overwhelming sadness. They had nothing left in them. They herded together into the Old Pen like farm animals, heads swaying, feet dragging. All that was missing was the moo.

Hearing Matha's blaring call, Peace, Livi, Max, and Arthur, who'd been in Max's room, joined the others. Peace was still unsure as to when and how to divulge the information the four of them now possessed. Livi, at his side, was loving every minute of it.

"We'll sit in the library as a final gesture of defiance!" said Matha. "If Beet must close, let the people do the closing!" Some few stepped forward to follow her into the building.

And it was then that the power of the press asserted itself. "Before we go any further," shouted Ferritt Lawrence to the crowd, "I'd like you all to hear something." Matha turned and stopped cold. Of course, he played the tape he'd made of the lovers at Sow's Motel. He had to. He was a journalist, and an investigative journalist to boot.

Just like that, the tape delivered the whole incriminating conversation at the highest volume, exposing both parties as conspirators against Professor Porterfield and the college itself. Students and teachers listened and said nothing in their outrage, until the tape arrived at "Oh! Mr. Bollovate!" when the crowd could not, and did not wish to, contain itself. If Matha thought she'd heard derisive laughter that day at the CCR meeting, what she experienced here would reverberate for a lifetime.

In terms of the case against Professor Porterfield, the tape only substantiated what most people suspected anyway; Matha had made the story up.

"I knew it all along," said those who'd known it all along.

But life was about to get considerably worse for the girl. From the middle of those assembled came a voice, clear and southern and declamatory in its emphasis. "Martha Stewart Polite!" cried Kathy. "What are you doin' with your life?" There was a terrible silence. "Martha Stewart Polite! Ah'm talkin' to you!"

"Why are you calling her that?" asked Bagtoothian.

"Because it's her name, silly!"

"Pass out the cookies!" Matha told Betsy Betsy. "Do it now!" But even her cohorts had deserted her. It was one thing to betray the college and try to screw Professor Porterfield, quite another to be named for Martha Stewart. Martha Stewart Polite! Her comrades ran from her, hoping to be absorbed in the community of peers they'd sneered at. Their peers were unabsorbing.

Yet Matha gave it the old college try. "Go ahead and laugh," she said. "But I have something to tell you that will make my little subterfuge seem like chicken feed. In the Library right now, Mr. Bollovate is stealing the Mayflower Compact! We saw him do it, him and La Cocque."

The two men appeared on the steps behind her. La Cocque, sensing danger, scuttled away. Bollovate didn't flinch. What? Are you kidding? Was Joel Bollovate going to be brought down by a tart like Polite?

He cast her a look containing murder. She caught it, fled into the crowd, and bounced off Arthur.

"Akim?" she said, hoping she had found the one in the group who would embrace her. She hardly recognized him clean-shaven and dressed like a person. She wondered what she had missed in him, while Arthur wondered what Akim had ever seen in her. He stood with his arms at his side. Kathy clasped her sister by the shoulders and led her away.

Bollovate reached into the large envelope and held the sacred document aloft. The crowd gasped. He chuckled. He was coddling idiots. "Why, I only took it for safekeeping," he said. "When the college closes, you wouldn't want this left lying around, would you? Who knows what sorts of people will invade the campus!"

He stared at the throng for which he had more contempt than ever and made some rapid calculations. What could they say about him and Matha but that he fucked her? So what if he'd wanted Porterfield out? Who didn't? He had a chance to emerge from this clean as a whistle if he acted with enough self-assurance. And he had stacks of that. It was time for his surprise announcement.

"My friends," he said. "I know how you feel. It's a sad day for all of us, myself and the trustees especially, who have tried so hard to keep Beet College alive. But unlike Ms. Martha Stewart Polite, I have news that *matters*. The college *is* alive. We're staying open!" No one knew what to make of that.

"You see," said Bollovate, "after observing that Professor Porterfield and his committee weren't getting anywhere, and were not going to get anywhere—Dr. Huey and I came up with a plan. Join me up here, will you, Lewis?" Huey took the steps two at a time and stood panting beside his master. "I hadn't anticipated telling you about this today. But now's as good a time as any, eh, Lewis?" Huey nodded and grinned. "Well! Dr. Huey and I are going to make Beet College the first online institution of its kind in the country! Totally online. Other places have gone this route without success, because they did not have the stature, the traditions, of Beet College. But we'll make it work, because we're going to be practical and prepare people for the real world. What do you think of that!

"And why waste four good years doing it? You can learn whatever trade you need to learn in six months! As for the liberal arts stuff, why make it part of a college education? Read Shakespeare on your own time! On your yacht! Meanwhile, go to college to earn the yacht!

"That's the future, boys and girls. Years from now, when Harvard and Yale have taken the same path and are online trade institutions too—for I promise you, the failing business of higher education will catch up with them all—they will look back and know that we at Beet were pioneers! Welcome to Beet College Online! You don't have to be there to be there!"

With each succeeding sentence he grew more exclamatory, but the crowd was sullen. Beet might be cold and sepulchral; what in New England was not? But at least it existed. It was real—real stones, real trees, real sterility, real gloom. Who wanted to spend six months parked before a laptop?

Six months? College was supposed to be the best *years* of one's life. Not only were they fun, and irresponsible, those years; they were joyously inner-directed. How could one possibly cram all that insistent self-indulgence into six short months?

What's more: the students kind of liked reading Shakespeare. A few even liked Plotinus.

Bollovate examined the situation. Had he misjudged? Had he judged at all? The idea of an online Beet College trade school was such a sweet deal. Ah, well. He could always scrap it. Or better still, attract an entirely new clientele outside the college who wanted to brag of a Beet degree. He'd come up with something, one could bet on that. And Beet College as currently constituted was going down the tubes, down the fucking tubes, except for the land, of course, all that gorgeous acreage just waiting to be free of students, teachers, books, bullshit. And Joel Bollovate would soon be free as well—good riddance—of wife and bonged-out children. How did he feel? This is how.

He had just caught the punt on the zero-yard line, and had tucked the pigskin (get it?) under his left arm, and with his right was stiff-arming the opposition, shoving the entire student body and administration and faculty of Beet College—including, oh dear, yes, the ever so high-and-mighty and preciously educated Professor Peace Porterfield—not merely onto the sidelines, but over the stands into the streets. And the green, beautifully green (get it?) field lay ahead of him like the stairway to heaven. And the crowd—millions of admirers—was chanting "Joel! Joel! Joel!" Oh, God! Was Joel Bollovate standing on the steps of Bacon Library, right there, in front of all those people . . . Was Joel Bollovate about to come? Oh, God!

CHAPTER

20

WOULDN'T IT BE SOMETHING IF THIS STORY ENDED HERE, with Bollovate in triumph, the students and faculty outfoxed, and Peace—exonerated of a crime no one believed him guilty of, or took seriously anyway—standing freezing and helpless with his freezing and helpless colleagues in the Old Pen, awaiting the certain collapse of their way of life? Wouldn't it be a hoot if Bollovate—whom Livi and Manning had called "a man like that"—wound up on top because, not in spite of, the fact that he was a bean counter, goddamn it, and an all-pro among bean counters at that? And as for those who looked down, all the way down their noses, at bean counters? Well, they would seem to have proved themselves as unfit for the world as Bollovate had said they were. And they had lost the little world they cherished *because* they were unfit? Wouldn't that take the cake?

It would. Things didn't turn out that way. But that was only because of two students who happened to count the beans, and their teacher, who learned that if one wants to make pigs fly in the real world, it helps to do the paperwork.

"Mr. Bollovate. How much in the slush fund?"

Recognizing Professor Porterfield, standing in his sweats, the crowd wondered if the strain on him over the past couple of weeks hadn't taken its toll. But Peace repeated his question. "Mr. Bollo-vate. The Homeland Security slush fund. How much money is in it, do you suppose?" Livi tossed the trustee a dark little smile.

"Oh! Professor Porterfield," said his nemesis. "The famous, do-nothing Professor Porterfield. You have something to contribute for a change?" Bollovate chuckled, still riding high.

"The Homeland Security slush fund, Mr. Bollovate." Everyone continued to stare. Why was Porterfield asking this seemingly ir-relevant question?

"The Homeland Security slush fund?" Bollovate hacked a dry laugh. "How the hell should I know?"

"Would you like me to tell you?"

"You're going to tell *me* about money, Professor?" He laughed out loud.

"The amount in the Homeland Security Department slush fund is $265 million, Mr. Bollovate. Check the Web site budget. I'll give you the code. A lot of slush, don't you think? Two hundred and sixty-five million dollars. A sum familiar to everyone here. Precisely the number of dollars in the college endowment you and the trust-ees said was all gone."

It took a moment for the crowd to catch up with what Peace was saying, so he made it easy.

"You stole the endowment, Mr. Bollovate. You and Huey most likely. Maybe the other trustees, too. You stole it, and you hid it. We were never broke. We never had to go through all this. The col-lege was solvent. What did you plan to do with the money, Mr. Bollovate?"

An old country adage: If you wrestle with a pig, you both get dirty, but the pig enjoys it. Which is to say, Bollovate was not at all shaken. He'd been in similar situations, loads of them, and he kept a portfolio of defenses in his pocket.

"Nobody stole a red cent, Professor," he said. "If the endow-ment wound up in Homeland Security, it was an accounting glitch. Happens all the time." He took stock of the crowd. "But I think we owe a debt of gratitude to Professor Porterfield. Let bygones be bygones, that's what I say. This means the college can go on as it always has!" He was banking on these sheep being as manipulable as ever. "A glitch," he repeated, an animal's wildness in his eyes. "I sure as hell didn't have anything to do with it."

Peace addressed the people around him. "You should know it wasn't I who discovered this crime. It was Arthur Horowitz, whom most of you know as Akim, and Max Byrd. They did it all. I'm merely speaking for them. We owe everything to these two young men."

The boys waved meekly. Livi clapped.

So, what had Akim né Arthur seen on his screen when he'd erred in his hot-link entry for Billy Pinto? OPERATING BUDGET. Only that. And at first, like the rest of the information on the Homeland Security home page, the budget seemed innocuous. There were ordinary line items—PAYROLL (FAC.), PAYROLL (AD-MIN.), MATERIALS (broken down into the big-ticket items like computers and the smaller necessities like lamps and office chairs). There was a line for TELEPHONE. There were lines for TRANSFERS in and TRANSFERS OUT, but they displayed no money because there was also a line for SLUSH FUND. The world of Joel Bollovate had opened like Kafka's gate before the Law.

"Holy shit!" Manning muttered to himself. He stood at the far end of the Pen, listening intently to Peace's story. "I was right!"

And why was the incriminating evidence out there for anyone to see? Because no one was supposed to see it, ever. Why go to a lot of trouble to conceal a slush fund if entry to the whole Web site required the breaking of hundreds of levels of codes? Bollovate was nothing if not secretive and careful when it came to money. How was he to guess his kingdom could be toppled by a temporarily crazy person, an "unsatisfied customer," obsessed with hacking into Homeland Security, of all things?

Where the two boys' fathers had been of help was in advising them to try to trace the accounts that went into the slush fund. Forty separate endowment accounts were involved, which is to say, forty funds earmarked by different donors for specific projects—tenured chairs, a new department, bricks and mortar. All were re-located into a lump sum called slush. It was hardly difficult for

Bollovate to hide what he'd done during the transfers, along with hiding the fact that there were no receipts for expenditures. All he needed to find was a bribable auditor in Massachusetts.

Call it a shell game, impure and simple, with the lives and livelihoods of thousands of people trapped under one of the shells and about to disappear. The cybertrail pursued by the two students led to the revelation that the college endowment remained intact, funds were illegally moved, and the books had been cooked. Now Bollovate ought to be cooked as well. What all that did not prove, however, provided him with one more gambit.

He blurted out a belly laugh that produced a small cloud of cold air.

"Oh, for chrissake, Porterfield. Who knows how that money wound up in the slush fund? It may have been a hoax. But if it was theft, the thief wasn't me. Anybody could have transferred those funds. No one expects the chairman of the board to deal with the day-to-day operations of the college. I'll check on it, that's what I'll do. And I'll get to the bottom of this, you can count on it. If there's a crook in our midst [a glance at the terrified Huey], he's dead meat!"

"That's funny, Mr. Bollovate," said Peace. "Because you've hit on an area of the investigation in which Max Byrd's expertise particularly came in handy. Max can find where messages come from." Peace held up a printout. "This is an e-mail to Dr. Huey from you, Mr. Bollovate, traced to your office in Cambridge. Shall I read it? 'Go ahead and set it up. Let me know when the money's there. Be sure the site's secure.'"

His hand played out, Bollovate said, "I'll sue you for slander, you son of a bitch!" As soon as he said "slander," one knew he was out of ploys.

He looked about for Huey as he waddled as fast as possible to his car, though not before Professor Porterfield cut him off and took back the Mayflower Compact. Excited by the turmoil, Latin broke free again, ran to Bollovate, and gave him his traditional salute.

Bollovate slapped the pig. The pig bit Bollovate, very hard, on the hand.

"The one that feeds him," said Manning.

"I'm bleeding!" cried Bollovate. Latin, frightened by his victory, gallumphed off.

Livi stood beside her husband, watched Bollovate writhe, and stalled. "Oh, what the hell," she said finally. She went to him and examined the wound.

Dog bites? Several. Cat bites? Plenty. But a pig bite? She'd never treated a pig bite before. She couldn't tell if Latin had dug to tendon or bone. A student offered her a bottle of Evian, and Livi cleaned the wound as well as she could. Her patient squealed.

"Get an X-ray and an antibiotic," she told him. She yanked the shirt out of his pants, tore off the tail, and made a compressive bandage, giving the hand an unnecessary and painful squeeze.

"I'll kill that animal."

"Go home, Mr. Bollovate," said Peace. And the trustee wisely took his advice.

In the uproar and confusion, Huey had gone to stand with the group from NBC, having decided on a career in commercial television. That was not to be. But eventually he would prove invaluable to the college by spilling everything about the hidden endowment, which, even with the cybertrail exposed, would have been hard to nail down in court without a confession. A plea bargain won him twenty months in a minimum-security prison in Dexter, Nebraska, where he served the pastor as an assistant confessor. He hoped to take over the ministry when the pastor retired.

Matha left the college, unsure what to do with her life. Kathy brought her back to live with her in the Hamptons. She felt her sister might fit in with the literary set, whose get-togethers always featured at least one very young person whose pretensions they could encourage for up to half an hour. Matha enjoyed the people at those events—once catching a glimpse of Martha Stewart herself, who flashed her a glance of empathy—but she liked the decorations more. Was it possible, she wondered, to forge a career combining radical poetry and party planning? Again she was torn. She spent a lot of time in Kathy's kitchen, baking pies, peach in particular. Within a few weeks, Matha was her old self—much as Kathy tried.

Nothing but good fortune followed the remaining MacArthur Four. Betsy Betsy won her "dream job" as a media reporter on a big-city paper, and there was no one who knew more about news-stand sales, to say nothing of what she understood of the ratio of ads to copy. After working the rooms at "more book parties than I can count," Jamie Lattice was finally named a Literary Lion, largely on the basis of his "irresistible" *Authors Who Have Talked to Me*. Goldvasser did get into law school, and he also got out. He teaches civil liberties procedures at the University of the Caicos. Bag-toothian invented the nuclear cluster bomb. He is reputed to be the wealthiest man in Montana, including part-time residents. All four retained youthful appearances, and anyone who had known them at Beet remarked that the years hadn't changed them a bit.

Ferritt Lawrence repairs air conditioners in Buffalo.

Max went on to graduate school, eventually to become a profes-sor of English as well as the country's leading mystery writer. His detective hero, Arthur, specializes in uncovering industrial espio-nage. The real Arthur never did make the How to Write for the *New York Times* course, but became the country's most respected theater critic anyway. Both young men remained close friends, graduating with highest honors—Max in English, Arthur in History, to which he'd transferred after Homeland Security. It happened that every-one transferred out of Homeland Security, because no department member could ever be found, including Billy Pinto. And the loca-tion indicated on the home page turned out to be a guns and ammo shop run by a taxidermist named Tod.

As for the college property, the Mayflower Compact and the pilfered first editions were returned to their proper places in the library, where—one is pleased to say—the librarian who had con-fronted Matha was appointed chief. To the relief of everyone, she knew not a word of French. (La Cocque, found not quite guilty of his part in the Mayflower not-quite theft, retired to Alsace.) The

Calder and the pieces of African art were gone forever, as were the furniture in Huey's house and the medieval knickknacks Bollovate had peddled (buyers would not be budged by sentiment). Gone, too, was the Steinway, which students were sure they saw in a bar in Revere, where they also could swear they saw Enron's Kenneth Lay, alive and drunk, playing stride piano, and crooning "Proud to Be an American."

The Moore *Two Piece Reclining Man* was returned; the man in Rockport who'd shelled out the $14 million found the sculpture made him drowsy. He wrote off what he'd recorded as his $16 million gift, and was content. The three-foot pig from the Temple was never recovered; Bollovate hadn't touched it, he swore on his mother's grave.

Sheila did not remarry, though several suitors proposed. "Joel broke my heart. That's it for me," she would tell them, giggling only occasionally.

And good old Ada Smythe, while her husband was looking around, had been doing the same thing. She'd wanted to stay with Keelye, but—and this was hard—she had to confess she found him boring.

Among inanimate objects, the happiest fate befell the Muncheonette fiberglass pig. Students wheeled it to the middle of the Old Pen green, where it provided the one literal bright spot on campus. When it was clear that Beet would survive, the students hung a sign on the pig's snout, reading: "That's Not All, Folks!"

But most of these events occurred after the Day of the Bollovate Part Deux (as the students called it thereafter) had come to an end. For the moment, on that night, one had the sight of some two thousand students, faculty, and staff—nearly the entire college—standing in the Old Pen, surrounded by the old trees and the old departments and Bacon Library. All were wildly grateful to two students and to Professor Porterfield, who, of course, would not hear of their apologetic embarrassment, and told them not to give it a second thought, though that might not have been a bad idea.

"Oh, no!" said Manning.

Chaplain Lookatme emerged from the crowd to a general moaning, even from the religious freaks. Was the night going to be crowned with another sermon?

Lookatme faced his unwilling congregation and lifted his arms skyward. "Our Friend," he said, "we have gone through a trying time and now we are free. Have You been watching over us? We know You have, just as we watch over You. We watch over each other. Dear Friend, if You are with us at this turbulent hour, could You let us know? Could You give us a sign? Could You?"

He, She, or It could. Lookatme had hardly asked this favor of his Friend, when . . . *KABOOM!* From the direction of the woods came an explosion that turned the night sky orange. The crowd remained where it stood, since the source of the blast was obscure. No one could tell that it had come from a cave somewhere behind the baseball field. Well, one person could, but he wasn't saying.

The trustees other than Bollovate got off without serving time, since it was determined they had not known of the hidden endowment. They did get probation, however, for being in on the plot to buy the college property. So they lost money, which some in the college called their "capital punishment." Their careers as developers were permanently impaired as well, since few people wanted to buy land from criminals who actually were criminals.

Joel Bollovate did not get off so easy. He received a fine of $900 million, most of his fortune after Sheila took her share, and was sentenced to five years in Boston's Walpole State Penitentiary, not a minimum-security facility. He'd been terrified that Walpole's residents would turn him into a sex slave, but they took one look and weren't interested.

What happened to Beet College? Who knows? It went on. It certainly went on. In the end, that may be the best thing about colleges. The opinion polls had no effect whatever on Beet or on any liberal arts institution. The crimes, the publicity, the civil wars of the faculty, the furious parents and alumni—none of it put a dent in the place. A good thing Bollovate had been discredited, or his idea of chucking four-year colleges in favor of jobs and trade schools might have taken root. But appealing as the idea may have been, it probably would have failed in the long run. When it comes down to it, nothing that happened at Beet that fall affected anything in American higher education. Nothing ever does. Good or bad, splendid or inane, colleges go on and on and on. There's nothing like them.

And Manning? He was named president pro tem—not by his colleagues, who decided he was "a marvelous fellow but, I don't know, a bit abrasive"—but rather by state officials, who stepped into Beet's business affairs after the Days of the Bollovate and judged the whole place "a cesspool." Manning asked Peace if he'd help him do the job. Peace said, "I only *look* crazy."

And Peace's proposed curriculum on storytelling? Another committee was established to consider it, with Keelye Smythe as chair.

Bliss House posted a notice: LET THE HEALING BEGIN.

What happened to Peace? He may have returned to work with the kids in Sunset Park. Livi had been right about his being happy there. He may have left teaching altogether, though it was hard to picture him in something like the law, for example, or in business. Politics? He wouldn't have lasted a day. People like Peace Porterfield don't go into politics. Social work? Maybe. A think tank? Doubtful. A think tank would have all the advantages of a college, minus the feeling of accomplishment.

He may have decided to cultivate a garden—not one of his own, but somewhere that had no gardens, and needed them.

One simply doesn't know what Peace's future contained. His present was good enough. He took her hand, and they walked together from that place.

About the author

About the book

Read on

Insights,
Interviews
& More...

Meet Roger Rosenblatt

© Chip Cooper

ROGER ROSENBLATT began writing professionally in his mid-thirties, when he became literary editor and a columnist for *The New Republic*. Before that, he taught at Harvard, where he earned his PhD, held the Briggs-Copeland appointment in the teaching of writing, and was Allston-Burr Senior Tutor and Master of Dunster House. At age twenty-nine, he was the youngest house master in Harvard's history. He was a Fulbright Scholar in Ireland in 1965–66. Five universities have awarded him honorary doctorates. In 1995, Long Island University appointed him its first University Professor of Writing; he held the Parsons Family Chair at Southampton College. In 2005, he was the Edward R. Murrow Visiting Professor at Harvard. In 2008, he was appointed

Distinguished Professor of English and Writing at Stony Brook University, one of five such appointments in the SUNY system.

William Safire of the *New York Times* wrote that Rosenblatt's work represents "some of the most profound and stylish writing in America today." *Vanity Fair* said that he "set new standards of thought and compassion" in journalism. The *Chicago Tribune* said that he turned "magazine journalism into an art form." The *Philadelphia Inquirer* cited his essays for "unparalleled elegance and wit." In its issue on "The Best" (January 2004), *Town and Country* named him the "finest essayist in the country." UPI called him "a national treasure."

Rosenblatt's pieces for *Time* magazine have won two George Polk Awards, awards from the Overseas Press Club, the American Bar Association, and others. His television essays for the *NewsHour with Jim Lehrer* on PBS have won the Peabody and the Emmy. His *Time* cover essay, "A Letter to the Year 2086," was chosen for the time capsule placed inside the Statue of Liberty at its centennial. When he was writing a column for the *Washington Post*, *Washingtonian* magazine named him "Best Columnist in Washington." Rosenblatt is the author of twelve books, which have been published in thirteen languages. They include the national bestseller *Rules for Aging*, three collections of essays, and *Children of War*, which won the Robert F. Kennedy Book Prize and was a finalist for the National Book Critics Award. He has written six Off- ▶

" William Safire wrote that Rosenblatt's work represents 'some of the most profound and stylish writing in America today.' "

Meet Roger Rosenblatt *(continued)*

Broadway plays, including *Ashley Montana Goes Ashore in the Caicos*, which was produced in the fall of 2005 at New York's Flea Theater. His comic one-person show, "Free Speech in America," which he performed at the American Place Theater, was cited by the *New York Times* as one of the ten best plays of 1991.

His first novel *Lapham Rising*, also a national bestseller, was published in 2006. ∾

Blueberry
The Play Behind the Book

Usually, when a writer has an idea, it takes its own form of expression, and that's that. Sometimes, however, one finds that a thing said one way can be said another. That happened to me with the following play. *Blueberry* was written after *Beet*, as part of an evening of two one-act plays. It contains some of the ideas in *Beet*, and many of the same satirical complaints, but it presents them dramatically rather than in a narrative. What interested me, once I had finished it, was how easy it was to truncate the theme of an entire novel into a brief one-act play. This suggests that either the play was too short or the novel too long. I must work that out.

Roger Rosenblatt
July 2008

Play takes place in the office of a college professor. Boxes, packed and half-packed, lie around the room, indicating he is in the process of leaving. In front of his desk is a chair. On his desk (could be a long table) are various papers, books about to be put in boxes, a telephone, and a CD player. He is in his fifties, not older. A young woman, a student about twenty, has just entered, and the door closes behind her. We hear it close before the action of the play begins. She stands at his desk, glowering and leaning aggressively toward him. She has said something to him, and he turns down the volume on his CD ▶

Blueberry *(continued)*

player to allow for his response. The CD is Ella singing "Stay as Sweet as You Are." The young woman is in a rage. The professor is irritated, but controlled.

PROFESSOR.   *(Turns off CD player, walks around the office, putting books in boxes. She pursues.)* Let me get this straight, Ms. McGowan. You're here to complain about a B. A grade of B.

STUDENT.   You bet I am! I've never received a B in my life! *(She brandishes her term paper.)*

PROFESSOR.   That's because these days everyone gets A's.

STUDENT.   Not from you, Professor Retro. Which is what we call you, you know. Professor Retro. *(He smiles appreciatively.)* Professor Retro! Everything old is great. Everything new is horseshit.

PROFESSOR.   *There* you go. You get an A for that remark, Ms. McGowan. For your paper on *A Doll's House*, however, you get a B.

STUDENT.   I don't think you understand. Since everyone *does* get an A these days, Professor, a grade of B looks like an F. It's a permanent blemish on my record.

PROFESSOR.   *(Goes to desk.)* And what do you wish to do with your record, Ms. McGowan? *(Looks over her folder.)* Oh, I see. You're majoring in Communications Arts. This blemish of a B may impede your quest to become an anchorperson in Buffalo.

STUDENT.   You have my file.

PROFESSOR.   I always look up who's coming to see me, in case the person may be armed.

STUDENT.   You think I'm crazy?

PROFESSOR.   The subject of this discussion is the monumental injustice of a grade of B. *One* of us is crazy.

STUDENT.   And what's wrong with becoming an anchorperson in Buffalo, or anywhere else, may I ask? *(He gives her a Jack Benny stare.)* And that's another thing. Every day we sit in class, listening to you make fun of Communications Arts.

PROFESSOR.   What would you suggest I make of it?

STUDENT.   What? There's something wrong with students wanting to be journalists?

PROFESSOR. Not a thing. They just shouldn't study how to do it in college.

STUDENT. Oh, Christ! That crap again. College is for *real* disciplines. Literature, Classics, Philosophy, History. What world are you living in, Retro Man?

PROFESSOR. You're right. Let's get rid of History. Let's have a walkathon. Together, we can make history a thing of the past.

STUDENT. *(To herself.)* What a freakazoid.

PROFESSOR. *(Returns to packing.)* Why are you so worked up, Ms. McGowan? After today, you won't have Retro Man to kick you around anymore.

STUDENT. Hallelujah for that. Only he leaves a trail of B's in his wake.

PROFESSOR. The great chain of B-ing.

STUDENT. Oh! Professor Retro! When I grow up, will I be as clever as you?

PROFESSOR. I doubt it. You'll be speaking journalese instead of English, so you can sound like your fellow professionals. Remember, Ms. McGowan, the question is.

STUDENT. The question is what?

PROFESSOR. The question is. That's what journalists say when they wish to indicate they understand something. The question is . . .

STUDENT. Oh shit.

PROFESSOR. And then you want to make sure that if there are rumors abroad, they're always "swirling." And if there's a protest, it always comes in "a firestorm." And the phone is always ringing "off the hook." *(Points to his phone.)* See that? When it's not ringing, it's still *on* the hook. And if someone disagrees with someone else . . .

STUDENT. Like you and me?

PROFESSOR. Yes—you've got it—that we're "no strangers to controversy."

STUDENT. You make everything seem so small.

PROFESSOR. I do what I can. I try to "push the envelope" without sending "shockwaves throughout the community."

STUDENT. I hate your bitterness.

PROFESSOR. It's all I have left. And you're wrong about my ▶

Blueberry (continued)

leaving a trail of B's. If you confer with your fellow students—
Buffalo's anchorpersons of tomorrow—you'll find that they all
received C's and D's on the Ibsen papers. Yours was the least
dumb of the dumb. Congratulations.

STUDENT.   *(Surveys him.)* You dump on clichés. *You're* the
cliché. Surrounded by your old books. Playing your old songs.

PROFESSOR.   I can't be a cliché. There aren't enough of me.

STUDENT.   Everything's a joke. Right?

PROFESSOR.   You came to *me*, Ms. McGowan. I didn't seek
you out.

STUDENT.   Because I thought I could reason with you.

PROFESSOR.   No, you didn't. You thought you could do what all
students think they can do these days—shame me into doing
what you want me to do.

STUDENT.   But you're too smart for me, aren't you? *(He smiles
to himself. Inexplicably, she tears up. Quickly wipes tear away.)*

PROFESSOR.   Oh, for Chrissake. This grade *can't* mean that
much to you.

STUDENT.   *(Recovers.)* God, you're warped. Such a mess.
You're full of meanness and sarcasm and nothing else. *(He
gives her an agreeing, pleased look.)* Well, you can't go soon
enough for me. I don't know why I took your course in the
first place.

PROFESSOR.   You're right. It was a waste of your anchorperson's
time. You could have been taking one of the invaluable and
demanding Communications Arts offerings instead—The
Media: Should It Police Itself? The Media: Can We Win the
Public's Trust? *(He continues to pack his book. Mutters.)*
Communications Arts.

STUDENT.   You realize Communications Arts is by far the most
popular major in the college. There are barely a dozen people
in your courses. The Renaissance. The Metaphysical Poets. The
World of Dr. Johnson. Modern Drama. Professor Wilson has two
hundred students in every one of his classes in Communications
Arts. Of course, you call him Professor Newspaper.

PROFESSOR.   Not to his face.

STUDENT.   He knows what you think of him—that he's the
most boring person on the faculty.

PROFESSOR. True. But absolutely the most boring. That's in some stiff competition.

STUDENT. He wants to kill you.

PROFESSOR. If he did, he still would not be considered a "person of interest."

STUDENT. Go ahead. Make fun of the new programs. But they're the ones that keep this college alive. You treat them as if they're made for idiots.

PROFESSOR. For and *by. (Reaches for a memo on his desk.)* But I'll be fair, Ms. McGowan. Communications Arts, while worthless, is hardly the least of the lot. The faculty has just received this memo from the dean's office listing the latest programs in the catalogue. It makes me teary with envy to realize I won't be around to observe their success.

STUDENT. Why are you retiring now, by the way? You're only— what—a hundred years old? Mandatory retirement can't set in till you're at least three hundred. I didn't think professors *had* mandatory retirement anyway.

PROFESSOR. We don't. I could stay on forever, keel over in class, and still hold my job for years, until my corpse disintegrated.

STUDENT. How could they tell? *(He likes that.)*

PROFESSOR. Be careful, Ms. McGowan. You'd better lose all that wit before you get to Buffalo. But, if you must know, I'm retiring because I can't take it anymore. You win. *(He packs more books and tapes up the cartons as he goes along.)* You and Communications Arts and all the thrilling, with-it programs initiated in recent years: Humor and TV Meteorology. Serial Killers of Color in the Northwest. Gender, Ethnicity, and Television Studies. Do you know I had a student who actually wrote an honors thesis called "No Transsexual Asians on *Will and Grace*: An Oversight or an Insult?" *(She turns away to suppress a smile.)* Of course, my favorite major—until I received this new memo, that is—was Nippocano Studies: Where Tokyo Meets Tijuana.

STUDENT. People are interested in these subjects, Professor, whether you know it or not. For minority students they provide a place in the curriculum. Stature. Recognition. They make these students proud. ▶

PROFESSOR. That would be lovely, Ms. McGowan, if it were true. What's true is that they just make them soft in the head. Proud of who they are rather than of what they might become. Not that the real purpose of higher education is to make you proud, anyway. It's to make you humble.

STUDENT. Well, you've mastered that.

PROFESSOR. *(Looks at memo.)* Wait! I have a new favorite. *This* one makes Communications Arts seem like a seminar in Catullus.

STUDENT. I suppose you're referring to Homeland Security.

PROFESSOR. Ah! You already know it. Yes! Homeland Security. A whole new major in Homeland Security. *(He reads from memo.)* Described as the "leading growth center in American education." Homeland Security! Where undergraduates learn such skills as making and installing one's own alarm system, SWAT team membership, hazmat expertise. "Hey, Dad! Could I have forty thousand dollars to go to college and study Homeland Security?" "Here you go, son. Your mother and I feel safer already." Oh, to be young again and head off to my Homeland Security class wearing my gas mask and my puffy white suit, with my term paper under one arm and a rifle under the other. What's my essay question this week? Manhattan is in greater danger than Baffin Island. True or false? Nine-eleven may happen again, and we must be prepared. True or false? *(Sits in chair in front of his desk.)* "Professor Bombshell? Here's my term paper: 'If You're My Mother, Where's Your ID?' " *(Rises, goes behind his desk.)* "Splendid, Willy! Thanks for the tuition check. Now, how'd you like to buy some land in Florida?"

STUDENT. I'll admit, Homeland Security does sound bogus. But it may get students jobs, Professor. Jobs, you know? The real world?

PROFESSOR. Colleges aren't supposed to be trade schools, Ms. McGowan. *Trade* schools are supposed to be trade schools. Colleges don't provide jobs. They provide lives.

STUDENT. Very noble. Very high-minded. Especially for someone who's about to ride off into the sunset. For someone who's legally dead.

PROFESSOR. You think I'm dead? *(Feels his wrist for a pulse.)* Could be.

STUDENT.   As dead as Ibsen.

PROFESSOR.   I'd *like* to be as dead as Ibsen. But tell me. *(Looking over her file again)* Why did you take Modern Drama in the first place? You knew about darlin' old Professor Retro. Did you think you'd convert me?

STUDENT.   I don't know what I thought. I haven't been thinking clearly lately. *(Appears sad and distracted.)*

PROFESSOR.   *(Looking at her file again.)* I see you belong to several extracurricular clubs. An a cappella group. One of twenty-three in the college?

STUDENT.   Sixteen.

PROFESSOR.   Number's down this year?

STUDENT.   You have something against a cappella groups?

PROFESSOR.   Not a thing. I get positively weepy hearing a dozen upper-crust voices from Scarsdale harmonizing on "Old Black Joe." *(Sings to himself while still looking at the file.)* "Nobody know da trouble I seen." But it's harmless. *(Reads.)* Ballroom dancing?

STUDENT.   I like it. It's something different. I suppose you disapprove of *that*, too.

PROFESSOR.   Actually, no. But what do *you* like about it? It's *so yesterday*.

STUDENT.   I don't know. It makes me feel elegant, ceremonial.

PROFESSOR.   "How but in custom and in ceremony / Are innocence and beauty born?" *(She looks curious.)* "A Prayer for My Daughter." Yeats. You probably know him as Yeets.

STUDENT.   Very funny. *(Sings "Stay as Sweet as You Are.")* See? It's a waltz. *(She extends her arms, inviting him to dance. He stays put.)*

PROFESSOR.   I won't dance. Don't ask me. *(Looks at her file again.)* Young Democrats. Equestrian Hillel. Equestrian Hillel?

STUDENT.   I'm Jewish.

PROFESSOR.   With the name McGowan?

STUDENT.   Half Jewish. My mother is Jewish. My father's . . .

PROFESSOR.   A horse?

STUDENT.   *(Bitterly.)* You're part right.

PROFESSOR.   Half and half. I imagine that accounts for your behaving like a half-Jewish American princess.

STUDENT.   *(Flairs up.)* You think I'm a JAP because I protest a grossly unfair grade? ▶

11

PROFESSOR.   And how is your B "grossly unfair," Ms. McGowan?

STUDENT.   My paper—if you bothered to read it—is on the closing door in *A Doll's House.* I wrote ten pages on the meaning of that closing door.

PROFESSOR.   Ten whole pages! And what did you conclude?

STUDENT.   That Nora is closing the door on the male-dominated world, on the oppression of middle-class women. That by closing the door she's entering the new world, the enlightened world. She *is* the new world. She's modernity itself. She changes everything by closing that door.

PROFESSOR.   Hooray! Bravo! Modernity itself! *(Applauds sarcastically.)* You're right. I shouldn't have given you a B. Where's my pen? I'll change it to a B-minus. My, my! I do declare! Nora closes the door on female oppression. Wow! Who woulda thunk it? The perfect answer for Communications Arts. Someone tells you something. You spit it back whole. *(She looks confused, annoyed.)* What you just gave me is not *original thought*, Ms. McGowan. Where is your *original thought*?

STUDENT.   It was right, what I wrote. Wasn't it right? *(He's so disgusted he starts to play the CD of Ella again. She turns it off.)* Wasn't what I wrote right?

PROFESSOR.   *(As news reporter, holding a mic)* Back to you, Chip. Right. Just right. And only right. The difference between the word and the right word is the difference between the lightning bug and the lightning. *(She doesn't understand.)* Mark Twain. Mark Twain said that about the difference between ordinary language and extraordinary language. You know? So you can *(Mocking.)* "think outside the box"? The *lightning*, Ms. McGowan. Here, in college, we're supposed to be in the lightning business. Original language. *Original thought. Your* thought. Thought that comes—and could come—only from *you*.

STUDENT.   What does original thought have to do with studying the great minds you talk about? Aren't we just supposed to fold our hands in our laps, sit on our asses, and worship them? Ooh and ah? Dr. Johnson. Ooh! Henrik Ibsen. Ah!

PROFESSOR.   *(To himself.)* Why do I bother? *(To her.)* They don't want your adulation, Ms. McGowan. They want *you*. They want to burrow in your soul and come up with *you*. Great minds exist to breed *other* great minds—people who think for themselves.

STUDENT. And where does thinking for yourself get you, Professor Retro? You're known around here for thinking for yourself. Look what you've got. A pile of dead books and a dead singer singing a dead song. You, Samuel Johnson, and Henrik Ibsen arm in arm, striding into eternity on your wooden walkers, thinking your original thoughts, and miserable to the core.

PROFESSOR. Happiness, Ms. McGowan? You want to be happy? Go to horseshit heaven where Tokyo meets Tijuana. Whoever said thinking makes you happy?

STUDENT. So why be original? To make yourself *un*happy? What if original thought is too much for you? Too scary? What if it takes you places you don't want to go?

PROFESSOR. The places you don't want to go are the only places you *ought* to go.

STUDENT. Oh, goodie! Another epigraph! And here I was, afraid you'd run out.

PROFESSOR. Epigram. Epigraphs are quotations at the beginning of something.

STUDENT. And epitaphs?

PROFESSOR. The end of things.

STUDENT. So you're an epitaph. *(She tosses her term paper on his desk.)*

PROFESSOR. *(Appreciatively.)* Nice.

STUDENT. If original thought got you where you are, Professor, give me unoriginal thought every time.

PROFESSOR. There's your B. *(He pauses, taking her seriously, holds up her paper, looks, shakes his head piteously.)* Nora closes the door on the oppression of middle-class women. Jesus. *Think*, Ms. McGowan. Think of the things one can close a door on. Sorrow. The past. Opportunity. Think of those on whom the door is closed. What does it mean to be on the other side of the door? Write about Nora *after* she closes the door. Write about her children, after they hear the door click shut. Nora says at the end, "Torvald, I no longer believe in wonderful things happening." I no longer believe in wonderful things ▶

happening. What does she mean? What does it mean to no longer believe in wonderful things happening? She closes the door on wonderful things. But she really doesn't. Even that— even that sentence—contradicts what it says. The sentence itself is a wonderful thing happening. In every heartbreak—Nora's, yours, mine—something beautiful intrudes. *Look* for it. *Dream,* Ms. McGowan. Dream into a scene or into your own life and come up with something wholly yours. That's original thought. *(He scrutinizes her.)* You seem to have half a brain. Why don't you use it? *(She looks away.)* Oh. Here I am being insensitive again. Too bad I'm leaving. You could bring me up on charges on Sensitivity Day.

STUDENT. *(Fired up again.)* Why are you always making a joke of sensitivity? As if people ought not to be sensitive!

PROFESSOR. Sensitivity Day, Ms. McGowan? Are you—pardon my French—are you shittin' me? When the college came up with Sensitivity Day a few years ago, I thought someone was making an ironic joke. A prank. At last, I said to myself, they've learned to laugh at themselves. Silly ol' me. They—you—were serious! Now every year we celebrate Sensitivity Day. We set aside a college holiday—a deliberate postponement of education—to be sensitive! Next to Christmas, Yom Kippur, Passover, Easter, Kwanzaa, and Ramadan, it's my favorite time of the year. That is, if you don't count How to Prepare for the Holidays Day.

STUDENT. You think that's stupid, too.

PROFESSOR. Stupid? What's stupid about trying to make so sure that no one is offended by anyone else's religious holiday that you wind up creating occasions with no meaning whatever? Did you know, Ms. McGowan—since you're half Jewish, half Christian, you might be interested in this. Did you know that our college chaplain, Mr. Gomez, has determined the crèche in the village square should have the figure of the baby Jesus removed because it's too controversial? That's Jesus for you— no stranger to controversy. Gomez proposes putting a menorah in the crèche to make everyone happy. I know *I'm* happy. How about *you*—or half of you?

STUDENT. Chaplain Gomez says he prays for you every Sunday. *(She smiles.)*

PROFESSOR. He's nuts.

STUDENT. I think he's sweet. He thinks of God as a Friend.

PROFESSOR. I know. I've heard him on the subject. You cannot imagine how grateful I was to have my old-fashioned views corrected. Here I was blithely going along, thinking of God as a superior being or force—that is, if I believed in God. But for those who *do* believe, I thought: Well, God. Okay. It's good to have something in one's life that one can look up to. A superior intelligence. Like mine. *(She sighs in mock despair.)* But along comes Chaplain Gomez, and I'm reeducated. Thank you, Yahweh! Thank you, Pal! Not a moment to soon! God is *not* to be considered a superior being, after all. God is our *Friend*. Just one of the boys. Or girls. An equal.

STUDENT. He means well. Don't you like thinking of God as friendly?

PROFESSOR. *Like* it? I *love* it. *(Clasps hands in prayer.)* "Our Buddy, who art in heaven . . ."

STUDENT. You hate everything.

PROFESSOR. Your point?

STUDENT. What's so wrong with Sensitivity Day? If we didn't have something like Sensitivity Day, a lot of students would feel . . .

PROFESSOR. Don't say it!

STUDENT. Alienated! *(She smiles mischievously.)*

PROFESSOR. *(Playing along.)* And what would they feel alienated *about*, Ms. McGowan? Their . . .

STUDENT. Otherness! *(They both laugh.)* Okay. It all does get a little PC.

PROFESSOR. A *little* PC? I can't wait to see what the Sensitivity Day panels will be this year. Reparations for enemies past and present? The Germans and Japanese? The Taliban? The British? Remember last year's panel on how to make amends to society's poorly-thought-of people. Dentists? Lawyers? Cable TV installers? Members of Congress?

STUDENT. Yes. And I also remember your motion at the meeting, when you proposed an addition to the list—white Protestants from New Canaan, Connecticut.

PROFESSOR. What about it? ▶

Blueberry *(continued)*

STUDENT.   They dismissed it as frivolous.

PROFESSOR.   You think so? This year, it's supposed to pass without opposition. Then, of course, there was the Slow Children sign debate. Maybe you didn't hear about *that* one. They voted to take down the Slow Children signs on campus for fear of offending slow children, I guess. They voted to replace the signs with *new* signs. The new ones will read, "Please Drive as Slowly as Possible as Children May Be Playing in the Roadway."

STUDENT.   What's wrong with that?

PROFESSOR.   Besides being stupid? Nothing. Only to make longer signs requires more steel and more paint. Twenty-eight thousand dollars more, in fact. Which they had to take out of the funds for the new wing in the children's hospital for the mentally impaired.

STUDENT.   You're making that up.

PROFESSOR.   *(Smiles.)* I am.

STUDENT.   You do that deliberately.

PROFESSOR.   I do.

STUDENT.   I should have taken your course pass-fail.

PROFESSOR.   That would have been a good idea—as long as one remembered that pass-fail offers two possibilities.

STUDENT.   How about my B? Be a good sport. Raise my grade. Make it your parting gesture.

PROFESSOR.   You're not being creative. Why not stage a protest with placards? **DOWN WITH B'S!** Why not occupy a campus building? An office! How about mine?

STUDENT.   You're so condescending.

PROFESSOR.   Aren't I? We haven't had a good college protest around here since the march to allow students to use iPods in class. Or was it iPhones? Power to the people of Verizon!

STUDENT.   *(Changing tack.)* I have an idea. Let's have an affair! Will you change my grade if we have an affair? *(He gives her an are-you-kidding, dismissive look.)* Okay. Let's have an affair anyway.

PROFESSOR.   No.

STUDENT.   *(Goes to him and puts her arms around his neck.)* Don't you feel the sexual tension between us?

PROFESSOR.   No.

STUDENT.   Neither do I. *(Brightens.)* But if we did . . . A torrid student-professor affair, with rolling around on the office floor, and sweaty trysts in the motel down the road, and boozy dinners in small, out-of-the-way restaurants where the tablecloths are checkered and the candles larded with wax and the owner knows our little secret and wishes us well?

PROFESSOR.   No. *(Tries to unclasp her arms. She holds.)*

STUDENT.   And we go at it every chance we get? And when we're finished we lie in the motel sheets and plan a brand-new life together—just the two of us, and the respectable world be damned—just the two of us, living by the sea, maybe, in a weathered cottage with a front porch with a swing and peeling paint and an old wooden rowboat named Retro?

PROFESSOR.   No. *(But tickled.)*

STUDENT.   *(Arms remain around his neck.)* But after a month or two, you tire of me. I've moved on from my sophomore year to my junior, and you're looking for a younger woman. *(He chuckles.)* And I beg you to stay with me, but you say your leaving is for the best? *(Again she grows sad, as if recalling something.)*

PROFESSOR.   What's the matter?

STUDENT.   *(Recovers.)* Nothing. I beg you to stay. I cling to your trouser legs. But you're adamant. You're off. I'm alone in the motel room.

PROFESSOR.   Alone with the print of Don Quixote above the headboard, and the ice bucket which you can fill at the end of the motel hallway?

STUDENT.   Yes! Don Quixote. The ice bucket. And me, alone.

PROFESSOR.   So sad.

STUDENT.   Tragic.

PROFESSOR.   Tragic.

STUDENT.   And yet . . .

PROFESSOR.   And yet you have learned something from this experience. The lesson of a lifetime!

STUDENT.   I've learned how to love!

PROFESSOR.   And I . . . I, too, have learned something. Something about myself.

STUDENT.   And what have you learned, love of my life?

PROFESSOR.   I've learned . . . there's always another ▶

Blueberry (continued)

undergraduate coming along. *(She pushes him away and laughs.)*
Anyway, now you won't have to worry about me. You'll be able
to pack up your B and head for anchor paradise in Buffalo and
forget about old awful insensitive Professor Retro. *(He opens his
right hand and places it above his left with the thumbs touching
and index fingers extended to make the letter "S.")*

STUDENT.   *(Looks chagrined.)* I know. The "S" sign.

PROFESSOR.   The signal for mutual recognition on Sensitivity
Day. Such a sensitive idea. A little cumbersome, to be sure—to
give the sign, mothers have to drop their babies on the sidewalk.
But so worth it. Not *this. (He makes the "V" sign.)* Or *this. (Two
thumbs up.)* Or *this. (He gives the air the finger.)* But *this. (The "S"
sign again.)*

STUDENT.   All right, it's silly. But there's foolishness in every
generation. I'd rather have the excesses of my generation than
the crimes of yours.

PROFESSOR.   Oh? What crimes are those? Civil rights? The
Women's movement?

STUDENT.   Now you're a defender of women?

PROFESSOR.   Of women, yes. But not of *(Reads memo.)*
"Postcolonial Women's Sports."

STUDENT.   Women! That gives me an idea. If you don't change
my grade to A, I'll accuse you of sexual harassment.

PROFESSOR.   *(Wistful.)* If only someone had done that years
ago. I'd be out of here by now.

STUDENT.   Not that I care, but what do you plan to do with this
early retirement?

PROFESSOR.   Well, first I'll stop by the college Self-Reinvention
Center. I'm thinking of reinventing myself as Simon Cowell.

STUDENT.   I should know better. But why Simon Cowell?

PROFESSOR.   Why not? He gives your generation everything it
wants. The American Idol! Instant success without working for it.

STUDENT.   You think we don't want to work?

PROFESSOR.   You don't. And my fellow teachers don't want you
to. They give you the big dreams—"Good morning, Buffalo!"—
because you don't want to earn the small ones. Yep. That's who
I'll be. Simon Cowell.

STUDENT.   That'd be an improvement. But I picture something else. You standing on the street corner with your fly unzipped. Unshaven. Disheveled. Drooling. Or going to special classes for seniors? Learning ceramics? "Why, Professor Retro, what a nice ashtray!" Or staring at the TV when it's off, but you don't know it's off? Or wandering about the house driving your wife crazy with your superior intelligence?

PROFESSOR. My wife died some years ago.

STUDENT. *(Chastened.)* Sorry. She must have been young. You never speak of it.

PROFESSOR. Young, yes. And I don't speak of it, of her, because unlike some of my colleagues, I don't think of my autobiography as part of the curriculum. *(Phone rings. He answers.)* Yes, Jack. *(No enthusiasm.)* Well, you know what I think. *(Listens.)* No, I'm not changing my mind.

STUDENT. *(To herself.)* As if *that* would ever happen.

PROFESSOR. No. My vote remains as it was. Expel him. Permanently. Expunge his name from the college records.

STUDENT. *(To herself.)* Disembowel him. String up the remains.

PROFESSOR. *(Listens.)* I'm sorry you feel that way. *(Listens.)* Yes, I know I'm a minority of one. *(Listens.)* It *would* look better if the committee were unanimous. But it's not to be. *(Listens.)* Bye, Jack. *(Hangs up.)*

STUDENT. What was that about?

PROFESSOR. None of your business. *(She shrugs.)* Oh, I don't suppose it can do any harm to tell you at this stage. You asked why I was leaving before retirement. *(Points to phone.)* This is why. This sort of thing. *(Packs more books.)* I sit on the College Honor Committee. I don't know why they asked me. Equal opportunity, I guess. Same reason they asked me to serve on a panel on diversity. They withdrew the invitation when I inquired if holding a different opinion constituted diversity. So, *this.* *(Again points to phone.)* A STUDENT was hauled before the Honor Committee last month for plagiarism. He wrote an ingenious piece of work. A first-class job. The kid plagiarized Emerson's "Self-Reliance." I'm not making this up. When I heard it, I laughed out loud. Of course, I was the only one laughing. The rest of the committee wanted to probe the plagiarist's ▶

Blueberry *(continued)*

motives, wanted to find out if he had been troubled, if there
were problems at home. His old man ran off with a yak?

STUDENT. It happens.

PROFESSOR. Wanted to know if, perhaps, he was ignorant
of the fact that one does not copy someone else's work word-
for-word and present it as one's own. Now, *there's* an original
thought! So I just sat there—cliché that I am. *(She winces.)* I sat
there while my fellow committee members "agonized"—their
word, "agonized"—over the plagiarist's fate. Remember, Ms.
McGowan, we are talking about plagiarism—the only thing
equivalent to a capital offense in an intellectual community.
Well, naturally, they voted to forgive the poor boy. Jack Umass
just called to ask me to change my vote.

STUDENT. Professor Umass of Native American Crafts and
Casino Studies? *(She stifles a giggle.)*

PROFESSOR. The same. And the author of *The One Hundred
Greatest Living Intellectuals in America*. He was disappointed
when the book sold only a hundred copies. So, Jack calls to
tell me that everyone else on the committee voted to let the
kid off. I'm stunned they didn't vote him a scholarship.

STUDENT. What was their reasoning?

PROFESSOR. Reasoning? *(He chuckles.)* Reasoning. Well, they
reasoned that we ought to see this matter from the plagiarist's
point of view.

STUDENT. What was his point of view?

PROFESSOR. He explained his paper as an *homage* to Emerson.
You know. The way a counterfeiter explains his work as an
homage to Ben Franklin.

STUDENT. *(Laughs.)* Well, at least he got to read Emerson . . .

PROFESSOR. At last! A sense of the absurd. Lucky Buffalo. Now,
why don't you go back to your dorm room with your B intact,
and let me get out of here.

STUDENT. *(Wildly melodramatic.)* Oh, Professor Retro! Don't
toss me out! Don't throw me to the wolves! I've seen the error of
my ways. I'll drop Communications Arts and take a triple major in
Classics, Philosophy, and Phys Ed. I'll study real hard and give up
journalism and get a PhD and become a professor just like you, so
that I'll be witty and wise and ride my high horse around

campus—backward, of course—and poke fun at Spanish people who want to know more about being Spanish and women people who want to know more about being women, and spread mockery and wisecracks wherever I go. And one day—if I'm lucky—a brilliant but misguided undergraduate will come to me to protest a grade of B, and I will show her the light. And I'll tell her, in every heartbreak something beautiful intrudes. And she'll believe me. And she'll be eternally grateful, as I am now, and we'll all move in reverse, until we create an entire race of Retros, and ride backward into the sunrise and set civilization back to the first dawn.

PROFESSOR. *(Continuing to pack up.)* Promises, promises.

STUDENT. *(Combative again.)* Do you think I'm here to be reformed by you? Like in the movies? I'm your Eliza Doolittle and you're my . . .

PROFESSOR. Professor Retro? *(Sings.)* "The rain in Tijuana stays mainly in . . ."

STUDENT. All I want reformed is my grade.

PROFESSOR. Thanks. I couldn't think of a rhyme for Tijuana. All you want is your grade reformed? *(Shrugs.)* If you say so. *(Thinks)* Marijuana! *(Nods, gratified.)* But you know how things work around here. Why don't you take your complaint to the dean? I'm sure he'll buckle in a second. Or to the Honor Committee? Maybe they'll decide you have trouble at home and give you an A. For your trouble. *(He's hit a nerve. She looks away.)*

STUDENT. I don't want that. I want *you* to change my grade. *(He smiles, indicating she'd have a long wait.)*

PROFESSOR. *(Studies her.)* You're a strange young woman.

STUDENT. You're a strange old man. What did she die of, your wife?

PROFESSOR. Creutzfeldt-Jakob disease. Have you heard of it? *(She shakes her head.)* Creutzfeldt-Jakob. Sounds like a Scandinavian beer. I'd never heard of it either. I wish I still hadn't. It's like mad cow. Comes from corrupted beef. She could have had a bad steak, a bad hamburger somewhere. I don't know. *(Looks lost.)* She began with headaches. They persisted, got worse.

STUDENT. You don't have to tell me.

PROFESSOR. *(He hesitates, not wishing to go into it. Then* ▶

gives a what-the-hell look.) The headaches led to disorientation. One night she forgot where our house was. She banged her fist on our neighbor's door until her knuckles bled. Then disorientation led to loss of motor function, then body function, then . . . Her dying took eight months, with no one knowing what caused it. It took an autops . . .

STUDENT. *(She touches his arm. After a pause.)* Let me ask you something. And I don't mean to be a smart-ass.

PROFESSOR. *(Lightening the mood.)* Why not?

STUDENT. All these books. *(She gestures around the room.)* All your learning. Did it do you any good when your wife was dying?

PROFESSOR. That's a harsh question. I admire it. No, it did not.

STUDENT. That's what gets me about traditional education. What does it have to do with how one lives in the world? Here's your young wife—ready to grow old with you—blindsided by a hamburger. So why believe in what you believe in?

PROFESSOR. Why believe in it?

STUDENT. All your smarts. You say it yourself. It didn't help when you most needed it. Something totally out of your control brought you to your knees and made you helpless. Left you abandoned. *(He looks at her skeptically, as if she's talking about something other than his wife.)* I know how you detest anything that smacks of practical thought. But what good has all that stuff you teach done for anyone?

PROFESSOR. What good?

STUDENT. What advantage has it given anybody? I mean, I liked your Modern Drama course. I'll admit it. And I liked reading Ibsen. But would the world be in any worse shape if Ibsen had never existed?

PROFESSOR. You tell me. Forget Ibsen. Would the world be worse off if *Shakespeare* had never existed? Or Vermeer? Or Beethoven?

STUDENT. I really don't know.

PROFESSOR. Neither do I. But I sure as hell wouldn't want to find out. Go home, Ms. McGowan. *(Phone rings again. He answers.)* Drop it, Jack. I . . . Oh. Sorry. *(Listens.)* Yes. The boxes will be packed by the time your people get here. May I ask you to deliver them directly to my home? *(Grimaces.)* No problem?

Thanks. *(Hangs up. To himself.)* "No problem." The guarantee of disaster. *(To her.)* The Maginot Line. *(She doesn't understand.)* I was just thinking of the Maginot Line. In World War II, where the French said they could hold off the Germans. "Hey, François! You sure you fellows can defend this line?" *(French accent.)* "No problem."

STUDENT.   Is there anything on earth that doesn't annoy you?

PROFESSOR.   *(Pretends to ponder.)* No. *(Reconsiders.)* E-Z Pass.

STUDENT.   You like E-Z Pass?

PROFESSOR.   It means what it says. It's concise. It's an improvement. It works. And it doesn't bother you. E-Z Pass.

STUDENT.   Of all that goes on in the world today, the one thing you approve of is E-Z Pass. *(He nods.)*

PROFESSOR.   *And,* it lets me get away from here faster.

STUDENT.   *(Studies him.)* Why *do* you hate this place so much?

PROFESSOR.   I don't hate it. I hate what it's *become*—what all colleges have become.

STUDENT.   Because they don't suit your way of looking at things. You're a bigot.

PROFESSOR.   I'm a bigot?

STUDENT.   Yes. A true bigot only sees things one way.

PROFESSOR.   *(Considers.)* That's good. Very good.

STUDENT.   *(Unmoved.)* But whatever you think of the new curriculum, and however ridiculous it may appear sometimes, we are still living in a more generous and—dare I say it—more sensitive learning environment.

PROFESSOR.   Gaah!

STUDENT.   Learning environment? You hate learning environment?

PROFESSOR.   This isn't a learning environment, Ms. McGowan. It's a school. One is supposed to get out of here a little smarter than when one walked in. That's the bargain. That's the deal we professors are supposed to make with you students. *(Pauses.)* Look. I'm going to talk to you as if I thought it would do some good.

STUDENT.   A stretch?

PROFESSOR.   A stretch. *(Sighs.)* Ms. McGowan, as difficult as this may be to believe, I actually approve of a more generous, ▸

Blueberry *(continued)*

more *(Gulps.)* sensitive world. When I was your age, I marched and sat in for just such a world. Many of the fellow criminals of my generation did the same. Do you think of yourself as a modern woman, Ms. McGowan? *(She nods.)* Well, here's a shock for you. We all were modern once. And at your age, I, too, hoped for an enlightened universe. But what higher education has become since then is pure horseshit. You are giving over your mind to Communications Arts. And you seem to have a pretty good mind. No genius. But pretty good. Yes. You're right. No amount of traditional learning can protect you from life's kicks to the stomach. But you still have the choice of things to learn. Choose the best. It's that simple. Study the masters.

STUDENT.　*(As Igor.)* Yeth, mathter.

PROFESSOR.　The canon!

STUDENT.　Boom!

PROFESSOR.　Given the fact that—at least for a while—you have within your reach, on this campus *(As he recites the names, he plucks books from the boxes around the room.)*, Aristotle, John Milton, John Donne, Goethe, Rilke, Einstein, Jane Austen, Van Gogh, Bach, Mahler, Dr. Johnson, and Ibsen and the best of the moderns—yes, male, female, black, white, and green. But the best *because* they're the best, not because they make you proud.

STUDENT.　*(As he holds up a book.)* Is that one Aristotle?

PROFESSOR.　*(Looks at cover.)* Dan Brown. *(Tosses it back.)* With the best that has ever been thought or felt at your fingertips, Ms. McGowan—do you honestly think Communications Arts makes for the most productive use of your time?

STUDENT.　*(Suddenly saddens.)* You sound like someone else I know.

PROFESSOR.　Well, I hope you listen to him.

STUDENT.　*(Softly to herself.)* I no longer believe in wonderful things happening.

PROFESSOR.　*(He looks at her, confused. Puts on CD of Ella singing "Stay as Sweet as You Are" again. Packs more books into the last open carton and tapes it shut. She stares at him. He turns off the music, looks up.)* Is your grade really so important?

STUDENT.　Would you change it if I said yes? *(He gives her a look)* No, of course you wouldn't.

PROFESSOR.   I can't figure you out. You waste a perfectly nice afternoon on a quest you always knew would come to nothing.

STUDENT.   *(Snaps at him.)* And I can't figure *you* out. If you believe all the high-and-mighty things you say about education, why are you quitting?

PROFESSOR.   Quitting?

STUDENT.   Quitting. You're running out on the college. You're deserting it. If you really wanted the place to be what you say, you'd hang in there. You'd fight it out.

PROFESSOR.   I've been fighting it out all my life, young lady.

STUDENT.   *(More agitated.)* You're quitting! You're a quitter! A quitter!

PROFESSOR.   What's wrong with you? *(Tries to calm her by touching her arm; she draws away.)*

STUDENT.   *(As if to herself.)* A quitter. *(She cools off but remains sullen. Looks at her Ibsen paper. He looks at her, concerned. She addresses him, but continues to look at her paper. Quietly.)* How do you find it?

PROFESSOR.   Find what?

STUDENT.   Original thought. How do you find your original thought?

PROFESSOR.   You've already found it. You have it in you. It's just a matter of letting it out.

STUDENT.   *(Angrily again.)* Don't be so fucking clever and all-wise for once! Tell me what you mean! Tell me! *Teach* me!

PROFESSOR.   *(He considers what she's just said, and wipes the wise-guy look off his face.)* All right. Okay. I'll teach you. *(He goes to his office door, opens it, and closes it again. With his back to the door, he looks at her.)* Listen to this sound. *(He turns back to the door, opens it, and closes it. The sound of the tumblers in the lock and the closing door reverberate.)* Listen. The door closes. *(He does it again.)* Here. *(He goes to his desk, takes a pen and a legal pad, and hands them to her. Gently he take her by the shoulders and seats her in the chair before his desk. He goes to the door again, opens it, and closes it.)* Now, write what you've just heard. The door closes. Write whatever comes to mind. Write about the closing of a door. Don't think. Don't hesitate. No throat-clearing. Just write. *(She sits with the pen and pad in her lap, stares into* ▶

25

*space a moment, and begins to write. He watches her. He walks
about. To the door. Back from the door. She continues to write.
There is as much silence onstage as the play can bear. It ought to go
longer than the audience thinks it can go. As she writes, he continues
to walk—behind his desk, back to the door, around her but not so
close as to disturb her. She is in her own world of thought, oblivious
to him. All is very still. Finally, she looks up and lets out a deep
breath as if she has emerged from under water. He goes to her.
She hands him the legal pad. He stands back and reads aloud.)*

PROFESSOR.   "My father stands at the door and looks us over,
as if he is taking inventory. We are all present and accounted
for—Mom, Michael, Jane, myself. He assesses us. He is wearing
a pressed tan suit and a white shirt and a pale blue tie, looking
very summery, very handsome in his pressed tan suit. He might
be a salesman. He might be a stranger come to report an item
of news, a bulletin. He might be returning home from a trip,
like Odysseus, returning home from a long trip. But he is not a
salesman, and he is not a stranger, and he is not returning home,
my father. Not returning. It is Sunday morning, and he is in his
Sunday best, dressed for the occasion of his leaving us, forever,
for good. That's an odd expression—for good. When the door
closes behind him, I go to stand where he was, just before it
closed. Mom, Michael, and Jane remain where he has left them.
It is as though he has hypnotized them, telling them not to move
until his hypnotic command permits it. But soon, Mom moves.
She goes to the kitchen without speaking a word. She makes us
pancakes. None of us speaks. We sit at our places at the kitchen
table and hand round the pancakes. Blueberry today. They are
blueberry." *(He looks at the pad a second, then at her. She sits
staring forward, not looking to him for a reaction. He goes to the
desk, puts on the CD player. Ella sings. He extends his arms toward
her and invites her to dance. She goes to him slowly, ceremonially.
They dance to "Stay as Sweet as You Are." He sits her down in her
chair again. He picks up a couple of books and asks with a gesture
if he may take the legal pad. She nods. He walks to the office door
and, without turning back, exits. She looks at the closed door.)*

THE END ∾

An Excerpt from Rosenblatt's *Lapham Rising*

Following is an excerpt from Lapham Rising, *Roger Rosenblatt's first novel (Ecco/HarperCollins, 2006). The book's hero, Harry March, is something of a wreck and more than half nuts. Up until now, he has lived peacefully on an island in the Hamptons with his talking dog, Hector, who is a born-again Evangelical and unapologetic capitalist. (The island is called Noman, so that when someone asks Harry where he lives, he can say "Noman is an island.") But March's life starts to completely unravel when Lapham—an ostentatious multimillionaire who made his fortune on asparagus tongs—begins construction of a gargantuan mansion just across the way. To Harry, Lapham's monstrosity-to-be represents the fetid and corrupt excess that has ruined modern civilization. Which means, quite simply, that this is war.*

"Roger Rosenblatt is one of the (intentionally) funniest citizens of our time and Lapham Rising *is a painfully funny comedy of manners. . . ."*
—Joyce Carol Oates

TEN A.M.: Kathy Time. Time for Kathy Polite to take off her clothes. She spells her surname Polite but pronounces it "pole-EET," to add that continental *je ne sais quoi* to her uniquely successful real estate operation. Whenever I talk with ▶

her, which is as infrequently as possible, I make a point of pretending not to know how she pronounces her name, and I replace it with that adjective of courtesy that mocks her existence.

"That's Pole-EET, as you perfectly well know, you old coot." She always speaks to me coquettishly, as though she had just returned from Savannah to her favorite old uncle's plantation, and is capable of reducing me to blushes and stumbles with the droop of an eyelid.

"Ah'm so sorry! I was just being polite."

"Ah don't know why Ah waste one word on you!" She puckers her lips like a grouper. "Ah'll never sell you *anything,* you old skinflint."

"That is *SKINE*-flint," I correct her. "And Ah would gladly purchase one of your delightful Taras, Miss Pole-EET, but the cotton crop has been so po' this year, we've had to eat the slaves."

That I would never buy so much as a lean-to from Kathy has had no impact, I hardly need to report, on her booming real estate business. Alongside the hundreds of "gems," "steps to the ocean," "priced to sell," and "just bring your toothbrush" houses for which she shills on both overladen jaws of Long Island, she also represents what grotesqueries are still for sale around Lapham's. She did not sell that particular magnificence, of course: Lapham had his own broker (a roommate from St. Mark's) and his own personal architect, an in-law of Albert Speer's, whose firm has been in the family for generations, and which had erected the dank mossy manses in Newport and Saratoga, as well as several more recent, bright mausoleums in Florida and Wyoming, near the Snake River—where, it is said, the whitefish committed a Jim Jones mass suicide in response.

But, as Lapham rises, Kathy is not far behind. Mainly she sells spec houses to Lapham wannabes, of whom there seems to be an endless parade. Thus, though without a contract, and herself but dimly aware of it, she is Lapham's silent partner in the destruction of the universe. She once told me that she was—and I quote— "very grateful to Mr. Lapham for setting the proper standard of architectural elegance in the area. As yet, Ah have not made his acquaintance. But on the day that Ah am so fortunate, Ah shall shake his hand warmly and tell him, 'It is people like you, suhr, who make the Hamptons the Hamptons.'"

Were it not for Kathy Time, I would have gutted her on the spot.

"Hah," she calls from her boat this morning—"Hah" being a conjunction of "Hi" and a sigh.

"Hah," I call back. She wants to assure herself that I am watching. She need not worry. I walk down to the platform of the dock facing the creek to decrease the distance between us, and improve my view. One does what one can.

She surveys me with a fatalistic shrug, as if I were a decision she regretted. "Harry, you need some new clothes."

I would say, "And you do not," but I don't wish to delay her from her appointed rounds.

On the stroke of ten, this is what she does every sweet drifty summer day. And here she is again, with her forty-year-old diver's body, standing like a soft little piece of vertical caramel in the bow of her Grady White with the dual 250-horsepower gunmetal-gray Yamaha engines lying at rest. The powerboat is anchored midway between Noman and Lapham's shore. It throbs. Who would not? I see her, clear as starlight, reaching for the heavens and stretching herself like some living figurehead on the prow of a New Bedford whaler.

On each side of her boat, port as well as starboard, facing both my island and the long line of developed and developing houses across from me, is a large red-painted sign: "Polite for the Elite, Realtors." The lettering is thick, high, and three-dimensional. One could read it from miles offshore. I imagine that the signs allow her to write off the boat as a business expense. But the real, unforgettable, visually ineradicable advertisement is Kathy herself, out for her regular morning swim.

She has been skinny-dipping off her boat for nine glorious summers. And there is hardly a man around here—including those who drive over for the occasion from as far away as Shirley and Mattituck, and including all the -ogues on both alligator jaws: Patch-, Cutch-, Haupp-, Aquab-, as well as Qui- and Qu- who does not stop whatever else he is doing at precisely ten o'clock to gaze in appreciative wonder at the wonder of Kathy Polite. ▶

"Hah, Hector!" He scampers down to the water's edge and makes a snowy flurry of greeting her. His manner with people other than me is to rush toward them exhibiting a frantic eagerness, wagging and levitating, as if he were a kidnap victim signaling for rescue.

"Hah, boys!" she calls to Dave and his construction crew. Dave and his son, Jack, give her a decorous wave from the waist. The Mexicans are more demonstrative.

In her way, she is a genius. Other realtors in the area spend a fortune on brochures advertising houses that are "this side of Paradise," or that offer "location, location," or that were "built in a unique style by the owner," meaning that they were designed by someone on whom German silent horror films made an indelible impression. The brokers need to print updates every week, because all of these houses sell in a snap and are immediately replaced by new listings. It is expensive to produce the brochures, and it takes both time and effort to distribute them around the sidewalks in front of the cheese shops and the basket shops and the shops that sell photographs of other shops, and to place them in the doorways of the "We have mahimahi!" restaurants, where they lie in stacks and gather sand.

What Kathy figured out was that it would be much more convenient, not to say more consonant with her own taste and character, if instead of having to seek out customers, she could devise an activity that would entice *them* to come to *her*. So without using a flyer, posters, a Web site with "such a cute name dot-com," or any other instruments of modern publicity, she attached her signs to her boat and began the practice of her mute morning sales pitch. She was, and is, her own Open House.

"Why don't you join me today, Wrinkles?" she calls from the side deck.

"No time," I shout back. "I have to water my duck."

"Your WHAT?" She clamps a hand to her mouth as if shocked. The last time Kathy was shocked was when her cousin said no. She heard me, all right. I say the same thing to her every day.

"What's wrong with your ear, Harry? Did you pull a Van Gogh?"

"Yes, Buttercup, I cut it off as a gesture of my love for you. Actually, I was trying to cut my throat."

"Not if Ah get there first. And what isthat under the tarp? It looks quite sinister—much lahk yourself, Harry March." She often says my first and last names together, as if she were addressing and classifying me in the same breath. She presents two even rows of large, newly whitened teeth.

The front of the Da Vinci lies to my right. A portion of the aft crosspiece is still showing. I cover it. "Why don't you just go on with your morning's work?" I try not to sound too eager.

She preens on her deck, her face as cute as neon. She turns first to the left, then to the right, as a much-honored actress might do onstage: the first lady of real estate, acknowledging an audience she cannot see but knows is out there. Distracted, she slips out of her green top and her beige shorts, displaying panties and a bra as white as glaciers against her autobronzed skin, which is russet-colored, or the color of unpolished gold. With the ceremonial prance of a Lipizzaner, she walks to the bow. She walks to the stern. Then to the bow. Then to the stern. Onshore, hedges jostle. Car windows open. Rabbits stiffen. Back to the bow. Back to the stern.

At last she is still again, and—as if lost in an ethereal reverie concerning plummeting interest rates or some newly minted millionaire just in from Rahway—she unhooks her bra and drops it at her side like a lace handkerchief. She looks out at the water. She looks at the shore. The shore's mouth is dry and agape. Now she slips off her panties. One can almost hear a sighing of the clouds. But there are no clouds.

"Why do you stare like that every morning?" asks Hector.

"You wouldn't understand." I never mention his first medical procedure.

She touches her forehead, then reaches up into her hair, a braid of browns and oranges that swings down to the middle of her back. She loosens the braid, and out spills plenty's horn. She touches her ribs and rubs them as if attempting to induce wings. She glows like a coal in ash. Though I would have no way of knowing this, I would put her normal body temperature at about 106. The water will hiss when she enters it. Though ▶

I would have no way of knowing this either, I imagine that she initiates lovemaking by leaping on a man from a great height, say a hayloft or a chandelier, and whispering "Surprise!" She touches her thighs and her knees as she steps to the side of the boat away from me and facing Lapham's. Now she straightens her body. Now she perches. Now she dives. The water opens its grateful arms and waits.

At this moment of her diving, as she is suspended in mid-jackknife, nothing happens on the East End of Long Island. Not a single nail is nailed. Not a single hedge is trimmed. Not a single bottle of Château Whatanamazingwine is sold. Not one compliment is paid to a tomato or an ear of corn or a peach. No one asks where the potato fields have gone. Likewise the duck farms. No Filipino housekeeper is yelled at for failing to position the fruit forks correctly. No year-round resident is pushed aside at a farmers' market. No one asks anyone else to a small dinner just for close friends, or wishes there were more time to spend reading quietly on the beach away from all the big parties. No one gives kudos. Or draws raves. No one embarks on an exciting new phase of his life, or enters the third act of his life, or comments that life is a journey. No one plans a benefit dinner dance for a fatal disease. No one lowers his voice to say "Jew."

Nothing moves. Nothing makes a sound. The universe lies in respectful silence as sex and commerce find their apogee in Kathy Polite and her morning swim. For one brief moment in this day, for what *certainly* will be the *only* such moment, I am at peace—all bitterness relieved, all burdens lifted from me. The wind kicks up. I bless her unaware. ᴄᴗ

....

Don't miss the next book by your favorite author.

Sign up now for AuthorTracker by visiting www.AuthorTracker.com.